MW01517425

To Ju
Thank you for sharing
and actually buying mine.
Donna

LEAVING PARADISE

Donna Wootton

Leaving Paradise

Tijean had always gone to bed at night certain that when he woke, every day was planned around him. There was more to this certitude than the simple domestic habits of hearing his mother waking early to do chores like preparing a meal of pigeon peas and rice before spending the day working at the resort, or his father entering his room to softly coax him out of sleep. By taking their roles for granted, his parents unwittingly accommodated this certainty. They knew that without maintaining peace and order the household could erupt into a pit of resentment. So on the night Tijean left home he found himself in the dark and overwhelmed by feelings of uncertainty. The small, white washed house he'd called home for nearly seventeen years disappeared behind him. The distance he had to travel to reach the boat was farther than he was used to walking. Normally he would ride his bike, but on this night, he decided to leave it behind, too. He couldn't risk the noise from the creaky gear box disturbing the stillness at midnight. The air was as heavy and humid as it had been all day, not a whiff of a breeze to relieve the heat. As Tijean practically ran along the broken pavement his thoughts kept pace with his feet. At his age every humiliation, every indignity, every setback cuts deeper than anything that can happen later in life. His mind roamed from his parents to school, back to his family only to return to the classroom. All these memories intensified his shame, but instead of making him feel small, he surged forward with an itch in his soles that fed his wanderlust. Over an hour later when he arrived on the dock to board the dive boat to leave the island "for good", he found he was not alone.

Jason Kearney was a marine biologist who walked with a slight limp. He arrived with two large Samsonite cases and a solid rectangular trunk, a burden that stood in sharp contrast to Tijean's only luggage, one worn out day pack. With both arms free Tijean immediately came to the man's aid. The cases were heavy, but Tijean was strong from lifting scuba tanks. "What have you got in these?" he asked the man who introduced himself as simply Jake. "Air?" It was Tijean's idea of a joke.

"Two computers, two hard drives, film, videos, microscope, telescope, flippers, marine gear," Jake said nonchalantly. He ended the list, "My clothes would fit into your day pack."

"Mine, too," Tijean said, making Jake smile. Tijean warmed to the man and, feeling comfortable, asked about the limp.

Jake allowed an interval to pass before replying while the two of them stored the cases. "Basically my right hip's shot.

Initially something showed up on an x-ray nearly ten years ago. A spur had grown on some cartilage. Funny thing, that. The doctor thought it was from a childhood injury." Easing himself into a lower position Jake sat. "So now I have to face the inevitable. I'm returning to Canada for a hip replacement operation. Just have to find a handiman to do the job."

"Canada? That's where I'm going. To Toronto," Tijean said, hoping to secure company on his foreign travels. Jake suggested they might be on the same flight out of Provo, and comparing itineraries, discovered that, indeed, they were.

"I can help you with your bags at the airport," Tijean said, recognizing that, although strongly built, Jake was at a disadvantage with his injured hip.

"Much obliged. I had to streamline my packing," Jake said, not so much to apologize or explain the contents of his cases, as to share a little life history with his new acquaintance. He laughed. "I must have stuff stored all over the world. I even left equipment at the Marine Centre."

"I've been to the Centre For Marine Resource Studies," Tijean said.

"To study?"

"No," Tijean said quickly. He grew flustered as he explained about the paper he'd written for high school after interviewing an instructor. "That was the assignment. To do an interview and write it. I had help," he said apologetically.

"So you're interested in marine studies?"

Tijean simply said, "I dive."

"Man after my own heart." Jake shifted his weight. "Are you planning on studying there, in the future?" Jake asked, making direct eye contact with the lad.

"No, can't. I haven't finished high school." Tijean let Jake's gaze hold him despite feeling exposed. He was revealing himself to this stranger, a man he seemed to instantly trust.

Jake could have started into a lecture about the necessity of getting a high school diploma, but he had experience in these matters, so, instead, took a different tack. "I've come from Grand Turk," he said. "Looking at the new Biorock structures. Do you know about that?"

Tijean shook his head "no".

"I've spent decades diving in the Maldives. The reefs here haven't suffered anything like the devastation of those in the Indian Ocean. The Turks and Caicos Islands support many restoration programs, but I don't agree with the use of Biorock. It's not as strong as natural coral." With that Jake launched into a description of the essence of the methods used to sustain meaningful marine management systems. "Early stages still, but a promising future for coral propagation. Of course not all development on the islands is sustainable but that's a whole other issue."

Jake's deep voice held Tijean's full attention. The tone was gentle, but with an authoritative masculine quality. "I'd like to go to the Maldives," Tijean said.

"Divers have been studying the atolls there for about 50 years. I've been revisiting them since the early '90's. Recently they've deteriorated badly. Bleaching is not new, but the serial effects of bleaching and local insults have greatly degraded the reefs."

"Do you see the same fish there as here?"

Recognizing Tijean's total inexperience outside the small pool of ocean at the lad's doorstep, Jake, to his credit, remained imperturbable. "Yes." With that, Jake regaled Tijean with anecdotes on the behaviour of Trigger fish. "Although they tend to keep their distance, sometimes a big one would come straight at me." Jake demonstrated, moving his upper body like a boxer ducking a punch. Then he spoke about the tuna.

While listening to Jake's detailed account, flashing bodies of great fish swam in Tijean's mind. Soon they were over the Fort George Land & Sea Park, midway to their destination on Providenciales. The night was unnaturally dark as low cloud hid the stars and moon. On deck, running lights cast a trail of reflective pools. Jake changed their topic of conversation by asking where Tijean was going in Toronto. "Do you have relatives there?"

"Yes. My cousin's meeting me at the airport. I have his photo. Otherwise I wouldn't know him because we've never met." Tijean failed to admit that he'd taken the photo from his mother's pile of correspondence she kept bound with an elastic in a drawer in her bedroom. Airmail envelopes regularly arrived from her sister, his aunt, with pictures enclosed. There was a time when Tijean took no notice of this far-off family. What were they to him? Only his mother always subjected him to their business as if it was his moral duty to know them. He thought it was absurd for her to try to establish bonds between them simply because they were blood relatives. To his mind it only complicated life with more obligations. Lately, though, he was glad she had a family bond because these relatives in Canada were his ticket to independence. His cousin, who was close to him in age, seemed genuinely excited to have him visit, especially clandestinely. "Don't tell your mother," Tijean wrote in a cautionary note with details of his flight plan.

"You won't be diving there," Jake warned, "at least, not in salt water."

Inhaling the sea air Tijean recognized the homesickness that would set in when the ocean was absent from his life. He was too disenchanted with his parents to sense any loss from their absence, but Jake had a point. "Will you miss the sea?" Tijean asked.

Jake nodded to where his luggage was stored. "I expect I'll live vicariously through film. I have plenty of work to sort through while I'm waiting for the hip op."

"Oh, I see," Tijean said, not fully understanding wait times for surgery. Yet he had heard that Canada had free health care from his mother telling his father about the health concerns of her sister's family. "You don't have to pay for this operation, do you?"

"Not if I wait three months to get back on the health plan, which I'll do. Better than spending my own coin."

Despite the darkness Tijean could make out Jake's features. He guessed the man was older than his father, probably in his sixties. He had a full head of hair that had once been blond, small blue eyes, pale skin, narrow lips and a thick build – completely the opposite in physique from Tijean. Although he had a full head of hair, his was black and curly. His eyes were discs with chocolate irises, his skin a rich brown, his lips broad. Tijean was tall with long muscles, not yet fully developed. "How long have you been away?" Tijean asked, curious about Jake's history.

"Well, let me see," Jake said, giving the question serious calculation. "Over thirty years."

"Did you learn to dive in Canada?"

"Yes, but I prefer tropical water. It's warmer. Better temperature for working in." Then Jake started telling Tijean how he stays down to film. "You have to keep your buoyancy, otherwise you bounce around the bottom. I take shallow breaths." Jake demonstrated his breathing technique. "It uses more oxygen, but I can keep the camera steady."

Tijean imitated Jake's shallow breathing. Holding his ribs Jake again demonstrated. Tijean tried the technique with improved results, imagining himself underwater. Within seconds the two were breathing together.

∾

On North Caicos, the bread basket of the Turks & Caicos chain of islands, Susan Borden, who has lived here for nearly a decade, drives a moped to work. She's not alone in her choice of transportation although there are more cars on the road now. This light motorized two-wheeler is still popular. Motorcycles are too big and heavy, also noisy. Feeling the freedom of the wind against her tanned face and the luxury of the effortless speed beneath her legs that are just starting to show veins through her thinning skin, she makes her way along the open road blissfully unaware that this routine is shortly coming to an end. The early morning air is already humid so the offshore breeze brings relief.

Outside the town of Whitby Susan sees a small group huddled together with binoculars lifted. Birders, she thinks, or listers as they often call themselves. Only the really serious naturalists make a special trip here for the sole purpose of bird watching. Tempted by their interest Susan pulls over and stops the moped at the side of the road. Ever since an earlier sighting of the bee hummingbird made on North Caicos, these enthusiasts have come to catch a glimpse of the male of this species which is the smallest known bird in the world. So small, in fact, it is only the size of a bee, hence the name. Spotting it in the wild requires enough expertise to be able to distinguish between the movement of a bee and the flight pattern of a bird. Tentatively, Susan approaches the five adults. One woman, sensing Susan's presence, drops her binoculars and turns her head. Susan stares into the ice-blue eyes of the elderly woman and quietly asks, "Any luck?"

This woman's face is small and flat, her skin tanned and wrinkled. She nods in the affirmative, and in a friendly gesture, lifts the neck strap over her head offering her binoculars to Susan. All this is communicated in mime. Mustn't disturb the bird.

Susan directs the woman's lightweight binoculars to the clearing where she's pointing and focuses the lens on the small purple flowers where she sees activity between the blossoms. The bird is no bigger than the end of her thumb. It is impossible to see its wings, but its crescent shape is distinguishable. Periodically the sun's rays catch its iridescent plumage, creating a sudden mini-rainbow of colour. The Taino, who were the first known inhabitants of the islands, associated the bird with the rainbow which forms a bridge between the land, sky, and subterranean waters: the three realms of the Taino cosmos. Their name for a hummingbird was Zum-zum, an obvious interpretation of the bird's sound.

Nodding her thanks to the small, kind woman Susan returns the glasses and, moving quietly, walks back to her machine. Wary of starting the motor whose noise would disrupt the peace of the naturalists, Susan pushes her vehicle along the side of the road until she crests the hill. She feels at peace with herself. Nature can do that, offer its remarkable gifts to soothe the soul. A car coming in the opposite direction slows, then stops beside her. The driver of the taxi is Guy who asks her if she is having trouble. "No, but thanks for stopping," she says and gives a clipped wave to Celianne who sits in the passenger seat, but the woman ignores her. Susan doesn't let that snub shatter her pleasant reverie, even though its sadness casts a pall of gloom so strong she wonders it doesn't shatter the car's interior. Luckily the windows are open. Anyway, for Susan the bee hummingbird sighting reaffirms this island as a paradise and the intoxication of that reaffirmation feels like an embrace.

Their son, Tijean, is a student in Susan's grade 11 class. His teachers have always suspected he has a learning disability, but his parents have consistently refused to have Tijean tested. They suspect that his problem is simply a matter of attitude and don't trust the proposal to label their boy, although they have accepted some intervention strategies as a means of helping him improve his grades. Still, his attendance is poor. In fact, he wasn't in class at the beginning of the week which in a way was a relief because when he returned yesterday he was disruptive and difficult. Guy is taking Celianne to the resort where she works and where Susan lives so Susan feels compelled to ask after the boy.

"He's gone," Guy says as he slowly accelerates away from her.

Susan watches the back of the vehicle disappear. Guy drives the taxi around the island for his livelihood. Wondering what he means Susan continues to stare at the emptiness. Has Tijean left home? Has he left the island? Maybe that's not a bad thing? Maybe Tijean needs to go away to get a perspective before he can appreciate his opportunities. Certainly there are other people still here taking advantage. In the distance Susan can see the foundation of the development being built along the shore. From the top of the hill it looks like a child's construction, but Susan knows too well that it is hardly small. Although the government strictly controls expansion, the pressure to build is changing the landscape. Susan sighs. "Yes," she says. "Times, they are a-changing." The march of time. Where are the Taino now? Gone, those people and their language with all their different words for bird life, but not totally lost. The aquatic bird that is a species of rail still bears its Taino name – Sora, as does the glossy black cuckoo named Ani. Like other indigenous Indians on the mainland, they, too, succumbed to disease, were killed, or taken into slavery. Like the Mayan they left their ruins – ball courts, utensils, stone monuments. It's people who changed all that; people can either preserve an unspoiled Eden or alter it. She recognizes how lucky she's been to live here while it is still paradise on earth.

Ms Mahala Mulrain originally comes from Middle Caicos where the population is counted in the hundreds, not thousands like on Provo where the population keeps growing. In fact, most of the other inhabited islands in the Turks & Caicos chain count their inhabitants below the thousand mark. Susan finds her colleague who serves as the Special Needs Coordinator in her office standing in front of the filing cabinet with the top drawer open. She rolls her nutmeg coloured eyes to the upper corner of their sockets to gaze at Susan who stands respectfully inside the door frame making Susan feel like an apologetic student. "Sorry to interrupt your work first thing in the morning," Susan says.

Mahala pushes the top drawer shut with the palms of her hands and drops her stick-thin arms to the sides of her slim body. She is a small, young woman with tightly braided hair that grips her scalp with the stiffness of a wire sculpture. "I guess you heard Tijean Williams ran away?"

Susan leans the bulky pad of her upper shoulder against the frame. "I just saw his parents on the road. His father said something to that effect."

"Come in. Sit down," Mahala says, gesturing to the chair in front of her desk where Susan assumes students sit when visiting. Mahala sits on the plywood chair behind her desk which is identical to the one Susan sits on. At this high school there are no stuffed chairs to distinguish administration from clerical or teachers from students. All the furniture is basic in design and made from lightweight materials, unlike the heavy oak furniture that Susan remembers from her years in high school. Even at the schools where she taught before coming to the island there were remnants of that 1950s style in back offices or storage cupboards. "I feel badly about Tijean," Mahala says. "I think despite his bad behaviour he has promise."

"I couldn't agree more," Susan says. "Although he's a nuisance in class, he's bright enough."

"Have you read his assignment yet?"

"No, I plan on marking the papers on the weekend."

"You know what's interesting about his?" Mahala is perched on the edge of her seat, resting her elbows on the top of her desk. She always appears intense. "How long it took him to find the topic."

The atmosphere between the two women is subdued. Despite the intensity of their concern there is a mutual feeling of defeat on the academic front and loss at their student's disappearance. Susan stares at the framed picture on the desk. It is a class photograph taken when Mahala graduated from primary school on Middle Caicos. She is easily identifiable among the small group of girls in their red checkered jumpers worn over white blouses as she is the tiniest. Susan looks up at Mahala. "So you helped him with his paper," she says.

"Yes, and I don't want to prejudice your marking scheme, but it's a good paper." Mahala sighs and then relaxes into the stiff chair. "Maybe he'll show up yet," she says.

"I expect so."

"Rumour has it he's left on the dive boat."

"Well," Susan says, somewhat surprised. "Eventually the dive boat will return to port."

Mahala lifts her eyebrows. "But will it return with Tijean?"

Exhaling Susan sighs and waits a second for the air to absorb her breath as if her sigh is a sentence communicating frustration. "When I saw the Williams this morning I wanted to ask them to come in to see me." Susan shrugs. "I don't know whether there's any point now? I thought it was time we talked about Tijean's future prospects."

"Yes," Mahala says, rejuvenated by the late proposal. "I've been thinking how perfect for Tijean if we could make accommodations for him at the Marine Centre."

Susan can't help looking skeptically at Mahala. " Do you think they would take him?"

"Maybe," Mahala says. "You'll understand after you've read his paper." She cocks her head. "I guess we should speak to Carl."

"Yes," Susan says. "Knowing Carl, he's probably already phoned."

Carl Musgrove, the Principal of Raymond Gardiner High School, is a native of South Caicos and has been at his new position for only one year. Mahala and Susan find the youthful man in his office, a space he crowds with his large body. He greets them both with a wide grin revealing a row of even white teeth. His clouded amber eyes narrow when his apple-shaped cheeks squeeze upwards. "Let me guess. You've come about Tijean?" he asks in a deep voice that often fills the halls, the cafeteria, the assembly room and the sporting field unaided by a microphone.

"You've heard, then?" Susan asks.

"The whole island has heard," Carl says.

"We were wondering about phoning his parents?" Mahala says.

"Yes, I was just thinking I should do that. Advise me what I should say. Is there something you want me to tell them?"

Susan watches Mahala and Carl while they exchange ideas for a script to deliver to the parents.

They are such opposites, not simply different sexes, but in size and temperament, too. Carl Musgrove is a friendly giant while Mahala Mulrain is an intense elf. Susan starts to fantasize them together as a couple, then chastises herself for letting her mind wander while these two are dealing with a serious matter. They ask her advice and she suggests they should phone the resort to invite the Williamses to come to the school to meet with them, hoping, as she's spitting out this suggestion, that she hasn't missed that same point in their exchange while daydreaming.

"Okay," Carl says and he negotiates a time that's convenient for all three of them.

As they leave the Principal's Office the students are entering the school. There is a strict dress code so the sea of young faces bobs above a uniform movement of colour: white shirts and blouses, dark green pants and skirts, black shoes. In the buzz of talk stirring the air Susan hears Tijean's name echo like a pulsing wave. She enters her room alongside Sharlene Saunders and Shanae Mundy who greet her in chorus before telling her that Tijean has run away. Mariejean Henry stops beside her classmates to join the discussion. Apparently her mother and father are friends of Tijean's parents. They fled the poor island of Haiti at the same time.

"Why is Haiti so poor?"

It is Rolston Martin who's asked the question. By now the room is full of students all standing in a pack at the front of the class listening to the girls talking to Miss Borden. The boy's question opens a gap in the assemblage. One hand rises above the silent group. Straining her neck to look over and through the crowd Susan sees Jean-Louis, a friend of Tijean's and also of Haitian descent. "Why don't we all take our seats," Susan says. "That way we can better listen to Jean-Louis."

Jean-Louis is a track and field star at the school. When he wears shorts his long legs appear under the loose fabric like spindly tree trunks. They are straight with no shape forming thighs or calves, yet they are muscular and strong. He rarely answers questions in class, but now he grabs their attention with his detailed explanation that recounts the history of coffee and how it came to the islands just like people from Africa. The island that prospered most from the trade in coffee was Santo Domingo, what is now Haiti and the Dominican Republic. They grew half the world's coffee back in the eighteenth century. "Can you imagine how rich they were?" Jean-Louis says. He's remained at the front of the class and is addressing his fellow students as if he's been given a speech to deliver. "Only it wasn't the Africans who were rich. They were slaves. It was the landowners. They made their fortunes off the islands and the slaves. Some of those families still prosper off the money they made there. But most of those people live across the Atlantic in Europe. Then, in 1791, the slaves revolted. It was the first successful slave revolt in history. The owners fled and ever since Haiti has been poor. By then the land was stripped and bare. When hurricanes hit, there are floods and mudslides and the people of Haiti continue to suffer."

Susan senses that his explanation is a story retold as oral history passed down to him through the generations of his family who trace their lineage to those very slaves. They are proud to be free but resentful of their economic condition and political state. Susan also realizes that there's no point following her lesson plan. The students' minds are elsewhere this morning. With a nod of her head she acknowledges Denzil Christopher who has his hand raised.

"He's right, Miss. Coffee is a very valuable crop, like gold. Or oil."

Susan could make a comparison to other countries like Guatemala, a country with problems that she could use to draw parallels, but she inhibits her pedantic role and, instead, lets her students have their say without questioning the credibility of what they're sharing. For that is what this conversation has become, a forum for sharing.

Somehow the class has split along gender lines: the boys are listening to a serious discussion between Denzil and Jean about the depletion of resources on the Caribbean islands while the girls are talking about Mariejean's and Tijean's families. How does this happen? Susan ponders the old nature versus nurture theory. She hones in on the girls' talk which isn't so much gossip as exploration. Their intent isn't simply to exploit the emotional landscape of the two families. They seem more to want to fully understand the dynamics between the family members so they can better explain this recent development. When they become aware that Susan has turned her attention to their discussion they ask for her confirmation to further enlighten their confusion. Of course, Susan can't reveal the nature of Tijean's learning difficulties without betraying her professional commitment to student confidentiality. Some think Tijean is more than a difficult boy – badly behaved in class, always getting into trouble in school, a worry to his family – and now the ultimate act of bad behaviour – a runaway.

Mariejean gains the attention of the group by raising her voice above the others. "But doesn't all this bad acting show who Tijean really is? He's got his problems, sure. Maybe he's got more problems than most of us. But he's just not cut out for school, is he Miss?"

There is a murmur of consensus. Sharlene Saunders tells Mariejean she is right. "And our class is better with him gone," she says. "Now he won't disrupt our lessons and make problems for all of us. Sorry, Miss Susan, but that how I feel."

Susan knows it's time to intervene. "I don't think that's what Mariejean meant. Everyone has a right to an education."

"But he done interfere with our education all the time," Sharlene says.

"Yes, I recognize that," Susan says. She senses she must pick her words carefully so as not to lay blame. "Maybe we should have offered him more alternatives? Maybe under different conditions he could have been more successful?" Is she blaming the system? Now she's thrown them into the quagmire of that debate – the system versus the student, the common good versus the individual need.

Best to change tack. "Where do you think he's gone?" Susan casts a glance over the girls' faces and settles on Mariejean. She has cocoa butter coloured skin, much lighter than Tijean's or, for that matter, the other girls in the class. A question flits through Susan's mind. Has Mariejean Spanish blood in her ancestral gene pool?

"He's with the divers."

Susan looks down on Mariejean's full head of hair that's like a senorita's, full and wavy. "So you definitely think he's left the island?"

Mariejean nods her head. "Oh, yes, Miss Borden. He's gone."

Suddenly Susan recalls a night image. "I saw him cycling along the road to Sandy Point."

"I know. His father said. By the night-time, he's gone on the diving ship. They know him well and they like him and they give him work all the time."

"Umm," Susan says. Mariejean sounds confident in her belief. Probably the families discussed the mystery of Tijean well into the night. Mariejean does have dark rings under her eyes. "I wonder why he first went to Sandy Point?"

20

"See his girlfriend."

"Ah," Susan says. She should have known. There's a girl. There's always a girl. This one got left behind, but not before the goodbyes. Did Tijean promise he'd return?

"Do you mean Caroline?"

The girls turn their attention to the group of boys. Rolston Martin comes from Sandy Point.

"Yes," Mariejean says simply.

Susan searches her mind. What Caroline? There's Caroline Musgrove, a niece to Carl. There's Caroline Wilson who lives in Whitby. Of course, Caroline Hamilton. She's from Sandy Point.

"She says he gone with the dive boat."

Rolston's confirmation bridges the separation between the boys and the girls. Hints of a romance will do that, especially an affair that's doomed. Susan can feel the hormones in the room rise and clash, ready to engage and defend. These teenagers want to identify with the suffering lovers. "Sorry," Susan says. "I didn't realize he had a girlfriend."

There is a communal groan. "Miss Borden. Where have you been?"

"Well," Susan says somewhat defensively. "Right here in my classroom." She smiles first at Sharlene, then at the boys. None of them share her humour. The romance between the now-separated couple is serious business and their earnestness makes Susan feel superfluous. Her eyes settle on

21

Rolston. "Did Tijean tell Caroline when he'd return with the dive boat?"

Rolston holds her gaze with his cocoa bean eyes while he shakes his head. "That's the point, Miss Borden. He won't return. Tijean told her he's going to jump ship and go as far away from here as he can get."

Mariejean is bursting with confirmation as she lets her voice reach a high note. "He took all his money. Tijean did. He made lots on the dives."

Shaking her head in a silent affirmation of Mariejean's statement, Susan tries to recover some semblance of credibility among the young students in her charge. "I see," she says finally, thinking of all she must remember to ask Celianne and Guy, sensing her role extending beyond being a teacher and counsellor to include some detective work. Along that line she throws out another question. "Did Tijean tell Caroline where he thought he might go?"

Mariejean turns to Rolston who shrugs. "No," he says.

"He told no one," Mariejean says.

That bit of information descends on the class like a confession. Tijean did not go off half-cocked, bragging about where he would go or what he would do. Instead the boy fled like a stealth fighter, keeping secret his whereabouts and destination. While Susan digests the seriousness of this revelation the class once again splits into smaller units to continue its discussions, only this time the split doesn't follow gender lines, but political ones. She overhears the heavyweights banter around names like President Aristide who left his country escorted by the Marines, hardly analogous to Tijean's leave-taking. But no conversation about the plight of Haiti can occur without at least one reference to the Catholic priest who remains the hero of the poor. Another group picks up the lead about the return of the dive boat and speculates the vessel could already be back and docked. Those with more domestic sensibilities wonder why Tijean didn't leave a note for his family as they can't imagine not telling their parents where they were going, especially if they were planning to leave the islands permanently. Susan can't help but feel a great sense of loss at Tijean's disappearance. It descends on her like the weight of a ten ton truck as if she's suffering a classic heart attack symptom, only she's not having any trouble breathing. In fact, her breathing is slow and measured. The pain of a sufferer, the breathing of a plodder. Picturing Tijean in her mind she starts making up adventures for him, sailing across vast and stormy seas, diving into dark and mysterious depths, encountering the risky maze of the unexpected. This mental effort of make-believe calms her and, replacing the weight of a great pain on her chest, she senses a slight nausea spreading from the pit of her stomach and catching her in the throat. Tijean could simply be sitting alone on deck watching the sun pass unobstructed across a blue sky.

While everything he knows in his life continues on without him, he could be feeling tormented, not adventurous. Here on the islands at school and at home, his friends and family are already living their lives without him, speculating about his whereabouts and well being.

"I'd get homesick."

Susan turns to Sharlene whom she can see in profile among the group talking closest to her. Now all the others are speaking at once as Sharlene's admission garners an immediate response. Shanae tells her not to be such a baby. Others demand if she plans to stay on the island for the rest of her life? "What about going to college?" "Aren't you going to get an education?" "You have to leave home sometime?"

"Yeah, I will. But I know when I do I'll be homesick. Maybe just at first," Sharlene says reluctantly as if she senses the need to accommodate the others' prejudices.

Suddenly Susan wants to mitigate their youthful hostility by confessing to her own experience of feeling homesick, a feeling that's newly aroused in her, something that seems to come with her onset of menopause in middle age. Ironic, here she is in a roomful of teenagers confused by the actions of one, hostile to the sentiments of others, wary of their future and she - the teacher, the adult - is on a par with them. I, too, feel homesick, she wants to shout. Sensing a presence at her side she looks over her shoulder into Herbie's mottled amber eyes. "Yes, Herbie."

"Can I ask your advice, please, Miss Borden?"

"Of course." Susan watches the young man bow his head as if feeling too shy to speak, but she knows that's not the real reason. He must be very troubled as he is usually so confident and forthright.

Directing his question to the floor Herbie says, "I want to speak to Mrs. Williams." He nods his head while lifting it to look at her. "I feel awkward about doing that. I think I should give her my condolences, but Tijean, he's not dead. Yet I should say something, otherwise I won't feel comfortable working at the resort with her."

"Ah," Susan says acknowledging his concern. Tomorrow, Saturday, Herbie will come to the resort where he works part-time. In comparison to the others Herbie stands head and shoulders above his peers, not in physical height, but in maturity. Before answering Susan thinks carefully how to direct him. While she's pondering his request he waits patiently by her side. Susan can hear him breathing, smell his manliness, sense his seriousness. She doubts that he has a girlfriend. Most of the girls at school are too frivolous for a boy of his sensibilities. "Ah," Susan repeats, striking upon an idea. "I'll be meeting with his parents later. Mr. Musgrove is arranging for them to come in. How be I talk to you after meeting with them? Then I'll have a better sense of their reaction to this business."

Herbie pulls his lips in a slight smile. "All right, Miss Borden."

"Check with me before you leave today."

"I will."

Herbie's little smile flatters his face and spreads his air of confidence with enough humility to make him very appealing. That there are no girls here falling all over him is their loss, Susan thinks. Sensing a kerfuffle at the classroom door she rises to attend to the commotion. There she finds Carl Musgrove greeting the students who rush to him vying for his attention. He laughs and bellows, "Excuse me, students. I need to have a private word with your teacher."

Susan steps through the gathered crowd into the hallway and closes the door behind her. "As you can tell, they're not in the mood for studying. We've been having quite the chat," she says, feeling slightly guilty for having to explain her lapse from teaching, but knowing rationally that Carl Musgrove is not likely to judge her harshly. In fact, he's more likely to approve of her heeding the needs of her students who are emotionally charged.

"I may have to call a school assembly later," he says. "To stop the rumour mill. Mr. and Mrs. Williams are on their way. I've arranged to have Mr. Singh cover your class."

Gathering herself together Susan stands tall. "Oh, so soon?" she asks. "Okay. I'll get the students started on their projects so they're working when he comes."

"We've arranged to meet in M.M.'s office." Carl nods, a gesture meant to seek confirmation and when Susan returns his nod Carl adds, "See you there then."

Clapping her hands loudly Susan enters the room. "Alright class." She has their attention. "I have to go to Mr. Musgrove's office now. Mr. Singh is on his way to cover for me." There's another communal groan. Putting her hands on her hips Susan addresses the students with a stern demeanor. "So here's what you're going to start working on."

When Mr. Singh arrives and is firmly in control Susan leaves. Then she enters the hall and again closes the door behind her, recalling as she turns the doorknob Carl's reference to Mahala Mulrain as M.M. If Mahala Mulrain married Carl Musgrove and took his surname she'd remain M.M. It would be bold of her to point this out to him, and simply adolescent to point it out to her, but Susan indulges the thought anyway. What's a bit of fantasy? Nothing more than projection, although it feels trivial and at their expense which is disrespectful, but she figures what they don't hear won't hurt them. She means them no harm. Susan recognizes it's that distinction that is so hard to get teenagers to understand. No harm intended as in mockery which is very much intentional jeering at someone else's expense. The young are precocious and want to expose their infatuations and are baffled when that exposure leads to mockery. How often has she had to counsel her students to juggle their emotions to fit them into a perspective that allows them to address other demands, like schoolwork?

Mahala is not in her room, but the door is open. Inside Susan can see out the window. Outside Guy and Celianne are walking toward the building. They look so dejected Susan's heart aches for them. Celianne is watching her feet with every step she takes. She is wearing flip-flops and her pale rimmed heels spread over the backs of the rubber soles. Guy holds his head high. He is wearing an old, faded turquiose T-shirt, much like the colour of the ocean on a cloudy day. Turning at the sound of Muhala entering Susan gestures outside with her head. "Here they come," she says.

Mahala comes over to Susan to stand beside her. "This is not going to be easy," she says.

"No," Susan says. "It never is when there's trouble." When Tijean's parents disappear from view Susan folds her arms under her bosom, ready to start talking serious business.

"You know," Mahala says in a confidential tone. "My parents are just the opposite of Tijean's."

Susan furrows her brow. "How do you mean?" Susan doesn't disbelieve her colleague. In fact, she can guess that Mahala's parents were ambitious for their daughter.

"They wanted me to leave the islands. For the life of them they couldn't understand why I wanted to come back here to work after I'd got myself a good education."

Mahala turns her nutmeg eyes on Susan. They show no expression, but her mouth does. It's wide open, revealing a healthy and attractive smile. "Well, I can understand why they wouldn't want you to return to Middle Caicos, but where did they expect you to go?"

"England. They told me to stay there, where I was educated." Mahala shakes her head at the memory. "You wouldn't believe the rows we had."

"Really?" Susan tries to picture Mahala shouting, but the image fades instantly.

Mahala cocks her small head. "Yes. My parents don't think much of those who stay on the islands. They think all the opportunity is elsewhere."

"Have they been to England?"

"No, never. They couldn't afford to go. They've worked hard all their lives and never been anywhere. Always here. Any money they had went to educate me and my sister."

"Where is she? Your sister?"

Mahala lifts her thin neck. "She's in the States. She likes it there. She says she's never coming back here."

"Don't your parents miss her?"

"Yes, and no. They're stoic. I don't think they feel that they've sacrificed anything by being parted from their oldest daughter. They accept it." Again Mahala shakes her head. "My grandmother says I'm the loyal one."

Susan holds the young woman's gaze feeling a tenderness pass between them. Mahala's confided a secret about a family feud that in another context would be too much information. In trusting Susan, she's seeking her reaction, knowing the older woman will offer comfort, not censorship. Susan recognizes she possesses a gift for listening as people often share their confidences with her. She must project an open air of tolerance. It's what makes her a good counsellor. She has to remind herself of that gift as a virtue and not beat up on herself over what's happening with Tijean.

There's a stirring at the office door and Carl Musgrove enters ahead of Guy followed by Celianne. They, too, look like they need comforting, but Susan senses that any attempt on her part to offer the sentiment won't be easily accepted by this proud pair. Besides, Carl is handling the affair and she must defer to his leadership. Under his capable direction they take their seats and listen to him paraphrase their purpose (and here Carl nods to Mahala and Susan acknowledging the roles the two women play for the well being of their son) for calling the couple to the school and offering whatever help they can give to assist them with Tijean. Susan finds Carl's choice of wording acutely politically correct, yet somehow totally sincere. He is genuine, a public servant willing to serve his community.

Susan feels the outsider in this round of talk. It's not just that she's the lone white face. It's more that the others have their own system despite having adopted a European model for schooling. Education is the construct. Family is the culture. It's like the separation of church and state. Education is adopted and applied. Family is a given: how they live; what they believe. And as every educator knows, it's what the student brings to the classroom. Although she's familiar with the system, she's not part of the family.

"It's too late for your help now," Celianne says. "You should have made him learn." Here she looks at Susan as if blaming her for her son's inability. Yet she doesn't get this past Carl Musgrove.

"You know, Mrs. Williams, we offered Tijean as many services as we have here to support him in succeeding. He has many learning difficulties to overcome before he can progress."

Celianne merely harumphs while her husband abandons his natural passivity to say that Tijean always gave them trouble at home about school because all he ever wanted to do was go diving. "He say school boring. I know his mother think you should have made him do his work, but Tijean, he a hard one to make do anything he not want to do."

The mood in the office shifts from the pragmatism of the bureaucrats to the passivity of the parents. Susan cannot accept that these adults will relinquish their responsibility, will yield to the willfulness of youthful rebellion. "I'm sorry," she says, barely concealing her impatience, "but the point here is what he wants to do."

"That no good," Guy mutters.

Mahala rises to the occasion. "What Tijean wants to do is good. He is motivated."

Again Celianne harumphs, a gesture that sends Susan over-the-top. "You're so small-minded."

"What Ms Borden means," Carl interjects, "is that we must put ourselves in Tijean's shoes. Try to think like he does."

"He not smart enough to think right," Celianne says.

In imitation of his younger role model, Guy says, "What his mother mean is that Tijean, he too young to think for himself."

Susan burns inside, but recognizing that she's already over-stepped her bounds, remains silent. She averts her eyes from Tijean's parents as she knows her look will tell them her opinion of their stand. What she wants to say is exactly what Carl expresses. Why, oh why, can't she remain level-headed instead of insulting people? She knows she'd make a terrible head mistress. These parents have struggled with a problem they don't understand. She's tried her best to be understanding. Guy always speaks well of the school and her role as his son's teacher. In his Caribbean dialect Guy tries to navigate the miasma that is an imposed and unfamiliar system. It's frustrating for all parties.

"Do you think he will return home?" Carl asks.

Here's the other issue, Susan thinks, and says aloud, "Aren't you worried about where he's gone? What's happened to him?"

"He gone away," Celianne says, keeping her eyes on the wall behind Susan. "He leave for good. I know that's what he think of doing for some time, now. On that boat making his plans."

Carl looks from the mother to the father as if seeking confirmation. "I understand you must be terribly worried?"

Guy only shrugs.

"Well, we won't drop his name from our register, Mr. and Mrs. Williams. If he returns home, he can return to school. We won't give up on him yet."

"Thank you, Mr. Musgrove," Guy says looking to his wife who now stands. He follows her out the door.

"Let me see you out," Carl says, following the despondent parents.

The two women are left alone in an atmosphere heavy with the unresolved. "Well, that could have gone better," Susan says. "I can't believe their attitude."

"No."

"I should have bitten my tongue."

"No, someone needed to say it. Don't be hard on yourself."

Susan sighs heavily and restores her posture to an upright position. "Now I've offended them. How will I face them back at the resort?"

"Don't even apologize. They have to understand that we had their son's best interest in mind. What do you think?" Mahala asks. "Will he come home?"

"I don't know," Susan says. Yet she does. She fully senses the flight of a fugitive, someone who lived through the immediacy of his school days barely tolerating the experience by holding on to the hope that if he could wait it out the opportunity would come when he could leave. Then all the waiting and dreaming would be worthwhile when he tasted liberty.

"Do you think any of the students know where he went?"

"No," Susan says, thinking about Caroline who is too young to redeem a wayward boyfriend. Celianne didn't mention her so Susan doesn't, either. Besides, even if Tijean does eventually return home, he won't be the same boy who left. He'll grow up on a different island, another country, maybe a foreign continent and return experienced in ways the others may not fathom. Because Tijean will have missed what his friends get to share he'll always remain an outsider.

"I just thought they might have said."

"Oh, they had lots to say." Susan shakes her head in a manner implying the intense interest of teens in each others' behaviour. "They're like any group of juveniles," she says before thinking of earlier social primates who wouldn't survive without their grooming rituals.

Mahala furrows her brow, and her skin creases in tight wrinkles. "How do you mean?"

Susan laughs, more at herself for revealing her far-fetched thought than at the situation she's comparing. "Oh, you know, the social whirl? Even animals are just as sophisticated in their social world as we are. When you read studies on their small groups, how they live together, they really do resemble groups of girls and boys."

Mahala nods. "Granted. All that intense grooming."

"Yes," Susan says, "And in teenagers, angst relieved by the mild euphoria of grooming."

Mahala laughs. "Their opiate. Are we onto something here?"

"Nothing that the social scientists haven't studied."

"I took a course on primate behaviour," Mahala says. "But what fascinated me most were the courses on kinship. Do you know about the Donner Party wagon train?"

"No," Susan says.

"The Donner Party wagon train set out in the mid 1800's to settle the West and, although there were many fit young men among their party, they didn't have the same survival rate as others were deemed weaker and when they looked at those who did survive the journey, they discovered that the ones with close family ties, other relatives traveling with them, were better able to cope."

"Really?"

"There have been many studies confirming that finding," Mahala says.

"I believe you," Susan says. "Is that what convinced you to return to the islands?"

"Yes."

The bell rings. Susan looks up at the clock. "That's the end of my double home room period."

"How time flies when you're having fun?"

Susan feels a slight discomfort at Mahala's comment that borders on cynicism. It seems unlike her, and unnecessary given the circumstances, yet probably meant innocently. "I'll leave you to your work, then." On her way out the door Susan carries her awkwardness with her like a bundle of sticks on her back. An antiquated weight, Susan thinks, like in a fairy tale with themes of poverty and ostracism. Those points make her aware that it isn't just Mahala conjuring this memory with her insensitive comment. It's also seeing Tijean's parents here, in a school setting where they appeared ill-at-ease. Seeing them in such a light makes Susan realize that, although she cannot identify with them, her heart still aches for them with the kind of empathy she'd feel for characters in a story. Somehow that little bit of sympathy makes her heart soar for discovering a connection between storytelling and the most human of emotions. She's looking at her feet as she walks down the hall thinking how everyone has a story to tell. Already she's conjuring adventures for Tijean and hopes that one day she'll be able to hear his tales. In the hall near her classroom she sees a group of girls huddled by their lockers. They're ego-bound, so engaged in their conversation they don't even notice Susan's presence, but overhearing them speak of Caroline, Susan's mind races to the other Susans in her senior public school class. She's back in her childhood where there were three Susans. One was known as Susie, the other simply Sue. Only she kept her full name – Susan. One day Sue made overtures to befriend her. Susan remembers being flattered by the other girl's attention, although befuddled as Sue was part of an in-crowd who ran wild in the streets and went to house parties that Susan didn't attend. Lois was Sue's best friend. When Sue invited them both to her house Susan should have been suspicious, but she wasn't sophisticated in the ways of girls and their intended meanness to each other. Lois specifically asked Susan to ride over to her neighbourhood on her bicycle to get her so they could go to Sue's house together which Susan did, only to find herself surrounded by a group of jeering boys from whom she escaped in a panic. But when she fled up Lois's driveway no one answered the door to her frantic knocks and bell ringing. Then she noticed a rustling of curtains at the bay window. That movement made her realize she'd been tricked into coming so Lois and Sue could witness her torment. That's when she learned there's a price to pay for being more studious than the others, but what she also learned was to stop envying the likes of Sue and Lois. Once she overcame her embarrassment and humiliation she was stronger, like someone who's passed a Biblical test.

Herbie is standing at her classroom door. "How did it go with Mr. Singh?" she asks.

"Alright, Miss. Did Mr. and Mrs. Williams come?"

Then Susan remembers what Herbie asked earlier. "Yes, Herbie. They are resigned to the fact that Tijean's left the island for good."

Herbie shakes his head. "Maybe that's for the best."

"Yes," Susan says, marveling at this young man's maturity. Was she so mature at sixteen? She recognizes that it's this characteristic that sets him apart from his classmates. Yes, she repeats in her head. He's emotionally mature, but totally lacking sophistication in the ways of others his age, as often their fun excludes him.

At the end of the day Susan leaves early, relieved that she has no obligations to supervise students or meet with her colleagues. As she straps her briefcase onto the carriage over the wheel of her moped she shakes the knot out of the back of her neck. In some respects it's been a long day. Gently she drops her head back and lifts her shoulders to her ears, working out the tension in her body. These movements offer enough relief to free her mind and she chuckles to herself. Her mother tells her she's too old to be driving around on a moped, only she doesn't use the British word. Her mother says "scooter". Doris never rode a pedal bicycle let alone a motorized one. Susan's sister, Sandra, thinks she's a bad role model for her children and has strictly forbidden them to operate a vehicle that doesn't have a roof over the driver's seat. When his mother announced that rule Susan's nephew, Kit, asked whether his mother intended that they couldn't drive a convertible or a car with the sunroof open. Sandra accused her son of being impossibly logical and asked him if he ever thought of joining the legal profession. When Susan suggested that having a lawyer in the family might prove advantageous to them all, Sandra shot darts at her while Kit reassured his mother that he never intended to do anything so practical as turn into a lawyer. Sandra seemed to blame Susan for that attitude, too. Now Susan holds her helmet with both hands while musing on why she readily takes the blame. It seems she's been groomed for the part. Shaking her head before fitting the plastic safety device over her skull she tells herself that she must rid herself of that habit. Maybe she's not too old to ride a scooter, but she is too old to be always taking the blame.

Straddling the seat Susan scans the panoramic view before starting the engine. Down the hill is the typical scrub brush that covers this island. It's a view she never tires of, nature as solace. The weather is glorious. Right now it's probably snowing across most of North America. Her mother and sister constantly complain about the weather, yet refuse to even consider moving to a warmer climate. They stay with what they know. Home is where the heart is. A platitude, Susan acknowledges, but in the case of her female relatives, the truth. An unsettling distraction accompanies Susan's meditation. Yes, this is paradise, but for how long? She pushes her foot aggressively on the pedal to dispel her weird doubts. With the hum of the motor sending a low vibration through her spine she exits the parking lot, but instead of continuing along the road out of Bottle Creek leading to the resort, Susan decides to take a detour at Major Hill to visit her friend, Leila.

Outside her pink stucco cottage Leila is watering the flowers in the window boxes. At the sound of the moped she drops the watering can, letting it hang at her side in her right hand, and with her left, shades her eyes. She's wearing long sleeves of a flimsy material to keep out the sun.

Susan turns off the motor and dismounts. "I've come for a visit," she says as she lifts off her helmet and shakes out her long, herbal-tinted, brunette hair.

Leila drops her arm and blinks her blue eyes into the sunlight. "What a pleasant surprise."

"It's been a long day," Susan says spreading her forearms in defeat. "Taxing." She takes note that Leila seems very relaxed, unlike herself who must appear overwrought, a condition that makes her think of damsels in distress in nineteenth-century novels.

"Come in. We can sit on the patio."

Susan follows Leila into the house. There's a couple coming down the stairs whom Leila introduces as Stan and Marie Kowalchuk from Chicago who are staying for the week.

Susan shakes their proffered hands. "Hope you're enjoying your visit to the islands?"

"Why, yes," Stan says effusively with a mid-western drawl.

"It's a little bit of paradise, isn't it?" Marie says in an accent distinct from her husband's, more colonial with its crisp, sharply enunciated, vowels.

"You could say that," Susan says by way of agreement.

Stan addresses Leila. "Don't know when we'll be back, but we have our keys."

"Alright then. Enjoy your evening." In the kitchen Leila picks a drink out of the fridge and displays the curvy, green bottle to Susan. "I have a few varieties. This one's elderflower," she says, showing the label on the front.

Susan takes the drink and reads the label. "Bottle Green." Curious, she looks inside the opened fridge door at the selection on the shelves. Reading the label again on the one in her hand she twists the cap. "Okay, I'll try this flavour," she says.

"Here, let me," Leila says producing a bottle opener. Then she offers Susan a glass.

Susan takes a sip. "Um," she says in a pleased tone. "A little sweet."

Outside they sit under the shade of an overhanging arbor of brilliant pink bougainvillea. "Are Stan and Marie the only guests you have this weekend?"

"No, another couple is due to arrive today."

"Ah," Susan says. "I was wondering if you were free to come to dinner?"

Cocking her chin in Susan's direction Leila laughs out loud. "Would I? I've been waiting for weeks to meet Marcel. Ever since he arrived on your doorstep." There's a glitter of the temptress in her eyes. "His reputation precedes him."

"Really?" Now it's Susan's turn to laugh aloud. "Tell me. What do you know about Marcel?"

"That he's rich. That he's handsome. That he's a flirt, in the nicest way. A man who loves women. And he's at that age, you know, been around the block, but still young. My age."

"Oh," Susan says. "But he worked at Club Med?" She's wondering about the claim that he's rich. Susan guesses that Marcel must be in his late thirties or early forties.

Leila coyly shakes her head. "So?"

Susan wonders at Leila's cryptic attitude. Marcel came to the resort on North Caicos after working a short period on the island of Provo. "Well, I see," she says.

"I'm not too sure you do. You know, Susan, he is quite the catch?"

"Granted, he's a charmer." Susan wonders about Leila's use of the term "quite a catch". Is her young friend that conniving, or is Susan's distaste of the term simply a generational difference between two women with twenty years separating them.

"Oh, he's more than that," Leila says in a voice that's turned serious.

Susan feels she's gone from having a girl's talk to a meeting with her bank manager. Of course, she never understands what her bank manager is telling her anymore than she understands what Leila is implying about Marcel.

Leila continues. "Do you know about his family?"

"No." Susan again recognizes that she is out of it, like she was with Tijean and Caroline.

"They're rich, like landed gentry. Have an estate in southern France where the family holidays."

"I didn't know that." Though Susan does know about that class of family from Mavis Gallant's short stories. Leila wouldn't know Mavis Gallant. Leila's American. Mavis

Gallant is an expat Canadian who lives and writes in Paris, like Hemingway and that earlier generation of writing giants. "I wonder how they got rich?"

"Coffee."

Susan becomes alert at the ring of that single word. In her mind she sings. "Black coffee."

"Sugar cane, the export trade. This was generations ago and that was just the beginning."

"Not nouveau riche, then?" Susan asks deliberately speaking the French in her educated accent. "A generation to earn, a generation to enjoy, a generation to spend." Though, Susan thinks, Marcel seems to be one of a generation to enjoy. If his family is still enjoying the wealth from earlier gains, then there have been many generations to accumulate. No need for him to work in an office in Paris or need to stick with a job at Club Med. No need to remain a cook at a resort, either, Susan thinks as she wonders how long he will stick with his job at the resort. "So, Marcel's a trust-fund kid?"

"He's hardly a kid, Susan."

"No, I didn't mean that," Susan says, recognizing again she's using a term that Leila mightn't know. "In the States what do you call the generation living off family money?"

"President."

Susan guffaws while leaning forward. "Good one," she says righting herself. Her mood switches back to the serious.

She mustn't hold a grudge or form any prejudice against a person like Marcel simply because he's turned out to be independently wealthy. "So is Marcel slumming it with us? I wonder how long he'll stay at the resort working as a cook for Ian."

"You'll have to ask Ian that," Leila says.

"Do you know something I don't?" Susan is suddenly suspicious. This morning as she was leaving for work Ian told her he was going to see his lawyer today. Why did he do that? There wasn't time to ask. She's been so preoccupied with Tijean she forgot about Ian and his pressing business. Leila is silently sipping her drink. She's not going to tell. Susan feels no urgency to know. In fact, she feels lethargic. It's as if this day has given her too much to think about so to inquire further is beyond her mental capacity. Her mind is mired in the problem at work. "Have you ever used a Ouija Board?"

Another question, but this one receives an answer.

"In college a bunch of us girls did. Why?"

"I was thinking today of some girls I went to school with who used to use a Ouija Board to predict who they were going to date and marry. I thought they were silly. I suppose I didn't hide from them how I felt. They took their revenge on me."

"For being superior?"

Susan frowns at Leila's assumption. "I guess that's how I appeared. Superior. When actually I just didn't belong.

45

I certainly didn't feel like I fitted into their group. I didn't want to, not really, so maybe I did treat them as inferior. Only, I suppose I wanted to be popular, like them. I envied them that, their popularity, their society, their engagements, their self-absorption. Whereas I was always studious, thinking, watching, not joining in. Yet I still wanted to feel like I belonged."

"Don't we all?"

Yes, Susan thinks. Yes we do.

In a gesture more fitting to a reversal of roles, Leila pats Susan's forearm with the palm of her hand. "You're so lucky to have Ian."

Sensing the touch on her skin as light as the feet of a bird Susan smiles while reflecting on her partnership with Ian, an expat like her from Canada.

"What about that young boy who ran away?" Leila asks.

"Tijean?"

"I guess you know him?"

Susan shakes her head to dispel the reverie of her relationship with Ian. "Yes," she says. "He's a student of mine. Was." She keeps her tone neutral, consciously not wanting to blame Tijean for all his problems. Again she thinks of Mavis Gallant. Her characters never fitted in, yet the writer didn't pass judgment on them. It was as if things just happened to them, events led them along by the nose. Yet, for Tijean, events and people seemed to conspire to eject him from home and school. "His parents aren't helpful," Susan says. There, she's done it again. Passed judgment. She knows she's being severe. It took so much for her to accommodate him. Can't she understand what his parents must have experienced? "A difficult student, I might add."

"I know the type."

"Do you?" Susan asks.

"Remember, I was a social worker in Florida where the majority of immigrants land, illegal ones, refugees from Cuba."

"Of course. They come with problems."

"And make problems." Leila gulps her drink. "It was too much. I remember once being phoned by a frantic school principal. A student was sitting in class in shock. His father had been murdered the previous night at his restaurant. They lived above it. Yet, the next morning, his family sent him to school. I couldn't help. What could I do? I was too busy doing grief counseling at a local high school where there'd been a fatal stabbing. Carlos Vasos. I'll never forget Carlos. He was an innocent victim. A bystander trying to help in a fight. The guy who stabbed him was violent. He'd only just returned to school after a month-long expulsion. Fat lot of good that did him."

Susan joins Leila in her bitter silence. She remembers the time the grief counseling team came to her high school. A student had had a fatal accident on the ski hill running a race over the weekend. Not quite on a par with Leila's experience. Although such violence did happen in Canadian schools, with more and more frequency. Susan shudders at the thought of what she's heard about situations there from her sister and the newspapers that sometimes reach them. Coming back to the present she lets those distant problems fade from her mind. They are a long way from the problem of Tijean.

"Apparently he left on the dive boat last night. It was making some nocturnal trip to Provo to pick up supplies. His parents don't think he'll come back. They think he's gone for good. I wonder when the boat will return?"

"Let's see." Leila rises, goes indoors and returns with a pair of binoculars.

Susan follows Leila. "I like how you've landscaped your garden," she says. There's comfort in looking at greenery, particularly the many variety of trees: flame, almond. They offer a respite from her worries about students like Tijean. Maybe she needs to get away, abandon the island, leave her problems to others to solve like younger teachers?

"It's small," Leila says by way of apology. Both women duck under the turgid leaves of the branches of a tree. "This is a lignum vitae, a tree native to the islands."

"It's beautiful," Susan says, brushing her nose against the bunches of purple blossoms.

"It can grow to a remarkable age, living up to a thousand years. As well as having an aesthetic value, these native trees have a practical use in preventing erosion, something I need on this property. Let me show you this," Leila says.

Susan bends beside Leila at the edge of the young woman's cultivated flower garden. Under the shade of the tree is a plant less than a foot tall with dark green mottled leaves. Following Leila's lead Susan examines the flowers that grow off the stem that has thorns like roses but petals like delicate snap dragons. "What is it?" she asks.

"Monk orchid," Leila says. "We have them in Florida, too."

"They're an orchid? I never would have guessed," Susan says.

"This one was rescued. They were growing wild close to the edge of a side road that a developer was clearing to widen. Margaret Jones found them uprooted."

"The journalist?"

"Yes, her."

"I remember reading about that. Did you help, then, in rescuing them?"

Leila smiles as she nods in the affirmative.

"Good for you," Susan says.

Leila rises. A few feet beyond the patio her property ends. The house is situated on a high point from where they can see Bay Cay. Raising the glasses Leila peers in the direction of Spanish Point. "If I'm not mistaken," she says, handing the binoculars to Susan, "There was a boat there earlier but I don't see it now. Maybe it's gone to Sandy Point."

Susan looks through the lenses and adjusts the focus while scanning the water until the view settles on the farthest point. "You could be right," she says. Handing the glasses back to Leila she turns and makes a hasty retreat. "I must go. If I find them there I'll see what they know."

"Buenas noches!" Leila calls in her accomplished Spanish accent.

When Susan gets to the dock and stops the motor a familiar sound reaches her. The piercing shrill of gulls is primordial and common to any ocean shoreline or large body of water. Susan sits spread-eagled, her legs splayed on either side of the moped, her feet firmly on the ground balancing her body and the machine, her arms open with her hands gripping the handlebars. Overhead the fat birds swoop and glide. Their sight and sound conjure a nomadic urge to join in that powerful desire to be somewhere else. Isn't that what she's investigating? Isn't that why she's here? Not just here, on this waterway, but here on these islands? These birds call up that longing. They take to the air and land on the earth and the sea, like spirited travelers satisfying the desire to be elsewhere, to experience flight and movement, to land and explore. Her own reverie comes to an end as she swerves to avoid the pot holes. Following the old coastal road she rides through Whitby, past Whitby Haven and the resort, then slows down to wind her way down to the shore. At the harbour she sees a boat docked. She no sooner stops when Guy walks down the gangplank. "Hello," she calls through the sea air while examining his facial features for any resentment he may feel, but he isn't the parent to harbour a grudge. That's more Celianne's personality.

Guy walks toward her. "Miss Susan."

"Any word?" Susan asks, still holding her position on her scooter.

A few feet before reaching her Guy stops and shuffles his feet in place, an act that disturbs the dry sand. Small puffs of dust clouds cover his shoes. "Yes. Tijean gone. He ain't never coming back."

Susan examines the top of his bent head. His hair is matted tightly and underneath the black frizz his bare scalp peaks between the knotted curls. "So he was on the boat?"

"Yes, Miss Susan."

Susan closes her eyes, not just at the confirming news, but at the tone this grown man uses with her, as if he, the father, is her pupil, too. "So he went on this boat?"

"Yes. Last night."

Now Susan feels exasperated. Will she have to pry every detail from his mouth, bit by bit? Can he not offer her some background information? She's imagined whole stories for his boy. What is the father thinking? "Where did they leave him?"

"Provo."

That's short and sweet and highly anticipated. Where else but the main island? "He didn't tell them where he was going?"

"No." Guy turns away from her. "I go now. Pick up Celianne."

Watching him saunter to his taxi Susan feels her impatience with Guy evaporate as quickly as the sweat on her forehead dries when the trade winds touch her skin after removing her helmet. What's the point of being angry, or even impatient, with him? He's doing his best; he's done his best and not only hasn't he reaped many rewards, his son's abandoned him.

Susan doesn't budge from her splayed position on the moped, but remains an observer, now focusing her attention on the activity on the dive boat where a couple of wiry men are moving like shadow puppets. Were these men role models for Tijean? She sits immobilized. How this inertia returns to sap her motor strength and leave her pensive. It's as if her brain is short circuiting out of the present and into the past for now a memory from her childhood returns. Susan recollects how Sandra resented her big sister always getting a brand new bicycle that then got passed down to her. Sandra complained she only rode on second-hand bikes while Susan got to ride on one that was gleaming clean with no scratches. It wasn't fair, but their father always reminded them that Sandra was right. Life wasn't fair and they should never expect it to be otherwise. Then he'd defend his position by saying that Susan rode more than Sandra. It was true. Susan would ride blocks to go to school, the park, the swimming pool, the library. Sandra preferred to get rides with her friends in their mothers' cars for by then families had second cars unlike her family since their mother wouldn't learn to drive. Susan continues to gaze at the busy men on the boat but she doesn't actually see them. Instead she sees CCM bikes in brilliant colours: red, blue, cherry – their fenders wide and ribbed, their tires patterned with deep treads, their chrome frames polished. Another world, another time, another life. It's good she's wearing sunglasses because tears start smarting her eyes. "Get a grip," she tells herself. These sweeping emotions leave her acutely aware of loss – her past, her family, her youth. It's a lonely and sad feeling. Only old age ahead. That awareness leaves her feeling ridiculous as she guns the gas to start the moped while looking down on the guano-spotted pier.

The vibration of the vehicle shakes her melancholy and she rides the coastal road to the resort with concentration. Making the turn off the main road she finds Ian standing beside Guy and Celianne on the path. By the looks on all three faces she guesses they are talking about the missing son. She cuts the engine and dismounts. As she removes her helmet Susan sees that Celianne is already inside the car. She must have run there at the sight of Susan's arrival. Ian and Guy continue talking in low tones. When she approaches the men she hears Guy's noisy breathing, each exhalation a reflexive blow through two small nostrils at the tip of his wide nose, each inhalation an automatic gasp of the lungs heaving his broad chest against his tight shirt. She hopes he's not going to suffer a heart attack over the stress of his son's disappearance.

"Well, he can't have gone far."

Overhearing Ian's appeasing response fills Susan with shame as she knows differently. She knows Tijean has indeed gone far. She looks down to the ground and as she does she sees Guy has his shoes on the wrong feet. Imagine the hurry he was in chasing after his son that he dressed so haphazardly.

"His mother think different."

Susan looks into Guy's eyes. Behind the black colour they appear deeply worried, so much frenzied activity on such a dark palette. His chest still heaves defining the solid padding of muscle. "Celianne, she think he leaving the island for good."

"But why would he do that?"

Again Susan turns away from Ian's innocence.

"He not happy." Guy lowers his head.

Susan feels a compulsion to interject her own desperate rationalizing. "Well, maybe not in school, but he loves it here – the ocean, the beach, diving."

"That the problem." Guy turns and saunters away to the driver's door of the taxi.

Catching up with Guy Susan touches his forearm. "I don't understand. Tell me. What is the problem?"

Guy continues at the pace of a resigned plodder unaware of how awkwardly he steps in the soles of his mismatched shoes. "The diving."

"But how can that be a problem? He's an excellent diver."

"Yes. He good at that. But not at school. We want him to get an education."

Susan feels a spring of energy to argue with this philistine. "He can. In diving."

"No, not that. A real education." Now Guy's eyes turn to the ground as if he's digging deeper.

None of this surprises Susan. Tijean's parents wouldn't think of learning to dive as getting a real education. She must convince them. Didn't Mahala say that he could? Just this morning she said that to Susan. But did anyone say it to them, to the parents? They seem so full of shame. Susan can't help but feel empathy for them. They are like the dispossessed. Her anger with them melts as she regains her role as educator. The parents, too, need educating. "But he can. At the Marine Centre."

Guy shakes his head. "No. We want him to get a degree. Not be like us with no education. He says it just a piece of paper. He don't understand how important it is. That piece of paper. It like having citizenship papers in the right country. It a ticket."

"But he can earn a diploma in marine studies and use his diving skills."

"That a waste of money."

"No, not for someone like Tijean. He's not cut out to be a lawyer or accountant, or even a teacher. He's not an easy academic. You know how much extra help he receives? But he's bright. He can do it. He can pass those courses. I know they'll accommodate him. And he's talented. He's interested in the sea."

"Yeah, in treasure. Like some pirate."

Susan watches Guy get into the driver's side of his taxi and start the engine. She leans into the open window. "Please, we need to talk about this."

Guy moves his head back in skepticism.

Without moving her head to acknowledge Susan's presence, Celianne speaks. "It too late."

Consumed by the confusion of Tijean Susan stands immobile for what seems minutes. Then she feels Ian's arm around her shoulders. "It's heartbreaking, eh?"

"I feel like a failure." Why oh why oh why hasn't she counseled him about attending the marine centre? It's no surprise that Guy and Celianne don't understand the future prospects of a diving career. They think in terms of the traditional professions that are secure and bring prominence to a family member. Many belongers are in education, politics, the law, as well as architecture and business now that there's a boom in development on the islands. Parents can feel proud that their offspring are filling such roles. The Williamses would not understand that even to be a professional diver in a career outside piracy or treasure hunting one needs to study the sciences of the ocean. Susan inhales deeply, smelling the briny air. Beyond the senses there's science, a whole world to explore, to comprehend, to preserve. How can she tell them to encourage their son in this direction knowing that even these studies would challenge his academic skills? Even at the Marine Center he'd need support.

"Hey, it's not your fault." Ian kisses the top of her head.

"Leila says I'm lucky to have you, and she's right."

"I agree."

Smiling at one another they offer their puckered lips in a kiss.

"I invited Leila to dinner tonight. She's very keen to meet Marcel."

"Is she, now? Let me guess. She's heard he's rich."

"Something I've just learned."

Turning Susan around, Ian looks into her face. "You look exhausted."

"I am. Maybe a swim will refresh me."

"Sounds like a good idea."

In her room Susan changes quickly. It is her own room, her private space for working and sleeping, separate from Ian's rooms which are attached to his office. At the pool she raises her hand, returning Ian's greeting from across the patio. Dropping her towel Susan dives into the deep end. Underwater she opens her eyes to the brilliant turquoise. She could be the Greek Goddess Hera renewing her virginity in the magical waters of a spring. Breaking the surface of the pool the goddess spews the chlorinated water from her mouth. Then she swims across the pool to the shallow end where she turns and, in a spread-eagle pose, falls onto her back to float to the middle of the pool.

Ian is still on the patio, probably playing lifeguard to her whim. He's an attractive man. Susan can feel proud that he's hers. How lucky she is to be here floating under this clear blue sky with a man like Ian watching over her.

Rolling over Susan starts into a crawl, back and forth, back and forth. In the suspension of that habitual physical exercise her mind relaxes and roams. She remembers the swimming lessons at the neighbourhood pool when she was a girl and felt awkward in her budding body. Everything showed through her junior swimsuit, and to add to the shame, she overheard her mother telling another mother that she'd have to take her eldest daughter shopping for a swimsuit with inserts. Sound, especially voices, echoed in the concrete changing room. Susan was standing in the shower stall, a common space with a few nozzles poking out of the wall, not like the shower heads of today with multiple holes circling the nozzle. At the time only a single spray at the end of a pipe. The water nearly hurt when it hit her back and she clamped her arms around her shoulders to protect her sensitive, growing breasts. Her new bathing suit was a Speedo, and she so liked the label, she rose to the challenge of its nomenclature, practicing lengths until she could roll over smoothly and stay within the lane. She won a few heats, earning her a number of ribbons, and for the few races she entered and won, some trophies that her mother kept. Now they are stored in boxes in Sandra's basement.

When she pulls herself out of the pool Susan is breathing heavily from the exertion of the swim. Patting her exposed skin dry with the towel Susan wraps it around her waist and folds the corners across each other, tucking in the ends. She does this knowing it won't hold but not knowing how else to tie it. The palm of her open hand rests on her stomach. Despite the fact that she has never born children she has a protruding stomach. Also, despite the fact that she swims regularly her stomach doesn't lie flat. Somehow this doesn't seem fair. "Life isn't fair," she hears her father's voice admonishing. Usually he was speaking to Sandra when he made that comment. Sandra was a whiner as a child.

Her head droops, not in exhaustion from the swim, but in weariness of the failure of people. They all need forgiveness for their mistakes. Susan notices that her toes are curled around the thongs of her flip-flops, clutching the loose footwear so tightly she must think she's falling. She smiles remembering Guy's mismatched shoes then gathers another memory to her consciousness. At their father's funeral her sister pointed out to her son, Kit, that he had his shoes on the wrong feet. Kit, short for Christopher, a name he was never called, looked down and declared that there was nothing wrong.

"These are my feet." They'd howled with laughter, embarrassing the boy and angering their mother, Doris, who thought her daughters had totally lost all sense of decorum. Weren't they supposed to be grieving their father? Susan had hugged her nephew asking his forgiveness and hiding her laugh tears behind his head. Now Susan breathes slowly remembering her relative. How different Kit is from the likes of Tijean. Her nephew studies philosophy, a real academic. And where will he find work?

Susan bows her head low, defeated by the weight of the irrational exchange. A waste of money to spend it on diving, but she knows this couple. They would make any sacrifice for their son's education. They hunger greedily for their son's accomplishment. Yet Tijean is no Kit. Her nephew earns scholarships that offset the exorbitant costs of studying abroad, next year in Malta. Susan knows the Williamses don't think of such freedom for Tijean. They picture him on the island doing them proud, not at some esoteric university cramming his head full of conjecture and theory.

Taking a deep breath Susan fills her lungs and lifts her head to catch the rays of sunshine full of tropical warmth. Tijean is built like his father with a great bulging chest that fills easily with oxygen. For such a boy there is promise of a full life here on the islands. He belongs. Surely his parents haven't driven him away with their unrealistic expectations? Where would he go? He's simply taken off at full speed to put some distance between himself and his family. He's probably sitting on a cliff looking out over the ocean wishing he were somewhere else or hiding in the salt marsh brooding like an abandoned animal. He'll return before the weekend's over. Then Susan will have the opportunity to speak to him privately and to his special education teacher, Mahala, so they can arrange a better future for him.

Once when she was a child she'd run away, although only as far as the hillside that overlooked the block of houses where her family lived. Before leaving the house she'd made herself a peanut butter sandwich. Such foresight while engaged in an act of fury. And she had been furious with her mother for laughing at a neighbour. This other woman had discreetly pointed out to Doris that she spent too much time in the kitchen engaged in unnecessary cleaning like washing the lids on pots. Doris wondered if her neighbour was blind. Couldn't she see the grime from cooking that accumulated around the rim of pot lids? Susan pointed out that their neighbour just wanted her mother to take some free time to join her for cards which Doris declared was the true waste of time.

Susan can still picture herself on that hillside where she sat eating her peanut butter sandwich, thinking how stupid her mother was to be so circumscribed by housework that she couldn't even go out to play a game of cards. She hated how domesticated her mother was. With a powerful surge of memory Susan instantly feels that her attitude towards her mother went a long way in explaining her own choices in life. Susan never did learn to cook, always bought meals at take-out counters or from the school cafeteria. When single, the appliance most used in her apartment was the microwave, before that, the toaster oven. Look where she's ended up? At a resort with her meals cooked for her by men. How liberating is that?

Susan decides to return to her room and change out of her wet swimsuit rather than join Ian on the patio. Her forearm still rests against her stomach. She's apple-shaped, not pear-shaped like most women. Weight collects around her middle like it does on most men. Her mind makes an association. She remembers her mother's voice. There was a saying Doris used that floats across her mind like mist rising from a waterfall. It's misty because it's not the clear common saying, "An apple a day keeps the doctor away," but something about eating apples keeping the tummy flat. Where did Doris come across that saying? Or did her mother confuse it with another old wives' tale. She was prone to malapropisms.

In the shower she rinses the chlorine out of her bathing suit and off her skin. Ian would like to convert the pool from chlorine into a low saline solution that resembles sea water – "salus per aquiem". However, it is an expensive technology.

In her room Susan turns on the floor lamp angled to illuminate the top of her desk where the pile of papers she still has to mark sits in an assembled stack. It's work that demands her attention. "Yes, okay," she says aloud to the urgent pile. These papers are from students who are very responsive and will demand to know their grade on Monday when they arrive in class animated in each other's presence. She pictures them arriving in a gaggle of activity, talking with one another about their homework, sharing what they did over the weekend, greeting her happily. At the start of the week they always have energy for what they anticipate might happen in school, but by the end they'll be anticipating their days off and becoming impatient with class. Easy beginnings, trying endings. What of Tijean? Will he reappear, or will he already be relegated to the past? The boy who used to be in their class.

From her briefcase she picks the file with the class lists and sorts through the sheets for the form she'll see first thing Monday morning. It shows Tijean Williams' name at the bottom. The top paper on the stack belongs to Denzil Christopher. She remembers she sorted the papers submitted into alphabetical order. While glancing over the names on the class list it strikes her how many of them have Christian names as surnames: Jean Louis, Rolston Martin, Shaan Thomas. They're European names, too, inherited from ancestors brought here by others. Then there's Tijean Williams – just an 's' added, as if he's more than one and in a way he is. Enigmatic. Who is the real Tijean? Larger than life, how will his life unfold?

Denzil's paper is entitled 'Gay Tourists'. Susan gave the students an assignment to interview someone on the islands about an issue that interests them. Denzil's interview is with a programme coordinator at Club Med. That international resort hosted a gay convention at its facility on Provo. Later the issue of gay tourists exploded onto the front page of the local paper. The government opposed the presence of a gay cruise ship landing on the shore of Grand Turk. Denzil is openly gay, has been since he came out on his sixteenth birthday, a fact he announces at the beginning of his paper. The programme coordinator, too, is gay and offers very convincing arguments for promoting tourism among the gay community, mostly to do with economics. It seems gays have more disposable income than other demographics. Denzil concludes with a rant against the hypocrisy of the sitting government that continues in the new millennium to consider gay relationships sinful. Not only don't they support alternative lifestyles, they're fearful of exposing their children to such immorality. Denzil argues that he is a child of the islands, yet he plans to live the so-called "alternative lifestyle" that the establishment condemns. He's a Belonger, someone born on these islands, and yet he's made to feel as if he isn't welcome. "Is this progress?" he concludes.

Susan is in a quandary as to how to grade his paper. Does she point out that the assigned format is an interview, not a persuasive argument? His writing is, as always, error free. She gives him an A-, not his usual A+, elaborating that he went beyond the guidelines, although she refrains from referring him to the pages in the textbook that describe how to write up an interview. This he clearly knows, but Denzil is way beyond the constraints of a textbook case.

Standing, Susan stretches by raising her arms over her head. It occurs to her that this is one of the tests for checking if a person has suffered a stroke. She goes to the mirror and smiles, the second requirement for a quick check. Then she speaks a simple sentence while still facing the mirror: "I am marking student papers." She passes all three items on the list on the test. Sandra advised her of this three-point quick check after Doris suffered a stroke. "It saves lives," Sandra said.

When Susan sits down again at her desk she leafs through the stack to find the paper at the bottom of the pile. To her surprise Tijean interviewed an instructor at the Center For Marine Resource Studies. No wonder Mahala spoke his name in the same sentence as that institution. Susan wonders, even dares to hope, that he had ambitions to attend. Maybe that's where he's gone? The Field Studies programme would suit his diving interests, but could he handle the academics? This morning she further questioned his Special Needs Coordinator about that and Mahala seemed hopeful. She'd helped Tijean with this report, as she does with all his written assignments. The marine institution would offer special need students similar help. With such academic support at their center he could succeed. They even offer financial aid, as does the government, especially to students who come from the Turks & Caicos.

With these questions begging answers Susan begins to read Tijean's report. He introduces the instructor, giving his name, background and qualifications. Further along Tijean describes the field studies which he clearly finds fascinating. So does Susan. The students complete three different field studies and submit a report for each one before writing their major Directed Research paper. One of the field studies examines the status of the Queen Conch stocks. During their field studies the students conduct underwater visual census that can provide comprehensive information on the distribution and abundance of animal and plant communities that often form the basis of coastal monitoring programs. Tijean concludes his report with the instructor's assessment that the school not only provides opportunities for students to study marine life, but is an adventure. Many students travel to the school from other countries and they find the experience socially satisfying, too.

Holding the paper at arm's length Susan assesses the impact of the report. Definitely an A paper, but more importantly, an opening for Tijean. There are possibilities here. Wouldn't it have been nice if he could be exposed to such a programme? It would turn Tijean around, give him hope for a brighter future. Yet he fled. He'd seen the possibilities, argued with his entrenched parents, and gone awol. If only she'd known. All she can do now is record his mark. How useless is that? So useless she feels her frustration mount while making the mark. The lead tip breaks and goes scurrying across her record sheet. "Damn," she says. "Shit," she concludes before reaching for the pencil sharpener.

The sad fact is that all the adults in Tijean's life failed him. She's not the only guilty party.

Susan goes back to the top of the pile. Cherine Gervin. She pictures the girl, tall and bony, a skeleton of a figure who won the high jump at the track and field meet. Her paper is smeared and messy. Probably she wrote it at the kitchen table. Susan keeps telling the students they can use the computer lab and most do. However, there's nothing about Cherine that caters to appearances. She doesn't worry about her hairstyle, fashion, make-up, and this lack of pretense carries over to her school work. She completes all assignments with great concentration, and when one goal is achieved, she moves on to the next job. Susan glances at the clock when her stomach growls. Best to keep her nose to the job and mark one more paper. Then she can feel that she's made a start on her marking before a social evening over a meal.

Ian wakes her. Looking over her desk and up at him Susan panics. "What time is it?"

"Seven," Ian says simply.

Rubbing her eyes with her knuckles she yawns. "I guess I fell asleep."

"Leila phoned. She can't make it tonight. Something about waiting for her guests to arrive."

"Oh," Susan says with disappointment. Looking down at Cherine's paper Susan sees that she's made it messier with her sleeping torso. "Maybe I should just go on marking papers."

"Sure you don't want to get into bed?"

"Maybe later, dear."

"Join me for dinner, then?"

Watching his back as he leaves her room Susan remembers sitting on the beach when she first arrived on the island. She was hypnotized by the scenery while looking out at the brilliant turquoise ocean and didn't hear Ian walking along the sand. When he sat down next to her she suspected he'd come to the beach because of her. A conceited thought, she knew, and it was so unlike her to feel conceit that she was afraid her vanity would show viscerally. Could he read her narcissism? If she'd been a male she'd swagger. Instead, she kept shaking her wet hair, adjusting the neck strap on her bathing suit, patting her beach towel smooth. She sensed Ian's eyes on her, studying her, not simply because she was a new arrival, more the way a man studies a woman who interests him. She was a female prospect. "You must meet a lot of people here?" she asked.

Ian's lower lip jutted out from a relaxed smile. "Sure do. Though it's not nearly as busy here as on Provo. That's where most of the tourists go. But I didn't come here for the crowds."

"No." Susan returned his gaze. "Me neither." She watched Ian shake his head in agreement and knew even then that she could easily adapt herself to him and his easy ways.

"Excuse me," Ian said, standing. "Business calls."

Susan turned to where he indicated with his head and saw Celianne standing at the edge of the patio. When she'd first arrived the woman had introduced herself and asked how long Susan would be staying. Celianne seemed pleased when Susan said indefinitely. Susan guessed Celianne had told Ian what she'd said.

No longer tired, but still feeling a little over-wrought by the day's events, Susan rises and walks to the window. She opens the shutters and inhales deeply. Ah, the natural aromatherapy of bougainvillea. Its sweet smell relaxes her. She sees Marcel walking along the path that leads from the bar. He disappears between the rows of bushes that line the walkway to the kitchen and the supply cupboard. Probably going for bottles. When Marcel first arrived he'd engaged her in small talk and learned she was formerly a teacher. He didn't know that Ian had been one, too, but had left the profession for the life of an entrepreneur. Marcel seemed content to accept a job without much responsibility. He was good with the customers. In France he'd worked as an accountant and joked that he was over qualified to run the cash register at the resort so he offered to help Ian with the books. Now she can't help but wonder about this French male. If he's as rich as Leila seems to think why is he working for Ian?

Later on her first day Ian had again sat down beside her when he found her on the patio. He seemed coolly contained. "Since you're the language expert, do you know the anagram for my name?"

"Am I the language expert?"

"Well, you're the teacher."

Wondering what else he'd already learned about her Susan laughed. Then she eyed him quizzically. "I guess you've never taught?"

"Yes, but in public school."

Susan was surprised to learn he had taught. "Well, granted I was an English major, but I only have an undergraduate degree. Don't assume I know too much." She shrugged her shoulders that were already showing a pinkish hue from too much tropical sun. "So what's the anagram for your name?"

"You're supposed to guess."

Ian kept his sunglasses on even though he was sitting in the shade. Susan learned to do the same as the sun constantly reflected off the water and stone patio which could tire the eyes after a long day of bright sunlight. Still, behind the dark shades he looked mysterious and she felt his playfulness. "What name is an anagram?" she asked cautiously. She hoped she wasn't pulling a faux pas and insulting him so early in their relationship.

"Cameron."

"Oh, right. I remember my father explaining the name Cameron to me. He was always reading snippets to me from the newspaper, like historical obituaries. You know, on this day in 1886. Anyway."

Ian looked bored. "You still haven't answered my question."

"I'm good at that." Again she looked into the dark where his eyes should be.

"What? Not answering questions?"

"So I've been told."

"Well, I'm not going to tell you. So you'll have to guess."

"An anagram for Cameron?"

He stood and started humming as he strolled away. Then he turned and walked backwards, serenading her quietly, "Maybe I'm right, And maybe I'm wrong, And maybe I'm weak, And maybe I'm strong. But nevertheless..." He reached into his breast pocket and threw her a pen before turning and leaving.

Susan caught it, and when she clicked it open and turned to look for a piece of paper, she noticed the menu on the table had the name of the resort engraved on its cover: Pumpkin Bluff Resort. Underneath it read

"Owned and Operated by Ian Cameron". No Meridian or Fairmount chain. An independent. Susan grabbed a napkin and printed "cameron", writing each of the seven letters clearly in lower case form. Then she started rearranging them. Finally she burst upon it: romance. Was she being had? Probably he used that come-on with every prospective female.

Later as it's turning dark Susan finds Ian in his office. He is a miracle, she thinks. So full of energy, expectancy, love, it's as if he senses her mood and wants to take the top prize in paradise. He gives her a welcoming kiss while folding her to him, his arms loosely crossed behind the small of her back. She reaches her arms around his neck. "What's this?" Susan asks.

"Come," he says, bidding her to follow him. While holding hands he leads her to his desk and turns on the lamp. There he disengages himself and picks up a bundle of papers that he hands to her.

Susan sees they are legal documents by the engraved stamp and letterhead. "You've been to the lawyers?"

Ian smiles. "I hope I don't shock you with this surprise," he says.

"What is it?" Susan asks. A frown appears on her forehead as she leafs through the bound sheets of long foolscap. She feels a rush of blood entering her skull. The information overwhelms her. "Is this...?" she asks not able to find the

73

words or the term that labels these documents although it's clearly obvious what they are.

"Don't be mad," Ian says.

"I'm not. I'm confused," Susan says. "Have you sold the resort?"

Ian holds his breath before answering with a hesitant nod.

"I had no idea."

Still watching her with his ice-blue eyes he reaches his arms toward her, then turns the pages of the document while she continues to hold it. With his finger he points.

Susan directs her gaze at a figure in numerals and translated into words. Her eyes flit between the two amounts, both the same, both reaffirming the other. "Are you serious?"

"About selling?"

"No," Susan says, trying to grasp what she sees on the paper. "I can't believe it."

"What? That I've sold the resort?" Ian looks pained. His hand is still on the document.

"No, no," she repeats, trying to clarify. "This is millions?"

Now Ian gives her his wide grin.

Susan returns her gaze to the amount. Then she sweeps her eyes to the signatories at the bottom. "Marcel is buying it?"

"That's why he came here," Ian says. He closes his hand around hers. "I think I'd better explain."

Afterwards Susan revisits this moment. It's while Ian is explaining his reasons for selling that a shift happens. In her mind that moment is disconnected from the past and the future. In the past they were the expats on an island, a couple intimate with one another, but strangers to their respective families. Ian kept a formal photo of his parents on his desk. It was taken on a special anniversary – one that he missed. His parents hadn't sent it. His sister had. She kept him in touch with his relatives, his extended family who lived in the Maritimes. Sometimes a formal card arrived acknowledging his birthday. Grudging communication. That spare-looking picture was a reminder of a lost context – his family, his home, his past. His parents had never visited the island so Susan didn't know them. She'd only laid eyes on them in the one photo. It sparked her imagination about them and she gave them a life, but she didn't know them. Yet while talking about where the two of them would go in the future there was no bitterness in his mood. When Ian described the change in their circumstances, the new direction their life would take free from the resort, in that moment his mood was tinged with sorrow. There was no sadness about leaving the resort. Instead, the sadness was a well from the past that Susan recognized as a permanent state of disappointment.

Naturally he missed his growing son from his previous marriage and his distant parents. Mostly his mood when giving her his explanation was one of longing. Sure the money supported his dreams. Who wouldn't be happy with becoming rich? The money set him free. Now he could return with his head held high. In spite of all the longing and disappointment he communicated, it wasn't just his relatives that bound him to the past. It was missing the person he'd once been. That's what Susan saw – another Ian, the one underneath the man she'd come to know. It was as if he was communicating by a means other than words. They would always share the same memories of their time together on the island. Only now they would have the opportunity to know the history of one another, not as fellow expats, but as two people who had a common connection both coming from the same country. She liked what she saw in him at that moment, having plunged to a deeper level of familiarity. Their situation was about to undergo enormous change. Why had she no twinge of premonition? Ever the worrier and analyst she wondered if Ian would continue to feel the same for her.

∽

When Tijean arrived in Canada he began to feel the freedom of his adventure. Jake insisted he wouldn't need him despite having to pick up his trunk from the over-sized luggage counter. "I expect it will take you some time to get through Customs & Immigration," he said, "so you better join the line." Then Jake gave Tijean his contact information, thanked him for all his help, and wished him well. "I expect to hear from you," Jake said. "I mean it," he added.

Buoyed by his independence Tijean grinned at everyone while walking over the carpeted floor of the terminal to take his place in the queue. A couple who were standing parallel to him in the queue alongside his returned his smile and asked if it was his first visit to Canada. "First time off the island," Tijean said. When they asked if he was from Jamaica Tijean quickly corrected their misconception, "No, North Caicos." They seemed not to recognize the name, but didn't admit as much. Tijean thought better of explaining to the couple that his heritage was Haitian. Instead he asked them where they'd been on holiday. That query started the couple off on a long description of their cruise around the Caribbean, including full details of meals, people they'd met, activities on board and tours on shore. Before long Tijean's line drew ahead of theirs and soon he found himself in front of an official behind one of the narrow counters that banked the back of the large room. The man seated was wearing a uniform, not as oppressive as a soldier's military rags, but a uniform nonetheless. His sweater was navy blue and made from wool knitted in a ribbed pattern. The airport official was a black man of similar build and features as Tijean. This recognition sobered Tijean. He immediately became aware that he never wanted to be in a similar position as this man, stuck inside working at a steady, dull job over an eight-hour shift.

"Landing card?"

Tijean handed over the item requested. Jake had helped him fill it out on the plane so he felt confident that it was in order.

"Passport?"

Before taking the document from Tijean, the official asked him to open it to his photo. As Tijean spread his passport flat he thought that this man was trying to intimidate him, pull rank, show his power and authority. However, once the man started to read the details of Tijean's nationality, he seemed to soften. "Where you living on Caicos?" he asked. Tijean told him. "I want to go there some time," the official said. "How long you staying in Canada?"

"I don't know."

The official looked directly into Tijean's eyes. "That you gotta know, boy. Tell me how long you planning to be here?"

"A month or two."

"Okay," the official said, picking up Tijean's landing card to have another look. "All that time you're at this address?"

"Yes, they're my relatives."

"Is this your first visit?"

"Yes."

"Fine. Welcome to Canada," he said, stamping Tijean's passport with a thud that echoed. Then he handed back the two documents. "You have yourself a good visit."

At that point Tijean was at a loss as to where to go. A group of four older teenagers came to his rescue by pointing to the overhead screen that listed flight numbers matched with pick-up locations. Tijean took the escalator that led to number 2. There he found a crowd gathered alongside a moving carousel stacked with luggage. People were reaching in to grab bags and hoist them onto the floor. It dawned on Tijean that he didn't belong here. He had no luggage. Now where to go? Making a 360 degree turn he saw a few fellow passengers departing. Above their heads he noticed a lit EXIT sign.

Ahead of him was another line, fortunately shorter than the ones leading to the Customs & Immigration counters. People pulling luggage on wheels mingled and shunted their way past another official. They were handing him their landing cards. For a second Tijean panicked, unsure what he'd done with his. He hadn't been told to keep it. Reaching into his pocket he found it with his passport. He felt a sense of relief when he passed by the bored official. No one asked him where his luggage was.

Another well-lit corridor brought him to a set of glass, automatic sliding doors which remained apart as the arrival passengers streamed through the wide opening. Ahead were crowds of people standing behind a roped barrier. Dazed by the unfamiliar surroundings Tijean walked past them trying to keep up with the movement of those who seemed in a hurry while scanning the faces for the one he could recognize. When he reached the end of the barricade he felt a hand on his forearm and heard his name. Turning, he looked into the face on the photo. "Hey, bro," he said, socking his cousin on the shoulder with a soft punch.

Sherlock Saintas held up a jacket. "You gonna need this."

Tijean laughed while taking the garment. "This really necessary?"

"You wait until you get outside. You see."

"Where my aunt?" Tijean asked, looking behind his cousin in anticipation of some surrogate wrath sent from his mother.

"She at home with the rest of them. They think I gone to visit a friend. You wanted this to be a surprise, right?"

"Yeah," Tijean said simply. Taking off his back pack, he gave it to his cousin to hold while he shoved his arms into the jacket. The lining was quilted making the garment thick, but not heavy. It was made of grey nylon with red markings indicating the logo of some team. "This yours, then?"

LEAVING PARADISE

"No, my Dad's. An old soccer jacket. He mad about the game." Returning the back pack, Sherlock indicated with a nod the direction they were headed.

Tijean looked down on Sherlock who was shorter than he was and much slighter. He was paler, too, like his dad who had some Spanish blood in him. His mother always reminded them of that fact when she got pictures.

Together the two stepped on a rubber mat that automatically opened the set of wide glass doors. The cold air that filled the exit space knocked the wind out of Tijean's lungs. He'd never felt such pressure, even on a dive. Instinctively he cupped his hands over his ears.

Beside him Sherlock laughed uproariously. "Told you," he said.

Outside the air was filled with the noise of honking cars. Traffic sped across the wide lanes in front of them. The road was covered by a cement bridge that served as a walkway to the multi-leveled parking lot. This structure seemed to intensify the noise of rushing cars, vans, taxis, limos. Who all these people, Tijean wondered, but dared not ask his cousin for fear of appearing like the country bumpkin. When an opening came in the oncoming traffic they made a run for it and crossed the four lanes. Once inside Tijean waited while Sherlock paid the parking ticket. Then he followed his cousin to the elevator. There he asked Sherlock how they were getting to his house. His cousin shook his head in amusement as he stepped onto the elevator. "How you think?" he asked. "In the car."

Tijean stood facing the closing elevator doors amazed that his cousin had been handed the keys to a motor car. Good thing, though. It was too cold for pedaling two wheels.

∽

Early Saturday morning Susan rises alone. Ian's already up and at work. He'd been up late greeting the new guests. She'd returned to her room to mark papers after a bite to eat with him, and after witnessing his signature on the sales agreement. Unbelievable, she thinks. He's rich. She's hitched to a millionaire. Who would have guessed? She dresses quickly and casually, then heads out the door.

She knows she's in a state of shock from the unexpected news of the sale, but soon, another shock greets her. Hesitating at the edge of the patio she glimpses two women sitting under a shade umbrella at a table beside the outdoor bar and immediately registers their profiles as familiar. Can it really be them? Underneath her curiosity a disquiet begins. Slowing her pace Susan stops behind a pillar where she's hidden from view. There she fiddles with the knot at her waist knowing she's not drawing any attention to herself. She's earned a reputation for not being able to efficiently tie a wrap-around over her swimsuit. The staff will assume she's coming undone again. Indeed, she does feel undone. Her disquiet has turned to panic. If she angles her chin over her left shoulder she'll get a better view of the two women. She can't ignore them. The resort, the town, the island are too small to remain hidden from view. Can the world be so small that after all this time her nemesis shows up here?

She knows she can't remain behind the pillar for much longer before she blows her cover and attracts attention to herself. What if Ian finds her hiding? Instantly she again recalls the day ten years ago when Ian Cameron first introduced himself. At the time she told him that her father had once read to her a short biography of David Young Cameron. Her father was always doing that, sharing clips of interest from his reading. "It says here he exhibited his work in Canada." Looking down on his daughter he had continued, "We must see if we can find some of his work, eh?" Susan had agreed and was not disappointed when taken on a cultural pilgrimage to the gallery at Victoria College where they found a painting by the artist. But Ian said he wasn't related. What can she say to Ian about these two?

Many tourists from Canada come to the island so, really, it is no surprise to see Kate Channing and Ruth Diamond here. Certainly, it is them. Now what is Susan to do? Life on the island has become blissful. Her Eden in the sun. Idyllic.

Enchanted. Unspoiled. Profitable, even. Now ruined. The accusations return. Her head is full of them. They repeat like the pounding waves on the shore in a storm. Gone is the bliss that quelled this malignant voice. How quickly she suffers a relapse. The slander worms deeper and deeper until it supersedes all other thoughts. No reasoning, no tempering, no shushing can still the calamitous repetition of accusations. She wants to cry out. She needs to get away. Where can she go? She is as helpless as a seabird tossed by a tropical storm. Yet storms are great equalizers. Especially here. Everyone is made helpless to the same degree. During the rare storms people on the island share the experience: the threat, the fright, the ruin, the rebuilding. And here is Ian.

"Come meet some Canadian guests."

"I can't," Susan blurts and, turning, flees. True to form her wraparound loosens. She stumbles over the fabric that clings to her leg. As she grabs it Ian holds her arm.

"Susan, what's the matter?"

"I can't tell you now." Susan wrestles her arm free, and holding the loose ends of her wrap-around, continues down the path. She is catching her breath as if from physical exertion, but she's not sobbing or out of control or anything like that. Which is good. She remembers what that is like. It's probably a bad mistake to abandon Ian like this, but she can't think of him now. She needs to triumph over this disturbance on her own. Without Ian this time. Initially he gave his support as one does by simply listening. She told him. He commiserated and accepted her situation as her story. Now the problem is made real. It's been given flesh and blood. No more distant hypothesis. Will he muster the same support right here in front of them?

She's panting when she enters her room. The sunlight is muted by the louvered shutters, but it's the silence that stuns Susan. She can't help thinking her presence has added to the quality of the silence. Her arrival makes it intense. Her eyes search the room. It's as if her mind is too big and busy for the room. This is not a room that has known such disquiet. This room is her sanctuary.

Standing with her back against the wooden door Susan feels her neck slacken allowing her head to droop. To try to explain her reaction to Ian would be too complicated. The truth always is. She could have just hugged him, right there, beside the bar. He would have understood that better than her fleeing. He'll question her lack of trust. She already saw that look behind his eyes when she pulled her arm away. It was a troubled look. Their love for one another melts differences. Her anxiety becomes his trouble, too. They're the 'Expats' on this island. He's nicknamed them that. They're not alone. There are other expats, but he fondly refers to the two of them with that nomenclature. Wherever you go on the Turks & Caicos you find Scandinavians,

DONNA WOOTTON

Americans and Canadians who are escaping the extreme
weather of the north. Or Brits who are escaping the rain. Or
French, like Marcel, who have a connection to plantations
whose borders are still marked by dry stone walls. Ian
bought the resort, originally with his first wife who quickly
grew tired of their Shangrila. When she returned home
she began divorce proceedings. "She continued to call
Canada home," Ian told her on the first night they made
love.

"You don't think of it as home?" Susan asked.

Ian eyed Susan quizzically. "This is my home." He
extended both arms to take in his surroundings. "Here." He
pumped his arms to emphasize the expanse of his domain.
Then he thrust a pointed finger at her. "If you're still here
in a year, I'll ask you that same question again."

Normally Susan disapproved of anyone who pointed at
her. She'd learned that from her father who often said to
speak with your voice, not your arms, or hands, or fingers,
whatever you were using to supplement the spoken word.
With Ian Susan just laughed dispelling all reservations about
this stranger, a man from Canada who lived in the outer
reaches of the Caribbean. Nearly ten years have passed and
Susan learned to call the island 'home'. Now that transition,
too, could change.

Again drawn by the sunshine filtering through the
shutters Susan raises her head and lets her eyes roam over

the room with its whitewashed walls. She feels a tiredness coming over her. The brain is like that. It becomes exhausted when given a problem with a far-off solution as it needs energy to start the wheels in motion. So she decides to lay down on her bed on top of the popcorn chenille bedspread that the staff wash regularly to a cleanliness that can make them feel proud and a whiteness that earns bragging rights. Flicking off her sandals she feels the coolness of the white ceramic tiles underneath her feet before she gives over to the lethargy that claims her.

Moments later Susan stretches expecting to feel rested, but no, whatever sleep she's snatched isn't enough to refresh. Her right hand hits the rattan headboard and she lets it dangle through a bent curve in one of the loopy scrolls that patterns the furniture. The ceiling fan is quietly slicing arcs causing the air to billow the mosquito netting that hangs at the foot of the bed. Earlier she tied the netting back at the side around the posts. Susan raises her left arm, bent at the elbow, and drops it behind her head. Her skin feels clammy. Wiping her wet hair that lies plastered against her forehead she allows this act to draw an association in her mind to the time Ian had water dripping down his face from his wet hair. He was singing while trying to keep the rain off her, "A fine romance, my friend this is." Then he apologized for forgetting some of the lyrics but picked up the song. "When tears come down like falling rain, You'll toss and call my name." Again he apologized. "Sorry, more snatches. You must wonder how my brain works."

"I'm curious," she'd said. "If you found it wet on the Maritimes, why did you move here?"

"This is paradise. Mostly it's hot and dry. Ask any of the Belongers. It's sun-dappled rain." He'd opened his arms stretching them in a wide embrace like some drought-driven preacher. "No cold snaps to chill the bones." He'd collapsed his arms as if he needed to preserve the heat in his body.

"But you're always claiming the oceans cause a moderating effect."

"Yes, here we get little humidity. Lovely breezes."

"Okay, the cold in the east is bone chilling and out west they don't feel the cold even at minus forty, right?"

"Oh, naive patriot. In a city of drunkards they don't feel anything." He picked up his feet and sloshed through shallow puddles in his soaked tennis shoes singing, "Let's face the music and dance." In a gesture of invitation he stretched his arms out to her and she accepted. They'd danced in the rain.

Is she conjuring these memories to remind herself that she's found paradise, that she can't be harmed by past wrongs, that her foes have no power here? She lets her left arm drop and notices the digitalized time. One minute has passed since she stretched. How can so much reverie pass in such a short time? One minute of reassuring love against the backdrop of ten months of persecution on the job. A brief rebound of love seems no match compared to the memories of the bad that unraveled her past working life.

She rolls over onto her right side and casually slides her arm away from the headboard letting it drop onto the pillow. So comforted is she by her reverie she allows her mind to revisit their dancing in the rain. She'd engaged him in further conversation speaking into his ear. "Did you ever experiment in the cold by putting your tongue on metal?"

"Of course."

"And did it stick?"

"It is easier to mumble my tongue is stuck than my heart is broken."

Recognizing Ian as a man who speaks in conundrums she leaned away. "I take that's a yes."

He pulled her towards him and they twirled. "Keep playing that tune, darling. Admit you did the same?"

"Yes, but I was a tomboy."

"You dance beautifully for a boy."

"Your tunes are out-of-date."

"We all are here. Haven't you noticed?" Then they'd kissed. Their first. And it didn't end with just a kiss. Susan moans. Oh for such innocence. She wants to return to that simple time. It was old fashioned. Falling in love at a Caribbean resort with a charming, eligible, handsome man.

This day dreaming is getting her no where. Avoidance. Avoiding her paranoia. What is paranoia but a heightened sense of her reality? The reality is that Kate Channing and Ruth Diamond are, at this very minute, sitting at the bar. Ian is probably entertaining them. In all innocence he's treating them like the other tourists only with the added attention due citizens from his country of birth. It's not envy she feels. It is pure and simple paranoia. She distrusts them the way they once distrusted her. She's suspicious. It's irrational on her part but she can't help but suspect they'll turn Ian against her the way they turned the other staff against her. Her suspicion brings tingles to the surface of her skin.

Susan goes further back in the past to another comfort zone. She's sitting on the floor at her father's feet. The brown slippers he wore rest on the bare wooden floor like sentinels, two parallel positions taken up by two long feet. She was in a made-up world playing with her sister's doll changing its clothing into a bathing suit. She covered the suit with a beach wrap of the kind worn then with a slit up the side revealing a length of thigh. It was made of terry cloth and fitted over the doll's head.

"Going for a swim?" her father asked over the top of the newspaper he was reading.

Susan didn't mind this invasion into her private, make-believe world. Her father was always a good sport to play along with whatever role Susan created. "I'm thinking about it," she said. "I don't need a towel because the robe is terry, just like a towel is." Her mother had sewn it from an old towel.

Ruffling his newspaper her father turned his gaze to an article he was reading. "It says here the Turks and Caicos want to annex their islands to Canada." He fixed his dark blue eyes on his daughter. "Can't blame them, eh?"

"What's Turks and Kite Goes?" Susan asked.

"Caicos," her father corrected. "The Turks and Caicos are a group of islands in the Caribbean under British rule."

"Really?" Susan said.

"Don't be astonished," her father said. "Imagine, a hot, sunny island part of Britain. We only know it as a rainy place, an island covered in fog because it's surrounded by so much cold ocean. But Britain once ruled the world. Cross my heart."

Susan paused. And hope to die. No, that wasn't what she hoped at all. She lifted the terry robe off the doll's head and held it up. "Does everybody have to die?" she asked.

"Yes." Her father laid the newspaper down on his lap accepting the seriousness of his daughter's switch in topic.

"Are you going to?"

"Someday."

Susan shook the terry robe. "I don't want to think about that." She hoped her father was wrong. Suddenly she was gripped by an overwhelming panic. What would happen to her if he died? What about her mother? And her little sister, Sandra? Who would look after them if her father died? Susan scrunched the terry robe in her fist, making it into a tight little ball. Then she threw it across the rug.

"Why did you do that, Susan?"

"It's a beach ball. See, it's bouncing into the water."

"Ah," said her father. "Into the turquoise ocean."

Susan knows when the dim past becomes clearer she isn't thinking independently. Instead she's gripped by memories. Some are safe and allow her to have a quieter life. Others are disturbing and send her searching through her past for answers. If she isn't careful she'll slide into another episode of depression. Her therapist told her after three bouts she's seventy percent more likely to experience more rounds of depression. Susan's maladaptive compensation strategy landed her in her second episode. Her first went undiagnosed. Now she feels she's fighting against the third round. Hippocrates recommended a regimen of nourishing food, rest, warm baths, support from friends and amusing activities to counter melancholy. She receives all that and more at the resort. They're merry company here and Ian offers good advice, soothing music and mirth with his boundless love.

Susan hears Marcel before she sees him. He's pushing the dolly along the stone path. Its wheels rumble and the cases of bottles clang. He's whistling while he works. Everyone here is happy but her. It's come again, that wave of paranoia, that depressing fear that she's inadequate, not good enough. All the reverie of romance hasn't squelched her nervousness. Her underlying anxiety isn't resolved. There's a whole swath in her brain holding out, keeping the memory of those unpleasant experiences in active service. A simple trigger – the reappearance of two women – and she's reduced to the role of victim.

Like Susan, Kate Channing was a former teacher in an uptown school that catered to the wealthy and privileged. When Susan arrived during the last days of summer to set up her classroom, it was Kate who showed her where she could find the staffroom and woman's washroom. "At my last school I had a private washroom off my classroom," Susan said after thanking Kate for showing her around the building. "Now look how far I have to walk?" Probably not the most diplomatic of responses. Certainly Kate took it the wrong way. "You won't be treated as special here." Her harsh tone made Susan laugh aloud. She laughed alone. Kate was not a woman who could laugh at herself. Also, she was very loyal to the school. Not only did she live in the neighbourhood and walk to work, she'd spent her entire career at Randolph Road High School coming straight to her placement after college. Susan had learned all this personal history in the small talk that passed between them during the school tour. Left feeling embarrassed by having put her foot in her mouth, Susan examined her new colleague. Kate was wearing an outfit by Della Spiga. Susan recognized it from a rack at a local women's wear store where she went browsing before coming into work as she'd wanted to check out the neighbourhood. The shops, like the houses, were upscale. Kate's outfit was brightly coloured in splashes of red poppies with black centres. On that first meeting Kate had put Susan in her place. She never fully recovered from feeling second rate. Once Susan bought a dress at that same store.

Susan thinks she must still own that dress. In fact, it may be hanging in the closet. Turning away from the window she opens the louvered doors to her clothes closet, then she pushes some hangers from the back along the metal rod until she finds the dress made from a soft, crinkled material in pastel colours. It 's still in good repair. That's the problem with high end clothing. It lasts forever.

What place on her cortex does the closet stimulate? Suddenly she's back to her first day in residence at university. Her wardrobe at college was sparse. In her single room she hung up the only items she owned on the few hangers provided. Susan must have had the closet doors open because when a fellow student came in and introduced herself she looked at Susan's clothes and said in a give-away surprised tone, "Are those your only clothes?"

Susan can't remember the student's name. They didn't become friends. Susan should have told her she wasn't Rosemary Clooney. When Susan was a child she had a cut-out paper doll of the singer who was her father's favourite crooner. Inside the booklet with the cardboard cover that she bought from Woolworth's were pages of clothing. These pages held a complete wardrobe that Susan found remarkable. Clothes for every occasion: shorts, tops, and bathing suits for the beach; formal dresses for evening wear; casual clothes for going shopping; suits for traveling. With sharp pointed scissors Susan cut out the tabs that fit snuggly over the cardboard doll's shoulders, around her waist and hips, along her arms and legs. Susan dressed the doll in all these different outfits and created a made-up life for her.

Later in life Susan learned that George Clooney was related to the singer. The singer had a real life that included relatives who were stars in their own right. So much for Susan's imaginings. They probably didn't come close to the maze of connectedness that made the singer human.

Softly Susan closes the closet doors. Are there skeletons in her closet? Does that saying have its origins in a similar act? Someone stands in front of an open closet and remembers the past - only it's horrifying and the images are not fully clothed people as Susan imagines, but bare bones. On these islands the first people, the Taino Indians, left behind only skeletons. Middens with a few ancient utensils, some words passed along in the oral traditions, but no other record of themselves or their way of life. They were replaced by another Indian people, the Lacayans. They, too, disappeared, victims of Spanish enslavement and imported disease. These are islands with skeletons in their closet. Beneath paradise lies the skeletons of ancient people, of slaves who perished from toiling the thin soil. Where are the triggers to spark memories of them? In a history recorded after the fact. Such is the way of the world. A false paradise. It's her paradise, but only on the surface. The beautiful landscape. Her lover. Still out there.

For all this instant doubt she has loved living on the islands. Yet when she arrived in April of 1996 the place was in an uproar over earlier comments made by the governor that the islands were becoming safe havens for drug traffickers. So the British government got tough and sent one of their warships. It was cruising the coast when she arrived. A specially trained branch of policemen landed on the sand, too. Ian and she still laugh about that. The Brits sent their special service and Canada sent Susan Borden. "You're really an undercover agent," Ian said.

"Actually, I'm heavily into money laundering," she still answers whenever the conversation turns to that time in the islands' history. A slight laugh escapes at the recollection of their jesting. She shakes her head, self-conscious of making a sound when alone, and turns back to face the room where she sees that it's still early. She could go for her swim, take a morning dip in the pool. Return her day to normal. Walk out there as if nothing has changed. Pretend she never saw those women. Maybe they won't notice her. But Ian will introduce her – a fellow Canadian. Susan now has dual citizenship. She applied in 2002 to Britain as these islands are part of the British West Indies holdings.

With a determined step she slips her feet into her sandals and walks outside. The view from the back is of a cactus grove. She smells the dry air and inhales deeply. There's a whiff of salt underlying the dryness. The breeze is coming from the south, the direction of the abandoned salt-drying pans. She is euphoric. This is her home. Why be afraid? She is a changed woman possessing dual citizenship living on an outlying Caribbean island as removed from the person she was at the end of the twentieth century as anyone can be. She can present herself to those two miserable women with pride because of what she has made of herself. They knocked her down and she rose and transformed herself here, in this paradise, into a happy, competent, lovable person. Who are they? Two women keeping each other company on an island in the sun. They continued to work, Kate teaching and Ruth administering. Yet they're not working now otherwise they wouldn't be enjoying lazy days in the sun at this time of the year. Why aren't they working? Susan doesn't leave her doorstep. She sits on the cushioned wicker chair under the pergola behind her room. She needs to sort this out. Could they be retired? Susan does a mental calculation. Yes, that must be it. They're already retired. Susan could be collecting a pension, too. Her sister, Sandra, told her if she'd stayed in teaching she'd be retired by now, under the 85 factor. Sandra is counting the days and knows that she'll reach her 85 factor just as her son and daughter finish university. They're twins, and the dual expense is straining the family's resources, so Sandra continues to teach even though she is tired constantly and the demands increase yearly. "You're lucky you're no longer in the system. It's all task oriented. The curriculum, the outcomes, the reporting." A mixed message: too bad you didn't stay to collect a pension; aren't you lucky you're out of it?

Entering the silence is the whine of squeaky wheels. Celianne is making the rounds with her laundry cart. Celianne is a Haitian immigrant while Guy Williams is an islander and, although they come from two different Caribbean islands, they believe they have the same African fathers. Susan listens to their stories knowing they mean generations ago, not one generation removed. There really is no ancestral predisposition for Tijean's difficulty. Maybe genetic, as both Celianne and Guy admit to having had difficulty learning to read and write. Despite this admission they don't seem to make the connection. Their minds travel in the realm of ancestors and spirits, a powerhouse of traditions more relevant than modern science. What would they make of neurology? If Susan told them it used to take 45 minutes to do a head scan and now neuroradiology can do one in 5 seconds, could they imagine the scope of the technology? The Williams wouldn't think what she said was relevant to them. And maybe it isn't. Maybe here all that advanced science isn't making an impact the way culture and tradition do. Maybe it's Susan's problem in trying to understand how best to teach Tijean. He's her responsibility. Was. Tijean's such a strong presence in her mind she continues to think of him as her problem. Aren't problems like that? Ever-present? A bubbling disquiet. Greeting Celianne Susan waits expectantly for the other woman's response. Does she still blame her for what's happened?

"G'Mornin, Miss Susan."

Susan is used to how Celianne and Guy address her. It's the same way her son does in class and the clerks in the local shops. "How are you today?" Susan watches her perform her maidenly duties with languid efficiency. She's a big-hipped woman dressed in gingham, her size belies her grace.

Opening the double doors under the cart Celianne pulls out a set of clean sheets. When she's upright she stops what she's doing and looks directly at Susan. "I can't help thinking that Tijean, he just gone out diving. Early this morning I forget and think that. No problem ever for him getting up on a Saturday."

"Not for diving. Just for school," Susan says knowingly. She also knows what Celianne is implying about a mother's expectations of her son's sleeping habits and that this morning she awoke half-forgetting what's happened. Yet a question about Celianne's well being always gets answered by news of her son. That's their shared interest. Celianne rarely tells Susan anything personal. Only now the woman is watching her as if she has something more to say, but doesn't know how to begin.

"You waiting to go for your swim?"

That's about as personal as Celianne gets. Why is Susan not following her regular Saturday morning routine? Why is she here when Celianne has work to do in the rooms? "I'm a bit slow today," Susan confesses.

Celianne nods and returns to the task at hand. Conscious of the awkwardness she's creating, Susan rises. It's time to face the outside world. When she gains a view of the ocean she sees the yawl at the dock. It arrives irregularly with local supplies, mostly fresh produce from the farm outside Bottle Creek. Ian is crossing the white sand beach with Herbie by his side, no problem with him waking up early as he's a responsible, as well as a studious and serious, young man. He's also ambitious and wants to leave the island to study abroad at a university, so he works part-time for Ian and saves his money. Not like Tijean who is physical and likes to dive for wrecks, doesn't even get himself a regular job with a diving outfit taking tourists, but goes with a local who has a boat and dreams of finding treasure. There is treasure to be found, by a few. No wonder his parents object to his choices.

A north easterly is blowing off the ocean. Susan welcomes the refreshing breeze against her face which is damp with beads of perspiration along her hairline. She hasn't had her hair cut in ten years, since her arrival. The curly strands grew past her shoulders then stopped growing. She can feel the ends now where they settle against her skin, then lift when the breeze builds under her neck. Lift and settle, lift and settle. It's a sensual experience. Her hair is darker and grayer at the roots, lighter where the sun bleaches it. Her sandals scrunch in the sand and she wiggles her toes against the gritty bits that get caught under her soles. She wore her sandals for the pool patio, not for the sand nor the wooden planks on the dock. She's in her element – the congenial activity of greeting Ian, Herbie, and her former student, Toto, who owns the yawl that he sails out of Sandy Point. Imported goods and supplies come via the road from the airport. Toto says he'd hate to be a truck driver, so instead he sails.

Ian stops in front of her facing her directly with questioning eyes. He sees all is right between them and kisses her forehead. She reaches her arm behind his waist. "Thought I'd come and help."

"Anytime. You okay now?"

"Yes, fine. A change of routine will do me some good."

Ian releases himself from her embrace and starts directing the stacking of supplies telling Herbie how to place the boxes on the dolly. Susan shields her eyes and looks up at Toto who has a young woman at his side. He introduces her as Cindi. "Fine day for a sail," Susan says.

"It is, Miss Susan. It is." Toto laughs the way Susan remembers him always laughing in class. There was never much that Toto took too seriously. "You want to come with us? Enjoy a day sailing on the ocean? You like, Miss Susan?"

Susan looks from him to Cindi and back. Is he serious? She's old enough to be the girl's mother. Would she see Susan as hampering her freedom?

Ian turns to her. "Why don't you go? It's a perfect day for sailing." He nods to Herbie that the dolly is packed and ready to be transported to the resort. The top box is loaded with fresh papayas.

Cindi is smiling down at Susan, her large straight teeth set against full pink lips on her pretty face. Her manner is welcoming, no awkward threat of being a third party intruder. Susan shrugs her shoulders. What a prospect! A whole day's diversion. The timing is perfect, so she accepts saying she'll need to get a few things from her room.

"We'll wait for you," Toto says agreeably.

On those words Susan flees down the planks thudding on the moorings of the old dock and across the shifting sand that rises to the the land where she heads between the cactus plants avoiding the prickly needles extending off their gigantic leaves. What freedom! What fun! A day's sail ahead of her instead of the gloom of those two women. What a comedy! For isn't that just what the situation is? Comic relief?

She's panting when she reaches her room with the door open. Why is it open? She's startled, then remembers Celianne's inside. "I'm going sailing," she announces.

"Not swimming," Celianne says in a somewhat disapproving tone of one who chastises the impulsive for their inability to make a decision and stay the course.

Susan ignores her. She must concentrate on her needs: a broad-brimmed hat, sunglasses, sunscreen lotion, Teva sandals with their rubber-soled grip, a long-sleeved light cotton blouse, a small carry-on bag with handles to haul her stuff on board. "That should do," she says while peering at the darkness inside the bag. Turning she starts to race back to the boat, but when the ocean comes into view, she sees that Ian is still loading supplies. There's no rush. Time has flown, but she need not. Only one hour has passed since she fled the pool. It seems impossible that so little time has held so much of her imaginings and threatened to change her fortunes. Yet here she is, striding to the dock swinging her bag with nothing more than a lazy day on a sailboat ahead of her.

There's activity on the boardwalk where Herbie has emptied the dolly and unpacked the boxes. Others are carrying the supplies on their shoulders to the back of the resort. All hands are out for this momentous occasion willing to help. They like the excitement and welcome the relief from the routine of their quiet days. Even people not employed by the resort turn up as they, too, like the excitement of the activity. Herbie is pulling the empty dolly back to the dock along the rickety boardwalk and Susan smiles to herself watching him struggle with the ungainly implement that starts and stops as its little wheels get caught in the ridges of the uneven boards. Following a Y path she meets him at the end of the wooden dock and gives way to him citing his purpose as more important than her own.

"Thanks, Miss Susan," he says imitating Toto.

Laughing at his idea of a joke Susan can't help but wonder if Kate Channing and Ruth Diamond are still sitting on the patio, or if the activity stirred their curiosity. Are they watching? Could they recognize her? Can they hear her student politely call her "Miss Susan"? What would they make of her being addressed by the formal, yet junior term, "Miss" followed by her given name? At Randolph Street High School Ms Diamond insisted that all staff be addressed properly. Susan was Ms Borden to the students and in the hallways to her fellow teachers, too. Ruth Diamond got rid of the left-over sixties liberalism of students addressing teachers by their first names. She preferred Ms as it wasn't any of the students' business if their female teachers were married. No man's status got delineated in that manner, so why should a woman's? Some women balked, and not just the old-timers. When Ms Diamond's second term as principal came around, those women were transferred to other positions at different schools. Conform or leave. Susan complained to her sister about the rigid atmosphere that the new female principal created in the workplace noting that in some ways it was worse than any man's rule. "That's the problem with women in authority," Sandra said. "You don't always know the rules. At least men are predictable. They learned the rules playing sports. Simple."

Here is a man unlike those others. In a ritual of affection Ian holds Susan's arm while he kisses her cheek telling her to have a good day. "You deserve a little relaxation," he says.

"I guess I do," Susan says accepting his care for her with generosity. No need to enlighten him as to the real reason behind her need for "a little relaxation". She knows he's referring to the problem with Tijean. All week her conversation at dinner was centered on Tijean's chronic absenteeism and on the problems in class when he did appear. Ian was helpful with suggestions of how to be firm without challenging the boy's self-esteem or embarrassing him in front of the others. "But don't fall for fads like behaviour modification," he said. "Those programs came from other disciplines." Marcel scoffed. In France such behaviour would not be allowed. "The problem with islanders," he said, "is that they're undisciplined. That's why they have no ambition."

Susan kept quiet. She knew better than to cynically ask if leaving home to work at Club Med in the Turks & Caicos, then leaving there to live permanently on a less populous island and work as a bar tender was an example of French ambition? Oftentimes expats are harsher on the islanders than on themselves. Now Susan knows Marcel is a creature made from a different cloth. His remarks are even more insulting than they first appeared. What does a man coddled in wealth know of the dispossessed?

Susan steps aside to let Ian move in front of the pile of boxes where he bends to lift them onto the dolly and sees that the back of his T-shirt is damp with sweat, the waistband on his shorts dark. Toto leans over the gangplank extending a helping hand and Susan climbs on board using the battens underfoot for purchase. Stepping over the gunnel she plants both feet squarely on deck before turning to give a slight wave of goodbye to Ian. But Ian isn't looking her way. He's pulling the long rope that leads from the stern to the bow helping to pull the boat ahead. Toto starts the engine leaving it in neutral and nods to Cindi. Susan watches Cindi who seems to know what to do. "Can I help?" Susan asks.

Cindi smiles at her. "We can manage. The wind is blowing onshore so we must get the boat far enough away so it will turn clear of the dock."

"I'll just watch," Susan says, acknowledging the young woman's higher expertise since Susan only has experience sailing with Ian on his centreboard dingy. They never sail beyond Pumpkin Bluff but stay inside the bay where Ian often takes guests for an hour's outing. If they want anything more adventurous Ian sends them to the marina where they can either charter a boat or join a tour. Marvelous how this young couple handle their big boat with confidence. Susan sits where she hopes she'll be out of the way of their activity, and as Toto gently opens the throttle, she feels the shudder of the engine underneath her. Cindi hoists the main sail leaving the yawl with the furled mizzen. In this manner they sail from the bay into the open ocean.

"Next stop, Whitby," Toto calls to her over the low rumble of the engine and into the dispersing effect of the breeze.

Susan nods as Cindi steps over her feet to get to the line. As Susan pulls in her toes her eyes catch the backs of Cindi's calves which are spindly but muscular; their thinness belie their strength. Susan lets her eyes fasten on Cindi and she watches the young woman coil the plaited rope in loops several times before making a final loop and slipping it over the top. Either Cindi grew up in a nautical family or Toto has taught her well. She moves with ease and Susan can't help but feel proud of her former student. Toto has chosen well, both in his line of work, and in his personal life. She knows she could never have felt such attachment to her students from Randolph Road High School. They were among the most privileged in the city, the country even. As much as they might gain laudable achievements, such accomplishments were expected.

On the open ocean the breeze feels cooler. These are the northerly shores of the Caribbean and it's winter. Even deep sea divers are warned to wear wet suits in these waters when diving off the wall. Beyond Caicos Passage is the Atlantic Ocean, not the Caribbean Sea. They're on the Turks & Caicos, not the Caymans. Tourists assume the same conditions can be found everywhere in the Caribbean, but that's not entirely true. Susan wonders what brought

Kate Channing and Ruth Diamond to these islands, to their island, to Ian's resort in particular? Probably word of mouth. There have been teachers from the city visit, but none Susan knows personally. Most travelers don't want to come to an out-of-the-way spot. They want nonstop travel to a major centre. Now that the question is in her head she can't let it go. Both women are conservative, hardly adventurous. They pursued their careers to the end never rocking the boat, playing the game uncritically, following directives loyally. Why aren't they on a cruise ship? Isn't that where they belong? Susan feels petulant enough to wish them gone on her return to shore, but realizes that's hardly likely.

"Keep a look out for whales," Toto barks in the tone of the captain giving orders.

Susan nods. At this time of year the humpbacks migrate through these waters. She touches her bag having forgotten to pack binoculars. Turning back to Toto who is standing behind the steering wheel in the recessed cockpit Susan decides against asking him. The task of navigating is fully occupying his attention. She looks at Cindi who is cleating a rope on the opposite side of the deck. "Do you have binoculars on board?" she calls.

"Yes, hanging in the cabin."

Susan starts to rise.

"Stay where you are. I'll get them."

Susan sits and feels matronly in a dignified way. Here the distinction has social status, unlike the negative connotations elsewhere. Once again the image of the other two women sitting on the patio materializes in her mind. They seemed matronly, too. They have that in common, age. She has to dispel their haunting interference. Cindi hands her the binoculars. Susan smiles in gratitude locking eyes with the youth. What a joyful pair of eyes they are. Pure white around large solid brown discs set in the middle with small dark pupils. "You're an experienced sailor?" Susan says.

Cindi nods. "My Dad, he sails. Has his own boat for the tourists."

"What's it called?"

"Island Princess."

"Nice."

"My nickname."

"Does he have a card? We'll recommend him to the guests."

"Yes, I'll get it for you before you leave."

Reaching the strap behind her head for security Susan faces the ocean focusing the lens on a distant vessel. It comes into view. A racing yacht with its spinnaker full, a bright yellow one with blue stripes. How exciting to watch the full speed, all the stay sails set flying. And how brave. Susan feels timid with speed. Always has. Since studying cognition in an upgrading course for teachers Susan decides her brain fires a delayed reaction compared to those who race whether on bikes or sailboats. Unlike other people she can't get the message fast enough to relax with the thrill.

"There's a blow."

Susan turns her head away from the eyepiece to see where Cindi's pointing, then moves the binoculars until she finds the spot on the surface of the water. She waits. Sure enough she sights a blow. Patiently she keeps the lenses on the ocean and is rewarded with the arched curve of a humpback with its distinctive backward facing dorsal fin. Minutes pass.

"No full breaching," Cindi says.

Susan looks to where Cindi is standing. "Sorry, do you want the glasses?"

Cindi shakes her head. "I've watched them lots of times. Sometimes they don't breach. They're traveling, not playing or putting on a show." She turns to Susan. "Looks like that's all you get to see for now. Maybe later we'll catch them when they're feeding."

"I'd like that," Susan says. She likes Cindi. Toto always was a lucky boy. Not a great student, but easygoing. She never worried about him. He has people skills, a useful kind of intelligence.

They're tacking at a different angle that puts Susan in the sun. She reaches into her bag for her sunscreen with an SPF of 15 and lathers her face, neck, upper chest, backs of her hands, thighs, knees, calves, a ritual she does more for the moisturizer than sun block. After wiping the excess lotion off her hands she returns the binoculars to her eyes and scans the coastline where Whitby is now in view. Beyond the shoreline is the low rise called Hollywood Hills with a resort on a pristine beach, bigger and more upscale than Ian's establishment. He purchased the land with his pension savings when he was forced out of teaching in the small Maritime town where he lived and worked. Building the resort was a whole other adventure. As an investment it's grown a thousand fold. Laughing to herself Susan feels the thrill of being rich. Funny because Ian never thought of his place as an investment, only as a way of life. He's grateful to own it outright as he couldn't afford to buy it in today's market. Think what he'd have to charge his guests if he had a mortgage to pay? What an understatement that's become. Ian talked that way when they first met. Susan feels she's bursting, but can't share their fortune, or news of their fortune, until after the deal is closed having promised Ian that much last night. Yet she can't quite comprehend how everything has changed for them. They've yet to make plans for the future. Turning her attention away from her inner thoughts she again focuses on the shoreline. It's the beaches that are phenomenal – mile upon mile of white sand and shallow turquoise water. Susan is taken aback by the sweep of the coastline, the sheer magnitude of clear beach. She strongly feels the element of wonder that seems to lie in the phenomenon, but really belongs to the person doing the observing. Still, looking through the binoculars, the sight of miles of sand presents as a phenomenon. Lowering the binoculars she turns her head to address the couple. "Isn't it amazing? All that beach?" Unpopulated, she thinks, but for how long?

"Paradise," Toto says.

Cindi's face lights up in a broad smile. "I think it's our heaven on earth. My Ma thinks it's blasphemous of me to talk like that."

Susan nods recognizing the belief of some islanders who strictly adhere to fundamental principals. Judgement based on faith, or dogma, certainly not scientific observation, or even human emotions. She approves of Toto and Cindi. They have a capacity for enjoying themselves, the best of all freedoms. Such a capacity is the hallmark of a clear mind and Susan is grateful to them for giving her that much, a clear mind looking over clear water at a pristine beach on a clear day breathing pure air. It is glorious. She is in heaven. This is paradise.

They are sailing towards the shore, heading for the marina. As they draw closer to land birds flock overhead – gulls screeching, terns diving, higher a pair of frigates, and standing in a row like soldiers on the supporting posts of the wharf, brown pelicans. Through the binoculars Susan admires the elongated beaks on the pelicans with their underlying pouch.

Cindi is unfurling the sails. They are coming in under power. Susan can understand why. The marina is a busy place, unlike the dock under Pumpkin Bluff. Susan volunteers to tie the stays leaving Cindi free to ready the mooring lines.

A local fisherman catches the line that Cindi heaves. Susan recognizes him. Like Toto, he, too, caters to the market willing to buy from a small, specialized merchant. A few resorts, B&B's, and some restaurants like to advertise that they serve local produce and fresh fish caught daily. Traditional farming isn't as extensive as it once was on the islands. Toto is from one of the few farming families. They trace their ancestors to the slaves who worked the plantations. Toto's created a niche market for his family's harvest allowing them to continue to work the land.

Seeing her friend, Leila, is waiting for Toto's boat, Susan settles her gaze on the woman who seems small boned at this angle, almost childlike dressed in a short, pleated skirt. "Ahoy there, Susan. Are you playing chaperon today?"

Susan tilts her head to indicate the absurdity of Leila's suggestion, then stands. Her friend often teases her about her relationship with her students calling her the den mother. "Did your guests arrive?"

"They did, which is why I'm here. Got here late, though, which is why I'm a little whacked out. The usual problem with Rufus."

Susan knows the pilot. He doesn't know time, at least as it relates to keeping appointments. Guests often shake their head at his mode of operation. "Kept telling us if he doesn't leave in the next ten minutes, then it'll be an hour or two." Susan's heard such musings many times. Yet entrepreneurs like Ian and Leila are dependent on small operators so they must remain committed to them. The charter pilots service more upscale establishments, places with long standing reservations and penalties for cancellations. As Ian would say, "You get what you pay for in this business; efficiency comes at a cost." Susan leans over the gunwale and raises her voice to Leila. "Drop around tonight if you're free?"

"Okay, I will. Sorry about last night."

"No problem. See you later." Susan remains at the side of the boat watching the activity. Toto is hauling boxes from the hold below the cabin. Gil, the fisherman, is helping Leila. Gil is short for Gilbert, but, of course, no one calls him Gilbert. Gil is too appropriate a nickname. He's dressed in cut-off jeans and his legs look skinny below the shredded hem. He'll sell Leila some fish, probably snapper. Leila never buys the conch like Marcel does for the resort.

Snapper for breakfast. Conch for the bar. "Are you heading to Pumpkin Bluff?" she asks when Gil's finished hauling and selling.

As he looks up at her he starts nodding his head and grinning. Susan sees a gap in his mouth where there should be a molar.

"Can you tell them I ordered a grouper for tonight?"

Gil continues to nod his small head.

"Did you lose a tooth?"

Gil closes his mouth and nods more vigorously in assent.

Although Gil is a man of few words Susan knows he can speak. "Are you going to the dentist?"

"Been. That's who took out the tooth."

"Ah," Susan says. What more can be done? A bridge? An implant? That's hardly likely.

Toto comes up from the cabin and stretches to his full height. "That's the last of the cargo. There's no more food, except for the picnic. Do you want to come on a picnic, Miss Susan?"

At this suggestion she feels a twinge of embarrassment. The two of them planned a picnic. They didn't plan for her. "I don't want to spoil your picnic," she says.

"Not spoil. It's in the ice box."

Susan smiles to herself. Toto isn't grasping her meaning. She tries again. " But I don't want to eat your food."

"Plenty of food. Cindi pack enough for ten people. She always afraid we won't have enough. She come from big family. Like me. Always afraid the others eat all the food and not leave anything for her. She eat fast, too. So afraid. I tell her, enjoy. What's the rush?"

Cindi walks by and slaps him on the shoulder. Susan senses their intimacy and thinks she should propose they drop her off before they go on their picnic, but Toto is pointing to the island offshore. "We sail there."

Susan recognizes a favoured beach. There are a number of islands off this shore like it, small and empty, where boaters go to swim, snorkel and picnic. It doesn't occur to her how they are going to moor until Toto drops anchor in the sand. She worries they'll drag anchor, but Toto seems fully confident of his maneuver. Cindi announces she's going for a swim first and gets the ladder to attach to the side of the boat. Toto says he needs a cold drink and asks Susan if she wants some juice. They drink together watching Cindi frolicking in the water. She could be a dolphin the way she dives and plunges. "You're a lucky lad," Susan says. "Having this boat and such a nice girlfriend."

"You think so, Miss Susan?" Toto cannot conceal his eagerness.

"Yes, I do."

"That makes me very happy. What you think is important. You are a good judge."

Susan laughs. "Really, Toto, you flatter me."

Toto is serious now. "What you think means a lot to me. My family like Cindi, too."

"Of course they do. Why wouldn't they?" Susan suspects something is not quite right. Toto remains very serious. "And what about her family? Do they like you?"

"That's the problem, Miss Susan. Her father not liking me. He think she can do better."

"Ah," Susan says. "Well, I think she's a very lucky girl." Susan suspects the father wants his daughter to get an education and a proper job. He'll want her to have a husband from a better class than Toto and with better prospects. Such ambitions are normal in a father with a beautiful daughter. Yet Susan can weigh the advantages of Toto over the unseen problems of another, even one who is educated and well placed. What's observable in Toto makes a longer list on the positive side than the negative. The father is striving for more, but that more is what's unseen and, hence, unknown. "When her father gets to know you better, he might change his opinion."

Toto smiles with a sense of relief that an agonizing lover hardly ever accepts. It isn't conceit he feels. His worry is more abstract. The greater proof of acceptance is in Cindi's physical response to him.

As if she hears her name mentioned, Cindi appears at the top of the ladder like a dripping mermaid culled from the depths of the ocean floor. "I'm hungry," she says and proceeds below to the cabin where the sounds of opening hatches echoes to the deck. She returns with sandwiches, salads, fruit and cold fish. After eating Toto stands. "Now for some serious sailing," he says.

His excitement is contagious, and in the hustle and bustle of setting sail, a gull lands on the boat where he seems content to perch seemingly waiting for them to take him along for the ride. "They always land facing the wind," Toto says of the bird.

"At least the wind hasn't changed direction," Cindi says.

"And the sky is clear. No clouds," Susan says knowing that they can depend on the good weather holding long enough to enjoy a sail. She is feeling useful being given the job of pulling the luff forward. By the time they're under full sail she is feeling daring. The sails are taut and full, their speed practically a race, at least that's how it feels to Susan who could never find the nerve to be on a racing boat, so this is the closest she'll get to clipping over the waves watching the shoreline recede and the horizon continue ad infinitum. What a dare, indeed! It is a heavy boat, not built for planing and surfing like Ian likes to do on his little craft. In many ways Susan enjoys the conventional speed of this vessel better. There's excitement in feeling the rush of wind at her back and seeing the water the boat displaces pounding the hull in foaming waves.

Susan turns her head to see Toto and Cindi trimming the sheets that are luffing when the wind catches her hat. It's a Tilly hat, a present from her sister that she brought when visiting from Canada. The toggle loosens allowing the string to slide over her esophagus. She turns back and grabs the hat from behind her head. When she has it securely in place Susan pushes the toggle up the string to fit tightly underneath her chin. Best to keep her face forward.

Ahead in the distance Susan sees two boats. Both seem to be very close together, a curiosity since there's so much ocean to travel. Why are they crowded together? Toto seems to be sailing directly for them. As they get closer Susan recognizes both vessels. One is a tourist boat that takes sightseers and the other is from the marine museum. Then Susan sees the attraction. They're watching the humpback whales breaching.

Cautious of her tricky hat Susan shifts her body to position herself so she can reach the binoculars. She gives Toto and Cindi a quick glance and smiles as if to ask permission to use them again. They are being very generous to her.

Looking through the binoculars Susan locates the whales. One tail is high and majestic. When it disappears under the water she scans the ocean nearby hoping to focus on another humpback that's breaching. Soon a great arched back rolls out of the water and rises showing its crooked hump. Then the whale lifts its tail presenting its double flukes which seem to hang suspended before slapping the water. The whale plunges and disappears. This spectacle elicits a communal awe. Yes, Susan thinks, people can only revere the power of this mammal. Of course, people do much more. They hunt and kill it, slaughter to the point of extinction. The human effort to counter such destruction is powerful, too. Susan recognizes the marine biologist aboard the research vessel. Everyone on the island knows this scientist and his team. He has their support. There is a will to save these whales by protecting their migratory route from Greenland past these shores. Of course, there's the selfish interest of the tourist industry, but Susan knows the populace also thinks in terms of the mammal's welfare.

Bobbing over the surface of the waves brings them closer to the research vessel. Calling to the scientist she asks if he's seen Tijean Williams, and when he nods in the affirmative, asks when. This one word gets knocked about in the air with the movement of the boats on the ocean and she has to repeat her question. When he answers, "ten days ago," Susan shakes her head in acknowledgment as she realizes he's referring to the boy's visit to the centre to conduct his interview. She notices that there are no divers aboard his vessel this afternoon.

Letting the yawl rock on the ocean Toto speaks to her query. Two nights ago he saw Tijean fly into Sandy Point on his bicycle, only he didn't stay long at Caroline's. "He shot out of town like a bandit," Toto says.

Trying to imagine a bandit on a bicycle Susan asks Toto if he has any idea where the boy might go, but Toto just shakes his head, as much in resignation as in his inability to give a firm answer.

Their boat changes tack. They are heading to shore. After dropping off Susan the couple will head back to Sandy Point. Respect for this couple fills Susan. They are going home. They do not run away from their origins or retreat from intimacy. This is the world they know and they embrace it with every gesture they make from loading the boat with supplies to sailing to different ports of call to making love. How she imagines them intimately reassures her that life will continue. She, herself, is coming to the eve of her physical powers of love making. This young couple are at their dawning.

Unlike them, both Ian and she sought to erase versions of themselves. In doing that, they found each other and created a different life together. Yet the memory of those former selves remains. No matter how distant, they are retrievable. Susan faces forward watching the shore draw closer knowing that her former self is there, on the land, in the memory of two other women, but mostly in her own mind. In an instant her brain can retrieve what is stored. The past is written on stone. These shores are mostly sand where people like Ian and she can escape and redefine themselves just like the sand changes with every coming and going of the tide. It troubles Susan that, ready or not, here comes the past. Before putting a foot on land she struggles with her position of rectitude. For that is how she now feels. Since spotting those women she's gone from feeling fearful and paranoid to being self-righteous. She needs to reassure herself that she was correct in her judgement of them, of what happened to her, and of what she's chosen to make of her life. She was right. Yet that's so black and white and life is grey She can't make life right anymore than she can make it fair.

The strong sun glints off the backstay of the departing boat when Susan last turns to wave goodbye. In a way she wishes she was still aboard. Sail away. Sail away. Sail away. A song. A longing. It takes her a full minute before she turns her back to the ocean.

There's a couple dressed in matching swimsuits sunning themselves on deck chairs beside the pool. They're guests from the States who are into the second week of their stay at Pumpkin Bluff. Otherwise the place is empty except for Herbie who is washing down the rest of the furniture. Susan waves, then sees Ian. He is in front of the panel that's recessed into the back side of the stucco wall holding the key that opens the metal door. "You look windblown," he says cheerily. "How was it?"

"Wonderful," Susan says and stops to stand beside him. "It's quiet here."

Ian shrugs. "You know how it is on a Saturday night. Everyone leaves to go into town. Catch the action."

Most guests treat Saturday night, certainly on their first weekend, as cause for celebration and take a taxi to go out. "Did Guy take the Canadians?"

"Yes," Ian says. "With the two guys from New York. They booked dinner at the French restaurant. Sorry you missed them."

"There's always tomorrow," Susan says, not feeling sorry at all.

"Gil sold us a whole grouper."

"Oh good. I asked him for that. I re-invited Leila."

"That'll make Marcel happier about cooking it."

"I'll tell him"

"Did her guests arrive?"

"Yes. Thanks to Rufus."

Ian nods. "So that was the problem?"

"As usual."

Ian opens the panel door.

"I think I should try to get some work done," Susan says.

"Marcel is taking a siesta in his room."

Susan decides to knock on Marcel's door before going to her own room. To get there she has to pass Ian's office at the back of the resort. The phone is ringing, so she enters and picks up the receiver. The caller asks to speak to Ruth Diamond. "She's gone into town."

"Oh," says the man. "Can I leave a message?"

"Of course," Susan says, and picking up a pen from the clutter on Ian's desk, she bends over the tall stack of message paper. The voice sounds like it belongs to an elderly man. When he gives his name, Dr. Gold, Susan recognizes the old vet. She censors herself from asking how he knows Ruth Diamond, although her curiosity is piqued. After hanging up Susan is in a dilemma as how to relay the message. She is holding the paper at eye level when Ian enters. "Oh," Susan says.

"I thought I heard the phone ring."

"I took the call." She shoves the message into his hand. "It's for one of the guests." For the second time that day, Susan flees from Ian. It's not unusual for her to help in the office, or the bar, or the restaurant, or even the kitchen. It is unlike her, though, to keep running away from him. What is Ian going to think of her? Feel concern for her level of stress and anxiety? Maybe excuse her as menopausal? Or worry that she is angry at him for selling the resort? There's so much to explain.

In her panic Susan forgets about Marcel until she is behind her closed door. "Damn, damn, damn," she says aloud. There is a soft knock outside her door. Then

Ian's voice gently calls her name. She cannot tell him to go away. Inhaling deeply she gains control of herself. "Come in."

Ian rarely enters her room. Usually they meet and socialize in his living quarters which are simply two rooms beside the office, a small bedroom with an ensuite and another small room that serves as a parlor. Susan's room, like Marcel's, is attached to the old games room that mostly sits empty. The rented guest rooms are at the front of the resort facing the ocean, as is the patio beside the bar where the complimentary breakfast is also served. "I know who Ruth Diamond is," Ian says.

When Susan sits on the side of her bed Ian joins her wrapping his arm around her shoulders. "Did she tell you?" she asks.

"She simply volunteered that she'd retired after serving as principal at Randolph Street High School for over ten years. I put two and two together."

Susan looks up. "She stayed as the principal there that long?"

"She kept asking for an extension so she wouldn't have to get to know a new school before her retirement. She volunteered that, too."

"Why is she here?" Susan feels defeated. Of all the places Ruth could go, why did she pick this particular resort for her retirement holiday?

"Sam Gold recommended it. He's making her his executor."

"What?"

"Old Sam's her bachelor uncle. He wants to talk to her about his will."

A bachelor uncle, Susan thinks. "So she's come here to get her inheritance?" That sounds unfair and cruel. Yet she wants to feel cruel to the woman.

"As executor she has to make sure the intent and wishes of the last will are followed. She isn't necessarily going to inherit anything. Apparently old Sam was estranged from his family. He's her mother's oldest brother. She says they're a family who don't get along."

"Why doesn't that surprise me?"

Ian squeezes her shoulder. "Now, Susan."

"Sorry, but you know I'm not loyal to that woman."

"I can't blame you there," says Ian.

"How did you learn so much?"

"We got talking. To be fair, she's really an okay lady."

Susan shrieks. "How can you be so unfaithful?"

Ian moves his hand from her shoulder to her ear. It's a comfort zone, a favourite touch spot. The heady days of their passionate sex lasted for the first three years of their relationship. Lately they've settled into a less carnal affair, more touching than thrusting. It suits both of them. Sometimes Susan can't believe she's got a male lover for her old age when she never had a faithful, steady one as a young, adult woman. "I'm not speaking out of disloyalty. I know what she did to you."

"Didn't do. She didn't stand up for me. Didn't defend one of her teachers. She sided with the parents instead of her staff member. She listened to them and their spoiled daughter."

Ian sighs. "Susan, why so much anger?"

"You know why."

"After all these years? No, I don't. Let it go. It's in the past. How can you let that anger come into your life now?"

"Because." Susan cannot add more to her reason. Why doesn't he understand? Yet, he's right. She's letting the memory of that bad experience colour the present. In a way, she's insulting him. He's given her a good life on these islands. Why be angry? Why isn't she happy?

Ian kisses the top of her head. "I've got things to do." He rises and stands over her. "Will you be alright?"

Susan peers up at him. "Yes, of course. But did you tell her I was here?"

Ian shakes his head. "No, I didn't think it was my place. Besides, I knew you wouldn't be pleased to see her. I'm just surprised at how disturbed you are."

"She's with Kate Channing."

Ian nods, recognizing the name of the other one in the infamous pair. "Why wouldn't she bring a friend?"

"Well she's not my friend."

Ian cuts an arc through the air with his chin in exasperation.

Susan hangs her head. "I suppose that sounds adolescent."

"No comment," Ian says as he retreats.

Susan feels her blood rushing to her head. Is she embarrassed by her thoughts and foolish talk? Or does her mind need more nourishment to sort through how disturbed she really is? Yes, I'm disturbed she wants to shout. She's consumed by a need to justify herself to those two women. And why? Because they held power over her? Because their actions changed the course of her life? Underneath this hysteria flows a tide of reason. Becalm yourself. Her own reaction caused the abrupt change in her life. Hers alone. How can they be blamed for her decision?

Susan wiggles. She needs to get out of this bathing suit. Take a shower. A refreshing shower.

Reason nearly succeeds in ruling her emotions once she is clean and dressed. Only sitting at her desk with student papers piled in stacks according to classes Susan remembers how fraught she was after the accusations leveled against her and how impossible it was then to focus on reading and marking. She came undone, her mind stuck in replay mode. The scene in the classroom haunted her. Susan hadn't seen Jessica fall. But she heard the wail and the commotion.

Jessica had a habit of drawing attention to herself in a negative way so it didn't surprise Susan to find the teenager on the floor surrounded by mocking boys. One of the other girls was solicitous and helpful. Susan let her take care of Jessica while she dispersed the boys and got the class back on task. Then she spoke to that other girl questioning her about Jessica. Apparently Jessica hurt her wrist in the fall when she was tripped. Jessica didn't know who tripped her. None of the boys admitted being the one who did it. Not one of them was responsible. Jessica continued to complain that her wrist hurt. The boys continued to mock and Susan ruled them to keep order. Then the bell rang and they were gone.

Susan remembers how relieved she was when they left. She was always relieved when they left. They were a particularly unruly mob. The class from hell. Actually a class from one of the smaller feeder schools. They had gone through the early grades together and somehow they all ended up in 9B. The whole staff complained about them, and at a meeting with their new principal, Ruth Diamond, asked that the class be disbanded. It was unhealthy for them to be together for so long. They were an incestuous bunch. It was not standard practice to keep students from the same feeder schools together in one form. High school was an opportunity to get to know others. Ruth turned to Kate Channing. Kate had helped with organizing the grade nine classes. Any reorganization would prove horrendous. Imagine the complaints from students and parents, let alone the timetabling readjustments. So they remained together, 9B, the class from hell.

In the evening Susan got a call from her principal asking what had happened in class with 9B. Ruth had just got home from a meeting at the school with Jessica's parents who had stormed into her office after six p.m. when Ruth was packing up to go home. Jessica was at home recovering, her wrist immobilized. Apparently she'd suffered a hairline fracture. Could Susan please give her the details so she could speak to the parents about the situation as an informed administrator? The parents had challenged Ruth. "It's usual to fill out an accident report," Ruth said to Susan over the phone.

Susan apologized. She hadn't realized the severity of Jessica's fall. Yes, she would come in early to fill in a report.

Now no natural light falls across the desk. Susan lifts her head and glances at the digital clock. Where has the time gone? It's been an hour since she returned from the sail and she's done nothing except have a shower and change her clothes. She should speak to Marcel. He was very disappointed last night when Leila failed to arrive.

Marcel has dark bags under his eyes making him look like he's just woken from a night of binging, not from a late afternoon nap. He is unmistakably French in his physical appearance, a gangly body and thin face with a long nose. He's wearing loose boxer shorts. "I bear good tidings," Susan says in apology for having disturbed his slumber. "Leila will be joining us tonight on the patio for dinner."

His face visibly brightens showing deep creases around his mouth and across his forehead. "Hence the fish," he proclaims. "I know a recipe. It's for cod, but it'll work for grouper."

"I knew I could count on you," Susan says.

"À ce soir." In a typical gustatory gesture Marcel smacks his lips against the tips of his closed fingers and winks at her as he shuts his door.

Odd how the thought of childhood keeps coming back to her Susan thinks as she closes the door of her room. Odd how the brain works in middle age with memories from the past barging upon the senses with more immediacy than the present. Could she be going senile? Does she have early dementia? Is this yet another symptom of menopause? Is it a sensation only women experience? For she is elsewhere, not in her little room at all. She can recollect everything about that moment in her past when she went to her father for help with an essay she was writing for school. Her father was sitting in the front room reading the newspaper with the television on, but the volume turned off. It was a habit of his that annoyed their mother. So typical of their household to find Susan in the front room with their father and her sister in the kitchen with their mother. Their father worked for the hydro company as a meter reading man. He got to walk a beat like the postal carriers. Andy Borden credited that daily slog with keeping him trim and fit. His wife, Doris, on the other hand, was rotund which she blamed on hours spent in the house. Andy didn't accept that excuse claiming that housework burned calories and the real problem was all the baking she did. Most evenings Sandra joined her. After the dishes and clean-up was done, the two of them would get out the Joy of Cooking cookbook and start into measuring, mixing and baking. Susan can smell the pineapple squares they made so distinctly she could almost believe there is someone in the kitchen at the resort who's trying the same recipe.

Susan had a much closer relationship with her father than her mother, unlike other girls in the neighbourhood who mostly ignored their fathers, or rather, their fathers ignored them to favour sons who played ball or hockey. Since there was no son, and since her father wasn't very interested in sports, Andy Borden doted on his eldest daughter. He had an intelligence that could have served him well if he'd been a professional man, but circumstances didn't offer him an opportunity for an education, although being limited by a blue collar trade caused him no resentment. Indeed, he treated his job as liberating as it allowed him to concentrate his energies on his hobbies which were mostly reading, gardening and forecasting the weather.

"So what's the topic?" he asked his twelve year old daughter.

"Well, that's the challenge," Susan said. "It's for our English teacher, but she teaches us another subject." Her father's eyes narrowed and locked with hers so she knew he wanted her to continue. "Creative Writing and Geography." Susan looked back up at him.

There was a moment's silence during which her father wrinkled his nose. "Creative," he snorted. "It's either one or the other. Either it's writing or it's geography. Can't she make up her mind? Why in my day."

"Please, Dad," Susan pleaded. She'd heard these criticisms from him a thousand times. He'd argued with the school staff during the parent-teacher interview. "You should run for school trustee. Then you could change things. But I need help with this now."

Sitting back he relaxed. "What are the guidelines?"

"It can be about any place in the western hemisphere."

Slapping his hand on his knee her father whistled. "By crikey! The Western Hemisphere!"

"Yes," Susan said apologetically. "Our teacher didn't want to limit our imaginations."

"No siree. We mustn't do that." Her father laughed indulgently. "Well, my dear, what part of the Western Hemisphere interests you?"

Susan shrugged.

"Just as I thought," Andy Borden said sarcastically. "It's too broad. Where's the facts to inform the imagination?"

Susan puckered her face in a beseeching manner.

"And is the imagination some organic entity outside our mind? What do they think informs the imagination, eh?"

"I dunno."

"Don't go soft-brained, Susan, just because your teachers are."

"Maybe I could write about that place you told me about once. Remember when you read the newspaper aloud to me? There were some islands that wanted to join Canada."

"In the Caribbean?" her father asked. "The Turks and Caicos?"

"Yes, Turks and Caicos," Susan said pronouncing the long 'a' sound.

Now, in her room on those very islands, Susan clearly remembers her father getting the atlas from the bookshelf and showing her the group of islands, her subject for a creative writing assignment using a place in the western hemisphere.

Susan closes her eyes and allows the presence of her father to reappear. When he first died she would sometimes feel him acutely and in such vivid detail she could almost believe he was still with them, still among the living. Over the years, though, his presence has become muted in her memory, not forgotten, simply less intense, less real. In the first year after his death she used to cry over his loss. Now she welcomes his recollection as a glimpse into a lost past. He died suddenly of a heart attack in February of 1996. He wasn't a typical candidate for heart disease being slim and active, but the doctor said it can happen that way when there's a history of heart failure in a family.

In the privacy of her room Susan allows melancholy to rule her emotions. Her feelings are a shadow of what she felt then. She recognizes how intensely sad she was after her father passed away and how, as a result, she was ill-equipped to handle the stress of the classroom. By the time she filled in an accident report, Jessica's parents were already threatening legal action. Susan could barely concentrate on the form with Ruth Diamond interrupting her to give advice about proper wording, all to lessen the school's liability. She called an emergency staff meeting at noon and reviewed the procedure for filling in accident reports emphasizing the need to use the form before dismissing an injured student. Then she called Susan aside and told her there was a supply teacher arranged to take her place for the afternoon while they went to visit the superintendent at his office where she learned of the possibility of having a letter put on her file about the incident. By the evening she was reeling from the threat of being labeled incompetent. A fellow teacher phoned to say that Jessica was back at school with a cast on her wrist and making the most of her disability claiming she couldn't take notes and needed a scribe. The union rep phoned to arrange a meeting to defend her actions against the bloody administrators, but before the end of term Susan handed in her resignation, cowered by the episode.

Susan shakes her head dispelling the pit of those events and wills herself to summon her mind to present matters. Then she goes into the bathroom where she splashes cold water on her face and raises her head to look at herself in the mirror. What a fright! It's a wonder Marcel didn't shut his door in her face she appears such an old hag with tangled hair showing grey roots and blotched skin wrinkled under the eyes. What can she do to improve her appearance? She mustn't show up at dinner in this state. She'll scare away the company. There's nothing for it but to put a colour rinse on her hair. Never mind that she's already had a shower and washed it. Squatting in front of the vanity she roots through the boxes and bottles until she finds the Herb & Tint, a quick and environmentally friendly way to colour her grey. Inside the box are two plastic bottles. She pours half the contents of these into the small plastic bowl provided in the kit and mixes the solution with the applicator brush. Then she starts sectioning her hair and applies the goo along the roots being careful not to miss a section otherwise her hair will be unevenly coloured with batches of her real colour highlighted by the artificial dark blond. Goo splatters onto the white porcelain sink and she leans forward trying to keep the mess inside the bowl where it can be easily cleaned. Afterwards she has to wait half an hour to let the colour set. During this time she trims and manicures her nails, buffing and polishing until they appear rounded and uniform in shape. Then she goes into the shower stall to rinse away the goo. Each strand of hair feels thick until washed and rinsed with an application of creamy conditioner. She wraps a microfiber towel around her head, then rubs her scalp before combing out her hair. In the mirror she sees only dark strands but knows by their uniform appearance that the rinse will successfully cover the roots and her hair will dry naturally with a full body. Her face already appears less haggard; a result, she can only guess, from the stimulation to the top of her head. Despite having worn a hat she can see that her face got some colour which may explain her earlier blotchy complexion. Her skin no longer likes the sun. In her youth she tanned nicely. Now, with too much exposure, she suffers heat rash and redness so she stays covered.

Susan rubs a hypo-allergenic face cream into her forehead, around her nose, across her cheeks and over her chin, which she then lifts so she can apply more cream to her neck. Stepping back she takes a critical look, concluding that the shape of her face has grown squarish with age. Nothing she can do about that. Then she moves close to the mirror and pulls the skin away from her eyes. They are blue like her father's only with streaks of yellow as if her mother's brown eyed gene tried to get mixed into the colouring, but failed. She squeezes some eye drops into the corners; then blinks. Deciding only a little colour is needed Susan pats some powdered rouge along her high cheekbones and applies lipstick from a tube using a small brush, a present from her niece who thinks her aunt needs modernizing.

The weight of memory returns. She loves her niece who is named Christine after Susan's middle name. Holding the thin handle of the brush in her hand Susan is surprised at how ashamed she feels. She was glad to leave the country in 1996, too overwhelmed by gladness to even consider that she was leaving behind members of an extended family like Christine who had grown very fond of her aunt. Twice Sandra has brought her children to visit for a vacation in the sun and both times Christine clung to her aunt when it was time to depart. Of course, Susan has been home on a number of visits, and now Susan realizes, Christine always made time for her. Her niece was never too busy with friends or her own activities. This awareness surprises Susan. She lost out on watching Christine grow from a ten year old girl to a twenty year old woman. It surprises and saddens her. An irredeemable loss.

That terrible sensation rises again in Susan with such heaviness she could be lifting weights. Her feeling of incompetence, that one line in the superintendent's report: An act of incompetence in not filing an accident report or informing her superiors on the day of the afore-mentioned incident. Here she is, ten years later, quaking in the bathroom from the indignity of that accusation. She could have appealed. She could have fought the judgement as the union wanted her to do. But they always like a good fight. Not Susan. She fled.

At first that line obsessed her. She spent hours reliving the scene in the classroom, mostly making endless renditions of her response to Jessica's wailing. If she'd only remained objective and not instantly judged the girl as having another one of her hypochondriacal fits. If she'd taken the time to at least examine the girl's wrist. If she'd spoken about the incident to another teacher who could have advised her and set her on the right path. If she'd only told Ruth Diamond.

Now Susan feels unsettled. All the fussing over her physical appearance and still she loses her wits. She has to get a grip on herself, on her emotions, on her mind. There's company coming tonight. She'll have Leila and Marcel for good conversation. And what is good conversation for but to further understanding? Susan can foresee the pattern the social evening will take. They'll begin with gossip. There's always lots of rumours going around the islands. Maybe there's an update on Tijean, although she immediately decides she's not going to raise the topic of his disappearance because that'll spoil the mood. Then they'll get political. There's plenty of that here, too. Besides, adults always like to think they can solve the problems of the world, especially at a distance, notably over a good meal and wine. Finally their talk will turn personal. Again, she won't raise the topic of the sale of the resort, although she can't help wondering if Leila knows. A social convention: gossip, politics, private affairs. Through building understanding and trust, conversation can raise the comfort level. Just what she needs.

Outside the overhead sky is turning orange. Susan loves the islands when evening settles. Darkness closes in without pressing. Here night doesn't make the world smaller, only more intimate. Brightness makes the islands public, opening them to the many blues of the sea and the sky. While the evening loses colour it brings different smells and sounds. Now there's a gentle breeze laden with the aroma of the sea with a hint of perfume from the orchid vines, a smell like nutmeg. She's become a connoisseur of the evening able to recognize the subtleties of smell transported in the air and to distinguish the noises buffeting against the breeze. The final squawks of the gulls desperate to prolong the day. The low-pitched throat calls of the night heron looking for its mate at the nearby pond.

When she reaches the open patio the ocean comes into view carrying the soft sounds of breaking waves rolling along the coast. The tide is going out adding depth to the broad beach. The final rays from the setting sun glisten off the wet sand attracting barefoot strollers.

Hands grip her hips. Susan shrieks and turns to see Marcel's grinning face. "Marcel," she says.

He moves his hands to her shoulders to stop her for examination. "But you are beautiful," he says in a thinly couched tone of surprise. He still has dark patches under his eyes.

Susan folds her arms under her breasts. "Not like the woman who knocked on your door this afternoon?" She sways, allowing her gathered skirt to swish around her legs.

"This afternoon you were lovely. This evening you are beautiful."

"Flattery will get you everywhere."

"With you?" He winks, then lowers his arms. "I will not betray my friend and present boss."

"Humm," Susan murmurs, thinking how he will use his charms instead on her younger friend.

"Now I go to the fridge to get that grouper you like." He turns and trots away like a gazelle.

There's a low murmur of voices. Susan turns, and out of the dusk, Leila and Ian appear. "I'm so glad to see you," Susan says. She kisses Leila on the cheek and catches the whiff of a fragrant bath gel.

"Thank you for inviting me. Again." Leila extends a bare arm to Susan. She's holding a paper bag with cord handles.

"For you." In her other arm she carries a white, knit, silk sweater.

"Thank you." Susan peers inside and pulls out a single terrarium with a tiny plant growing under the glass lid.

"It's a dwarf hosta," Leila explains. She laughs. "I didn't see the point in bringing a bottle of wine."

"No," Ian says making a broad sweep with his arm in the direction of the bar. "What will you have to drink?"

"Oh, I don't know." Leila looks to her friend, the hostess, for direction.

Ian walks over to the bar and both ladies follow him with their gaze. He's wearing a collared shirt with the top buttons undone so it hangs loosely down his back exposing his bony vertebra.

"Wine, spritzer, vermouth, a beer?" he calls over his shoulder.

"Okay, a spritzer," Leila says.

"And you, Susan?"

"Pimm's. With tonic, please." She's grown fond of Pimm's with tonic. It seems a beneficial drink as an anti-inflammatory to her developing arthritis. Since Leila looks confused, Susan explains, "It's a liquor from Great Britain. James Pimm opened an oyster bar there back in the eighteen hundreds and developed this drink to go with the oysters."

Leila raises her eyebrows in acceptance. "There's a lot here that's British," she concedes.

"You've changed your hair," Susan says, examining the short crop of highlighted hair that stands gelled on the top of Leila's head. It's a modern style which suits her round face. "I like it."

"Thanks," Leila says to Susan and again to Ian who hands her a large stemmed wine glass. He hands Susan an old fashioned glass with ice cubes clunking against the sides.

"Thanks, Ian," Susan says.

Marcel makes an entrance carrying food. He's wearing white linen pants and a black cotton polo shirt. There's a platter with a whole fish that he's holding by the two end handles. Under one arm he clutches a net bag with red potatoes and brown onions. Under the other arm he cradles a small sack of flour and a box of breadcrumbs. "Bon soir," he calls before dropping the food on the counter behind the bar. Then he comes around the corner to where the other three are standing together.

"Leila Sarton, this is Marcel Dubois," Susan says.

Leila extends her hand. "Pleased to meet you."

"Enchanté," Marcel says. He lifts her hand to his lips and kisses her fingers.

Susan gives Ian a look of amused tolerance and Ian smirks in response.

"Do I understand you're cooking for us tonight?" Leila asks.

"Yes, I am preparing the meal. I use a recipe from my homeland that is for salt cod, but grouper is only a bottom feeder, so it will do for this inferior fish. Cod is so much superior, yes?"

"Heh, I'm just an American. What do I know about gourmet cooking?"

"Not much, I agree," Marcel says with utmost sincerity. "Like the bottom feeders of the ocean, your country is at the bottom of the culinary chart."

"Marcel," Susan says in protest. "That's insulting."

Leila is laughing. "I think the French lost the 2012 Olympic bid with that attitude."

"Yes," Susan says, taking a turn at sincerity.

Marcel shrugs. "I can't help what's true." He turns. "Come, sit at the bar. You can watch a master at work."

Ian shakes his head in amusement and follows. Susan stares at Leila wide-eyed with apology.

"Don't look so shocked, Susan," Leila says. "Remember, I'm used to the arrogance of American men. You're overly protected with the likes of Ian to take care of you."

Susan sees Leila's present sitting on the table. "What should I do with this?"

"Put it in your window, and when it's grown to where it reaches the top of the glass, transplant it to the garden."

"You said it's a dwarf? I thought hostas were enormous plants."

"The common variety are. This is just a little border plant. It'll bloom, though."

"How lovely. Where did you get it?"

"My father. He's obsessed with hostas. Even attends week long conferences on them."

"Really? Who would have guessed?"

"I took it from my garden. I hope that's okay?"

"Of course it is." Susan takes Leila's arm, propelling her to the bar. "I just hope I don't kill it."

"You won't. They're a hardy plant and can grow in almost any conditions."

They place their drinks on the counter and sit beside each other. "So you'll never guess who's leaving the islands?" Leila says. She peers over the narrow counter to watch Marcel finely slicing the onions on a wooden board that he usually uses for cutting lemons and limes.

"Who?" Ian asks as he opens a bottle of cold beer for himself.

"Rufus."

Marcel stops his slicing and stares directly at Leila. "The pilot?"

"The one and only."

"But I rely on him," Marcel says in a complaining tone. "How will I get to Provo to visit my friends?" Turning to Ian he continues, "How will guests get here?"

"Where is he going?" Susan asks.

"Thailand."

"Thailand?" Ian says. He reaches for a bottle of wine which he displays to Marcel. "Is this what you want?"

Marcel nods and resumes slicing.

Ian takes the corkscrew from the tray and opens the red beaujolais wine from Cote-De-Brouilly.

"Why does the old codger want to go there?"

"He's not so old," Leila says. "Just weathered. He's only my age."

"He can't be," Susan says.

Leila nods in the affirmative.

Marcel pushes the pile of sliced onions to the side of the board and turns on the tap. "And how old is that?"

"Really, Marcel. I didn't know French men had such rude manners," Susan says.

"You are wrong, Susan. French women are flattered when you ask them their age. Then they can impress you with how youthful they look."

"Thirty-six," Leila says as a matter-of-fact.

"See," Marcel says to Susan then turns to Leila. "You look twenty years younger than Rufus."

"You're right." Susan directs her comment to Ian. "I always thought Rufus was our age," she says, picturing the man in her mind with his weather-beaten face.

"So did I," Ian says. "How has he done all he says he's done in only thirty-six years?"

Marcel plunges the potatoes in the water. Then he sprinkles a couple of tablespoons of flour on the onions. "So why does he want to go to Thailand?"

"He says tourism has picked up again, only not everyone wants to work there in case another tsunami hits, so they need pilots. Besides, he has a friend there."

"Was his friend affected by the tsunami?" Susan asks.

"No, he's not on the Andaman Sea. He's on an island in the Gulf of Thailand, the other side from where the tsunami hit."

Marcel takes a garlic from the bottom of the net bag and minces a clove on the wooden board.

"Is his friend a pilot?"

"No, an architect," Leila says.

"Maybe they need a chef?" Marcel mixes the garlic with the onion and seasons the mixture with salt and pepper.

Ian huffs. "Hope you're not changing your mind about where you want to settle?"

"I'll talk to him," Marcel says. "But don't worry. I won't go anytime soon. I like to hear how it goes for Rufus first." Marcel takes the pot of potatoes to the outdoor range at the back of the bar and lights the burner. Then he jaunts back to the bar and raises his glass of wine before taking the first sip.

"To friends," he says.

"Friends," they chorus.

Leila finishes her spritzer and Marcel offers her the red wine. "Try some of this," he says.

"Don't you drink white wine with fish?" Leila asks.

Marcel shakes his head. "Such parochial rules," he says. After pouring some wine in her glass he lathers a slab of butter onto a large copper pan. "It's good wine, no?"

"Yes, very good wine," Leila says.

"You drink good wine with food. That's the only rule." He carries the pan to the other burner, then returns for the board and drops the onions and garlic into the sizzling butter. Immediately he picks up the brass handle and shakes the pan. "You must open more wine," he says to Ian.

"Another bottle of the same?"

"No, I spare you the expense. We drink this Domaine de la Madone. A cheaper beaujolais for cooking, please."

"Well, that's a relief," Ian says, uncorking another bottle.

Susan turns to Leila. "Isn't it nice just to watch?"

"It certainly is. But I feel I should be helping in some way."

"I suppose we could set a table."

"That would be helpful," Ian says.

Susan gathers the cutlery and shows Leila where to find the napkins. She picks a table near the end of the patio with a clear view of the ocean. The sound of the retreating tide serves as a soothing backdrop. "Don't feel obliged to like Marcel," she says quietly.

Leila giggles. "He is a charming character. How can you help but not like him?"

Susan knows Leila's too old to shelter from any match-making stratagems. Still, she feels protective, even though Ian and she arranged this meeting. Returning to the bar Susan picks up her drink, cautioning herself to sip slowly. Sometimes it seems the Pimm's goes down like pop.

"And what about your guests? Ian said there's a couple of women from Canada staying at the resort. He and Marcel got talking with them briefly late Friday night when they arrived. Have you had a chance to meet them?"

Susan knows Leila's not to blame for her ignorance, yet somehow Susan registers Leila's unwitting question as the height of innocence, even callow. "Actually, I know them quite well."

"Really?" Leila remains perplexed. "Ian didn't mention that they're friends of yours. But then, they've only just arrived."

"Actually," Susan says, repeating that single word, "actually" - a leader to right any false interpretation. "I know them from teaching."

"Ah," Leila says.

Susan knows Leila hasn't guessed the half of it. "They were unaware I was here."

"Oh, I see," Leila says.

No you don't, Susan thinks, but explains, "The one, Ruth Diamond, is Sam Gold's niece. That's why they're here."

"To visit Sam?"

"Yes," Susan says, keeping her explanation simple.

"So, Sam does have relatives who care." Leila turns her torso to face Susan. "At least about his money. I bet Sam thinks his niece is a gold digger."

Thinking how well his surname suits his character Susan says so to Leila. Laughing together they rejoin the men at the bar. While the potatoes and fish simmer Marcel chops greens for a salad. They watch his hands in action mesmerized by his easy skill. "Did you have a nice sail today, Susan?" he asks without lifting his eyes from the chopping board.

"Yes I did," Susan says. She readjusts her position on the stool so she can rest her feet on the bottom rungs, then looks across the bar at Ian. "Do you know Toto's girlfriend's father, Dick Ellis? He runs a tourist boat out of Grand Turk?"

"No."

"Sorry," Susan says. "I meant to give you his card. Cindi gave it to me this afternoon. I wonder how they met?"

"Probably at a jump-up," Ian says.

They laugh remembering their own times at those dances. "Probably," Susan says. "Anyway, I thought you could use him for the guests, but obviously, he's too far away."

Leila leans further into the bar and rests her elbows and forearms against the edge. "He's such a nice young man, Toto," she says.

"Yes, he is," Susan says. "Unlike the yappy dog in OZ, he's very quiet, though adorable."

Marcel twists his lips and hums. "You ladies have a crush on the young man?"

Susan does not hide her disdain as she turns to Leila. "I think Marcel is jealous of younger men."

Leila shakes her head in agreement. "Yes, he's probably threatened by them."

"He's quite an entrepreneur," Ian says. "You have to admire the kid."

"Okay, I surrender," Marcel says. He asks Ian to hand him a bowl from the cupboard. Clanking and shifting the bottles he retrieves the dark, basil vinegar and the extra-virgin olive oil. "A simple dressing," he says as he mixes the oil and vinegar with a squeeze of lemon. He looks up at Leila. "You still want to help?" he asks.

"Sure. What can I do?"

"Toss this." Then he turns to Ian. "We need four dinner plates and four salad plates." After giving the order, Marcel turns down the burner.

Leila cocks her head at Marcel. "Shall I take this to the table?"

"S'il vous plait."

Leila turns to Susan. "I don't know what he said, but I think it's yes."

Susan giggles. "Please, Leila. 'S'il vous plait' is please. Yes is a simple 'Oui'."

"Si," Leila says as she lifts the bowl. "I only know English and Spanish."

Marcel drains the water from the potatoes down the sink. "Spanish isn't much of a language."

Dropping her head into her hands Susan rests her elbows on the counter top. "I'm glad she didn't hear that," she says quietly, then faces Ian. "He's a snob."

"All French men are snobs," Marcel says.

Picking up the salad plates Susan follows Leila to the set table. The sky over the ocean has turned royal blue, the warm colours of orange, red, pink and violet sink with the last rays of the sun. "Look at that," she says. "Not a cloud in the sky."

"It's perfect," Leila says.

"Sorry," Susan says, indicating the men at the bar with a flick of her head.

"Don't apologize," Leila says. "I'm glad you introduced me. I've never met anyone like him. But then, I don't think I've ever met someone who's French. Certainly not in the Keys, or at the B&B."

When Leila and Susan return to the bar Marcel has the hot food arranged on the plates. He gives them each a hot plate to carry and picks up one for himself, as well as the bottle of red wine.

"Shall I bring the salt and pepper?" Ian asks.

"No need, Ian. It's spiced to perfection."

When seated Ian proposes a toast to the chef and they raise their glasses. Marcel turns uncharacteristically modest and suggests they eat before singing his praises. It seems he speaks out of confidence, though, not modesty, because on taking their first bite all three diners start praising the food and congratulating him once again.

Leila swallows noisily. "This is so succulent. How do you keep the fish moist? I've never tasted anything so good, even at home on the Keys and there's plenty of seafood restaurants there."

"Well, you Americans are dedicated to life, liberty, and the pursuit of happiness," Marcel says. "We French demand the right to good food, fine wine, and many holidays." He raises his glass to Leila. "We define happiness through our culture, not our organizing political principles."

Susan raises her glass to her lips, but before sipping, looks at Ian who is sitting on her right. "And what's our organizing principle?" she asks.

"Peace, order, and good government," Ian says pithily.

"How dull," Susan says. "Aren't we Canadians a sensible lot?"

"That sounds very sensible to me," Leila says. "I wish my country put peace first."

"Yes," Marcel says. "I agree with Leila. What's wrong with sensible? Especially when it comes to politics?"

"Well, sober then," Susan says. "It sounds so sober compared to the Americans."

"And adult," Ian says. "A young country with adult intentions."

Susan stays her knife and fork. "How eloquent."

Ian broadens his smile. "Thank you. I love it when you admire my mind."

"I must visit your country sometime," Marcel says. "I'm interested in seeing the French part."

"Quebec," Susan says. "That's the province. It's only hot in the summer months."

"It doesn't need to be hot," Marcel says. "I am used to the cold and the rain. I ski, too."

Ian swallows before speaking. "Actually, you'd like Quebec. You can go skiing at Tremblant during the day and enjoy fine dining at night. There are good restaurants in Quebec. It's that French thing, you know."

"I've never been to Canada," Leila says. "But I've been told by Canadian tourists who come to Florida that it's cold."

"You can come with me, cherie," Marcel says. "I will keep you warm."

"Don't miss a beat, eh Marcel?" Ian says.

"What beat?" asks Marcel. "I'm not a musician."

Leila turns to him in earnest. "It's a saying, a colloquialism. Ian means you take every opportunity to flirt with me."

"Yes. Is that okay with you?" he asks seriously.

Leila and Susan look at each other.

"It's part of the dinner, yes?" Marcel says.

"Very good, Marcel," Ian says. "You cook, you flirt."

Marcel grins at Leila. "It's just the beginning of the night."

Now Susan and Leila laugh out loud.

Ian turns to Susan. "I'm so glad we didn't arrange a blind date?" he says.

"Blind date?" Marcel says. "Date, I know. Why blind?" He turns to Leila. "Do you say this, too, in America? Blind date?"

"Yes," says Leila. "I've been on blind dates."

"So what happens?" Marcel asks.

"Friends arrange for you to go out with someone you don't know, but who they know, if they think you might like each other."

Marcel seems pleased. He wipes his mouth with the side of the napkin, then returns it to his lap. "This is better," he say. "I cook for you. You cook for me." He looks at Leila directly. "You cook breakfast, yes?"

Susan grabs her napkin to cover her open mouth while she laughs.

Leila remains sober. "I will be cooking breakfast tomorrow morning," she says. "For my four guests."

"Four? Five?" Marcel asks.

"Five including me."

Marcel turns back to the last scraps of food on his plate. "Maybe more," he says. He rises. "We need bread. And more wine."

Ian leans across the table towards Leila. "We didn't mean to set you up like this," he says.

"It's okay," Leila says. "It's been awhile since anyone's admired me."

Ian returns to an upright sitting position. "Oh, is that what it is?"

"Leila," Susan says. "He's blatantly hitting on you."

"Don't worry, you two. I can take care of myself."

Marcel plops the opened bottle of wine that he used for cooking on the table. "Now our mouth has acquired taste buds for fine wine, but we no longer can taste so well, so we won't know the poorer quality of this bottle." He remains standing as he cuts the bread on the board.

Raising the bottle to the ladies to indicate if they want more to drink Ian offers to pour. Leila nods in the affirmative. "Susan?"

"Just a half a glass, please."

Ian extends the board with the bread. "You'll need wine to go with the cheese," he says.

"What cheese?" Susan asks.

"The cheese I am now getting," Marcel says.

When Marcel is out of earshot Susan leans over the table in a conspiratorial huddle. "Guys, can we get this conversation heading somewhere that doesn't dead end in sexual innuendo?"

Reaching a hand under Susan's hair, Ian massages the back of her neck. "Relax. He's just having some fun."

"And being a flirt," Susan says.

"What's wrong with that?"

Leila watches Susan throughout this exchange with narrowed eyes. "You seem a little up tight tonight, Susan? Is anything wrong?"

Susan shakes her head vigorously. "No," she says, as she leans her back against the patio chair.

"If I didn't know better, I'd suspect you were jealous," Ian says.

"Don't be silly," Susan says.

"Or maybe I should be jealous?" Ian says.

Susan raises her hands and forearms in surrender. "I won't say another thing."

Marcel returns with a plate of three different cheeses and stands over the table holding the two-pronged cheese knife. "Ladies, what is your preference? A soft, ripe camembert? A sharp, blue cheese? Or a hard, white cheddar?"

Leila interlaces her fingers and pulls her arms against her chest so her hands rest between her separated breasts. "Can I have a small piece of each one?" she asks.

"But, of course." He slices three sections of cheese and hands each one separately to Leila on the end of the knife. She takes them in her hand and puts them on the side of her salad plate cum bread plate. "Susan?"

"The same, thanks."

"So, Ian," Leila says without raising her eyes from the selection of cheeses. She seems to be pondering the dairy products with the kind of intense interest a researcher pays to a specimen. "How is your son doing at college?"

Marcel looks from Ian to Susan. "You have a son?"

"Ian's son," Susan says.

"I was once married," Ian says. "A long time ago. Just some cheddar for me, Marcel." He turns to Leila. "Dartmouth is actually a university. He's loving it and doing very well. At least, he got high grades in first term. He's in residence. First time living away from home, or from his mother." Ian makes a stifled guffaw, feeling the indignity of his ex-wife's overly protective practices.

Marcel sits. "What's his studies?"

"It's just gen. ed., a foundation year."

"Gen for general?" Marcel asks.

"Yes, sorry," Ian says. "General as in unspecific, not military. It's good for him because he doesn't know what he wants to focus on. Maybe Fine Arts. Maybe Poli. Sci. Who knows?"

Leila asks Marcel to pass the bread. "I met him last Christmas," she says. "He looks a lot like Ian, same frizzy brown hair and pale freckled skin."

"He comes to visit?" Marcel asks.

"At least once a year."

"And do you visit him?"

"Rarely," Ian admits. "I encourage my relatives to come here. It's hard to leave this place. Who would run things?"

"Not me," Susan says. "I have a job. And I hardly feel competent to fill your shoes."

Voices reach them, carried by the night air. "The guests are returning," Ian says.

Susan feels a jolt run through her nervous system. She settles when she recognizes the Copelands, the couple from New York. Tonight they're both dressed in whites. "Hello," she calls.

The Copelands walk over to their table. "We've just had a picnic on the beach," Arthur says.

"Did you enjoy it?" Ian asks.

"Oh, very much," Sharon says. "We felt stuffed from eating so much this past week so we decided to lighten the fare this evening. Just fruit, bread, cheese and a bottle of wine. Much like what you're eating now."

"We've had a fish feast," Leila says. "Cooked by Marcel."

"I bet that was good," Sharon says.

"I saw you strolling along the beach earlier. How far did you go?" Susan asks.

"Just to the dock," Arthur says. "We sat on the end of it watching the setting sun."

"And feeding bread crumbs to the pelicans and gulls," Sharon says. She reaches her arm through her husband's elbow. "Well, we won't interrupt you any more. Good night."

The four diners wish the couple a mutual good night. "Why don't we take a walk along the beach?" Marcel asks.

"That sounds like a fine idea," Leila says.

"You two go ahead," Ian says. "We'll tidy up."

"Yes," says Susan. "That's the least we can do. Thank you for cooking dinner, Marcel."

"My pleasure." Marcel and Leila insist on helping to carry the dishes to the bar before leaving.

The dishwasher is a British model, half the size of North American appliances. Yet the capacity is generous. It's quietly chugging along doing its job when the electricity goes off. "Damn," Ian says.

In the total darkness Susan can see Ian's shadow groping for a cupboard handle. She guesses he's looking for the emergency kit. She remains immobile knowing to move would only result in knocking into something. Then a strong beam of light shines across her face.

161

"There you are," Ian says, lowering the light. "Here's the small flashlight."

Susan feels the metal handle and finds the switch.

"I'm going to turn on the generator," he says. "Can you stand guard and help any guests unfortunate enough to arrive in total darkness?"

No sooner is he gone than Susan hears a commotion. She lights the way in front of her feet to where the sounds of giggling and cursing come. The voices are recognizable. It's the gay couple, Ted Morrall and George Smitherman. For a few seconds she listens to their spirited responses before stopping in her tracks. They're with Kate Channing and Ruth Diamond.

"Over here," Ted calls. He has a loud, booming voice with a hint of an Irish brogue.

"Is that you, Ian? Shine that light in this direction."

Susan recognizes Ruth's bossy voice. "No," she says simply.

Ted's voice again penetrates the solid darkness. "Oh, it's you, dearie. Come to our rescue, have you? We're so grateful."

Susan wants to reply in like gratitude, so long as he doesn't say her name, but keeps calling her "dearie". She met Ted and George briefly last night and instantly liked them. Ted is the talkative one and had them in stitches within one minute of sharing their travel stories saying they went from being coddled like they were still in kindergarten on board the jet from the States to being bounced around like no-good scoundrels on the tiny plane from Provo. Cautiously she steps in their direction.

"You're a saint," Ted says when Susan shines the light on his person. His face is red either from too much tropical sun or too much tropical booze. He stands frozen with the dim light on him.

"Suddenly we were in darkness."

Susan recognizes Kate Channing's voice. "Ian's gone to turn on the emergency generator." The reality of his action hits her. When he starts the generator the lights will come back on. "Sorry about this. Ian has the big flashlight, but I'm sure I can guide you to your rooms."

"You lead, duckie," Ted says. "Let's form a line by holding hands."

Susan is game for any helpful suggestion and reaches for Ted's hand with her free hand. "Ready?" she asks. The congo line sets the four others giggling. Behind her they stumble and shriek.

"My foot!"

"Sorry."

Ted accompanies their nocturnal jerk with a tune. "Ta, ta, ta, ta, ta, ta, tum." Soon all four are humming along with him.

Susan heads straight for the ladies' suite. She feels in a panic to get there and has to remind herself to go slowly so no one will trip in line. There are no visual markers and she has to rely on the small pool of light on the ground. Hesitantly Susan lifts the flashlight to check for the building. The only natural clue to the senses to help her orient her position is the distant sound of the ocean, that eternal tide keeping the waves in motion. It provides a reassuring backdrop to the raucous noise of the congo song behind her.

"We're in Room Four," Ruth calls when Susan again attempts to lift the light.

Suddenly the lights come on with a seeming brilliance, although it's only the recessed room light above the doorway that shines. Susan steps aside into the cover of darkness and turns off the flashlight.

"Here we are," Ruth says eagerly holding her purse under the dim light while searching for her key. Turning to the men, she says, "Won't you come in for a night cap?"

Ted laughs. "It's way passed George's bedtime. And I'm still feeling a little jet-lagged. Thanks, just the same. We had a grand old time tonight." He turns to where Susan is standing. "Thanks, dearie, we can find our way now."

Susan waits while the ladies offer their thanks to her and the men, then go inside and shut the door to their room. Like a timid mouse she scurries back to the bar following the ground lights along the path. The resort sits in gloom as only the working light above the bar sink is on. Ian's turned off the strings of lights that decorate the front of the bar and the overhanging lights around the patio. "You need to put in solar cell lights," she says.

"I know," Ian says. "Did some guests return, then?"

"Yes, four of them."

"That makes six safely tucked away in bed. Six more left out there in the darkness."

Ian has his back to her. She notices the top of his scalp where his hair is starting to thin. The pink skin showing through reminds her of a baby's head. It occurs to her that people carry their beginnings with them all their lives. She feels they are returning to those beginnings as they age – losing hair, losing memory. It's like coming full circle. Ian doesn't ask who were the four guests and she doesn't name them. It's not like they're their parents. "Marcel and Leila are out there in the dark."

"I'm sure they'll manage."

She feels self-conscious about her reactions to their coupling and in need of explaining herself. "I don't know why I reacted to their interest in each other the way I did."

Turning to face her, Ian waits for her to explain further. He is a good listener. His patience makes him a good listener, as well as his genuine interest in other people.

"It's silly because today I was thinking about when I first came here and met you."

"What were you remembering?" he asks with the tone of someone used to giving a gentle prod.

Susan smiles. "Remember you challenged me to find the anagram to your name?"

Ian laughs, showing his small, pointed teeth.

"Did you ask all the ladies you met to figure that out?"

"No, honest," Ian says. He approaches her and drapes both arms over her shoulders. Again he laughs at the recollection. "I remember that. I'd come across it in some magazine I was reading." He snoggles her nose. "You have to believe me. You're the only one who I ever challenged."

"Whom."

"What?"

Susan leans her head back. "You're the only one I challenged."

"Why do English teachers always spoil the fun?" He pulls her back close to him. "So why didn't you want Leila to like Marcel?"

"Oh, I don't know. I thought they'd only just met. Then I remembered our instant courtship."

"Love at first sight."

Susan leans her forehead against Ian's in a silent gesture confirming their mutual feelings. "I'm not too sure I totally trust Marcel."

"You're kidding me?"

"No. Maybe I just don't know how to read him."

Ian shrugs like the French man. "There's more to Marcel than meets the eye."

"I'm glad to hear it."

"I hope he's not thinking of backing out of buying this place."

Susan looks at Ian quizzically. "How do you mean?"

"Well, he did seem interested in Thailand. Maybe he wants to run his own resort there, too."

"Ah," says Susan comprehending. "Like a chain. Turks & Caicos. Thailand."

"Sounds ambitious."

"So I guess he came here more like an apprentice?"

Ian nods. "Something like that. Maybe he'll rebuild one of those places in Thailand destroyed by the tsunami."

"Thank you for telling me that." Susan's mind enters another realm of disquiet. Ruth Diamond was always saying that. "Thank you for telling me," or, "Thank you for asking." Susan yawns.

"Yes, it's that time," Ian says. He releases her and jiggles the bunch of keys in his pocket. "I hope the electricity comes on soon because that generator is very noisy outside my office."

"It will," Susan says. "Doesn't it always? The Saturday night blackout from too much energy consumption. It's like peak hours at home between six and eight weekdays when everybody returns home from work and turns on their lights or air conditioners and stoves or other appliances. Only on this island peak consumption coincides with Saturday night's entertainment, not the work week."

"Very clever, my lady. Do you want something before we retire?"

Lifting the inexpensive bottle of beaujolais, Susan tilts it. "Shall we finish this?"

"Okay." Ian takes two stemmed glasses from the overhead wrack. They hang upside down along a groove cut in the wood. He turns and follows Susan who again turns on the flashlight. "You know, I first saw this system for storing stemmed glasses when I traveled to Europe as a student. They had them in all the bars."

"Yes, I know. You've told me a dozen times."

"Have I?"

"Um, humm," Susan says thinking how much they've become like an old married couple. How do other people do it? They stay together for decades listening to the same stories repeated ad nauseam.

When inside the parlour Ian suggests playing some CD's to cover the sound of the loud generator. Susan lights some candles and holds a candle dish by its pottery handle above the storage rack so Ian can make a selection. He shows her the score from the Cole Porter movie. "Okay?" he says.

"Sure. Why not?" Ian claims Kevin Kline can't sing so Susan is a bit surprised that he's chosen the CD which she bought after they saw the movie De-Lovely. They saw it on Provo, the only island with a movie theatre. Ian rarely leaves the resort so it was a special treat and, of course, he knows all the lyrics. Susan defended her purchase saying the other performers could sing. Besides, Kevin Kline can dance and act and she thought he was brilliant in the movie.

Ian rises from his squat as the first strains of music play. He beckons. "Shall we?"

They dance cheek to cheek in the dark room with Ian humming in accompaniment to the opening strands of Robbie Williams' rendition of "It's De-Lovely." When he sings, "Do Soh Me Lah," he loosens his grip on her shoulder, steps away and begins to serenade her, " The night is young." Then he twirls her under his arm. She joins in the refrain, "It's delightful. It's delicious. It's de-lovely." She's ready again when he sings, "To the pop of champagne Niagara Falls." "Canada," Susan adds in a mock toast. Then he pulls her close and again they dance cheek to cheek. Ian continues to hold her throughout the second track as he sings along with Alanis Morissette. When he gets to the middle of the song and sings, "Even lazy jelly fish do it," Susan thinks of the ocean at their doorstep and how easy it is to relate to Cole Porter's songs. Near the end of the track Ian again steps away from her to serenade, "The most refined ladies." Then she joins in the lyrics, "Let's do it. Let's fall in love." He's back to humming the third track accompanying Sheryl Crow in "Begin The Beguine." In her head Susan sings along to the words, "Of tropical splendor, It brings back the memory of green under the stars and down by the shore an orchestra's playing and even the palms seem to be swaying when they begin the beguine." By the fourth track Ian's broken out and is upping the ante on Elvis Costello singing "Let's Misbehave." He steps away and starts dancing a Charleston. They're used to the darkness now and elegantly avoid the furniture in the cramped space. Before the song ends he leaves her and reaches for the remote. Susan knows what he's doing, skipping "Be A Clown." She walks over to the end table and pours the left-over wine into the glasses, then sips the oxygenated liquid to the introduction of "Night and Day". Ian joins her, picks up his glass, and after taking a long gulp, finishes off the small portion of wine. Setting down the glass he looks into her eyes and accompanies the exaggerated call on the CD track, "You, you you." Again Ian sings along with the lyrics, "Night and day you are the one." Sometimes he stretches the vowels in a parody of conviction, "Spend my life making love to you." She sips slowly and smiles at him under the rim of the glass. When that track ends he takes her empty glass and puts it on the table. Reaching for her he holds her tightly singing the words to the beginning of the next song, "Oh how lucky we are. While I give to you and you give to me. So on and on it will always be."

The computer in the office beeps.

Ian pulls back. "Could that be the electricity back on?"

"I hope so," Susan says watching his shadow leave the room.

"Yes," Ian calls from the office. "It's back on." She hears him opening the office door. "I'm going to turn off the generator," he calls.

Letting the candles burn Susan sits. Why spoil the mood? She feels permeated by Ian – his physical presence, his distinct smell, his easy dancing, his pleasant voice, his true love. He is wonderful company and has been a loving partner these past ten years. She knows how very fortunate she is to have met him, to have fallen in love, to have him offer her this – a place in the tropics that is an unusual, but very comfortable home. Yet she doesn't dwell on that, but on the only story Ian ever told her just once. It was why he felt he had to leave the little town in Nova Scotia where he was born, raised, married, and taught school. A nine year old girl in his class accused him of sexual abuse. The principal hauled him out of the classroom and told him he had to go home. At the time the principal apologized, saying he knew the girl was white trash. Ian was surprised to hear him use that term, "white trash". The girl's word was unreliable coming from a family like that, but the law stated that when accused a teacher could not remain in contact with pupils. Either Ian had to prove his innocence, or the girl had to retract what she'd said about him. Of course, Ian was devastated. He knew where her family lived on the other side of town and he knew one of their neighbours, an old school chum, who came by the house to offer Ian his moral support, telling him how unbelievable the girl's accusations were. Everyone in town knew he was incapable of such behaviour, just as everyone knew the girl was more than capable of lying. Ian understood the situation, but as he said to Susan, once accused he felt he could never hold up his head again without feeling that everyone in town felt something toward him, either sorry or suspicious. He may never have been an abuser, but he was an accused one and it amounted to practically the same thing. So he made up his mind not to return to teaching, but to leave.

The CD stops playing. Susan looks over at the machine that is flashing a digital display. Leave it, she thinks. Ian must have turned off the generator. When Ian confided this slander to her he admitted how difficult it was to leave the only place he had known. "It was the humility I felt, like a terrible blight. I was unable to step out of myself. I just couldn't shake it off. I had the support of family and friends, my colleagues. The place where I lived, where the Camerons have lived for generations. Not just the town, but the whole county. Camerons everywhere. Some of them prosperous. Some of them still eking out a marginal living.

Not anyone had left the county, let alone the country. I was paralyzed by the accusations. I no longer trusted the system. Not when it could throw me out like that."

Susan remembers the look he gave her then, his eyes haunted and bulging, still terrified. She recognized his plea. What have I done wrong to be so abused? Indeed a contagion it was. The abuse that the girl suffered transmitted to him, her first male teacher. The spread of abuse infected all innocent victims. He had a much rougher go than Susan did. The accusation against him became public through word of mouth. Hers remained on file, hidden, only known to a few. He lost his immediate, as well as his extended, family, watched a son grow up from a distance of thousands of miles, risked a new start in life at a strange business in a foreign country. She admired how he seemed to put it all behind him, despite the heavy cost; how he welcomed each new day with optimism; how he rebounded with energy from such a set-back; how he gave himself to the life he'd chosen by default.

Susan looks at the clock wondering why Ian hasn't returned. Probably there is more to do than just shut down the generator. Stretching her arms above her head and yawning, Susan stifles the desire to close her eyes. Her sleepy mind continues to analyze her negative response to her old colleagues despite her better sense which tells her to listen to Ian. Unlike her, Ian never got a negative professional report placed on file. He never returned to teaching. He left. Both of them came here seeking asylum. Most people come to the islands looking for utopia, a place in the sun where people live peacefully. At least, that is the sentiment that used to draw residents. Now more visitors come simply as tourists. New residents are mostly investors or asylum seekers from Haiti. How the politics and dynamics have changed over the decade. There are still a few characters around who originally came seeking paradise, like the old vet, Doc Sam Gold. Susan's mind is a spiral. It ends up where it started. With them. They're giving her a persecution complex simply by being here. It's an idiotic reaction. She knows this. Yet she can't help herself. Maybe she should have faced things head-on. Maybe running away wasn't such a good idea. Maybe she should have fought back. But with what? She had no energy then. She has no energy now. She simply wants to go to sleep. Where is Ian? Why hasn't he returned? She pushes herself off the chair and stands.

Outside she finds Ian at the far end of the pool talking to Marcel and Leila. Over the ocean the dance barge is silhouetted against the sky, its twinkling lights moving across the horizon like a ghostly pirate ship, its rhythmic music floating along the air like the chords of bellowing bagpipes. "There's the dance barge returning from Parrot Cay," Susan says. The others look.

Marcel puts his thumbs through two belt loops while he continues to stare. "The young couple from Canada went with the four Brits."

Ian cocks his head to look at Susan. "Remember when we used to do that?"

Susan smiles. "How was your walk?" she asks.

Leila is still holding the heel straps of her sandals. She turns her head to look at Susan with an expression suggesting she's seeking confirmation from a friend. "Wonderful. Marcel's giving me a ride home." Leila turns her head away to look at Marcel's profile.

Susan wills herself to a position of generosity. "Better than cycling at this time of night," she says, although she knows Leila's bike is equipped with a powerful headlamp.

"Her bike will fit in the back of the jeep," Marcel says.

Susan guesses they won't see Marcel again tonight. He doesn't work Sundays. When the couple leave Ian tells her he needs to cover the pool for the night so Susan offers to help. She does so absentmindedly thinking about the day and trying to retrieve some of the memories of her father that loomed large periodically. If only she could hold them to her longer then she could keep some of her father with her. After he died she was swamped with memories that came in alternative chronologies. It seemed to be part of the grieving process; as the grieving subsided, so the memories faded. Remembering him today was like receiving a gift. Although the grieving is over, she's left with many fond memories of him and her childhood. The good memories are a support. Even in death he is her support.

"Okay," Ian says.

Susan snaps out of her reverie. They're finished.

"You look very tired, Susan."

"I suppose I am," she says.

"My place or yours?"

Ian looks radiant to her. In the artificial light his hair shines like a halo. His eyebrows and eyelashes are luminescent from being sun bleached. If she opts for her place she'll spend the night alone and she doesn't want that. She wants his company. "Yours," she says.

Ian puts his arm around her shoulders and they walk side by side.

Feeling safe in his embrace, Susan speaks softly. "I think I must have been at my most vulnerable when I arrived here."

"Are you insinuating I took advantage of you?"

Susan chuckles. "No, Silly. But I now realize, like my father, you are a great support."

Ian kisses the top of her head. "So I'm a father figure?"

Susan twists her neck to speak directly to him. "You're too young to be a father figure, or my substitute father."

"You were grieving."

"Yes, the loss of my father and my job. Well, to be more precise, I'd left my job."

Ian inhales deeply. They reach the office door and Ian holds it open for Susan to enter.

Inside Susan stops and turns to look fully at his face. "There are so many different ways to relate to people. I mean, my father and mother were married to each other and they were in their own separate hemisphere in the family, but I had a special relationship with my father."

"And where was Sandra? There can be only two hemispheres. Which half was she in?"

"She was with mother in her other half."

"I remember your sister saying you were closer to your father than she was." He walks past her and into the next room.

Susan follows Ian with her head bent. His shirt hangs loosely over his buttocks showing only royal blue cloth. She knows underneath there's a defining shape of his small, but strong muscles. The memory of holding them during love-making almost tempts her to passion.

Ian turns on the bedside light, and reaching for the blinking digital clock, looks at his wrist watch before resetting the time.

"I guess Saturday's over," Susan says.

"Umm," Ian says. "It's Sunday morning now."

Only in Susan's mind Saturday isn't over. Somehow, the long-lost life that's haunted her all day and that she let go of when she moved here, clings while she brushes her teeth in Ian's bathroom where she keeps a set of personal items. Unlike most adults who never change their way of doing things, she did. What's bothering her is the aftermath of that change. Should she have adjusted to the problems of her earlier life? Could she? Does it even matter? She's closer to the end of her life than the beginning. Is that what's scaring her? How does it matter now what decision she made then? It's already taken place. Her life. What she missed. What she changed.

She pats her mouth with the soft hand towel that smells of the fresh sea-salt air and marvels at how Celianne gets the laundry done to such perfection on this small island with its limited public utilities, water caught in a ground cistern, and knows that others don't always appreciate the unique beneficence of something so simple as a perfect towel.

When she returns she finds that Ian is sound asleep which is not surprising considering the late hour and the long day he's had. Tomorrow he will rise early to make his special Sunday breakfast for the guests on the cook's day off. He will not disturb her in the morning, leaving with the quiet grace of a domestic cat, and she does not disturb him now getting into bed with the cautious movements of a welcome guest. Just lying beside him offers the comfort of belonging. She knows she is spoiled. Life is so much simpler here, not just on the island with its sun drenched pace, but at the resort where all her needs are met – meals, laundry, cleaning. No errands even as simple as shopping interfere with her teaching life. The way she lives and works resembles how nuns live in a sanctuary with few distractions and circumspect obligations. Compared to Sandra's busy life, hers is privileged. Her sister runs a household, raises teenagers, cares for their aging mother, manages a long-term marriage, and works as a professional teacher. Her sister is a super woman. Susan feels liberated by comparison, if a little guilty about not being there for their mother. In the darkness Susan smiles to herself thinking about the story that Sandra told her over the long distance phone line about their mother's creeping confusion. She's still a regular church goer, and after one service, the minister asked the members to contribute items from their households that the Sunday School could use to make props for the children's recital. Their mother collected all the blue candles she could find in her cupboards and drawers and took them to the church where she was greeted with surprise. It wasn't blue candles they wanted, but broom handles. In bed Susan shakes with contained laughter at the mental image of her mother arriving with a handful of blue candles. It says something about the woman that she even has blue candles. What special occasion could prompt their need?

Blue candles. Broom handles. It's too funny. Susan feels the need to censor herself from laughing out loud. She mustn't wake Ian. It's all so sad really. Like Sandra, Susan worries about the deterioration of language skills that her mother is experiencing. She falls asleep not knowing whether to laugh or cry.

∽

It seemed to Tijean that he was greeted by his relatives in Toronto with a mixture of animosity and enthusiasm. Sherlock's parents made it clear that having Tijean around didn't excuse his cousin from attending school. On the contrary, they even suggested that Tijean accompany Sherlock to register in class at the local high school. Apparently the Vice-Principal there would temporarily turn a blind eye to his lack of papers. Tijean resisted their encouragement. He hadn't fled the island to land in a foreign school. So in the morning when the children arrived on his aunt's doorstep, a half dozen infants and toddlers who needed daycare, Tijean made himself useful. He peeled the oranges for snack and poured apple juice into tiny cups. One little boy, named Rashid, took a liking to him, staying by his side while he ate, sticking to his legs while Tijean cleared up the dirty dishes, helping him carry the orange peel to put into the compost, and pulling a chair to the counter to stand on while Tijean washed up at the sink. His aunt suggested Tijean read Rashid a story before nap time. There was a selection of children's books in a bin on one of the shelves where toys were stacked. Mostly they had threadbare covers and dog-eared pages, well read and handled. Tijean rightly guessed that they had once belonged to Sherlock. He recognized one. It came from the islands, "My Grandpa and the Sea", by Katherine Orr. Probably his mother sent it to her sister in the mail. She'd bought a copy from the Unicorn Bookstore on Provo for Tijean when he was a boy.

Tijean made himself comfortable on the floor. Rashid stood beside him and put his arms around Tijean's neck. The boy's chubby, short limbs felt light against Tijean's hard, bony body. He opened the book, but instantly Rashid grabbed the cover and closed it pointing at the title. "Ah," Tijean said. He read the title, then opened the cover. Again Rashid closed the book, but this time he pointed to the name written on the bottom. Tijean read the author's name, then looking at Rashid for approval, opened the book to the dedication page. He decided he better read that, too. The illustration on the first page showed a folk art painting of a small hut on the edge of a lush forest with mountain peaks in the distance. A small figure, the grandpa, was pointing, and clinging to him was the grandchild. Like us, Tijean thought, equating the fictional relationship to himself and his charge. Tijean started to read aloud, "My grandpa was a fisherman on the island of St. Lucia. He had never been to school, but he was very wise. He could read the sea and sky like most of us read books." Instantly Tijean recognized why his mother had chosen this book to buy. It wasn't like her to spend money on reading material. This story must have reminded her of her own father, Jean, who had been a fisherman in Haiti. As Tijean continued to read and turn the pages, Rashid stood listening attentively. His small body grew warm against Tijean's side. The grandpa in the story had a dug out boat that he repainted every year. He didn't want to join the fishermen who were competing with bigger boats because he felt the bigger boats were taking too much fish out of the sea. He remembered when there used to be plenty of fish. Even seamoss was getting scarce because people were taking it by the wheelbarrow full. Before long, Grandpa could not make a living by fishing. Yet he yearned to be on the sea where his heart was. Eventually, shrewd Grandpa came up with the bright idea of farming seamoss. "The new business prospered and so did Grandpa, for he was back on the sea where he belonged," Tijean read. When he finished the story Rashid let his head rest on Tijean's shoulder. Not having any siblings, Tijean was unused to being around children. He was touched by the boy's warmth and felt protective of his tiny physical presence. Soon he realized that Rashid had fallen asleep standing up. Cautiously, so as not to disturb Rashid, Tijean rose while holding him and carried him to his cot. Then he quietly walked out the front door and sat on the porch steps. Although the air was cold, the sun was bright and shone directly on him.

Sitting alone Tijean began to wonder where he belonged. It wasn't here in this cold climate among people who came from all over the globe and lived jammed into a neighbourhood of mismatched houses, for that was how the buildings looked to Tijean, all assembled higgledy-piggledy. He longed to be back on the island, but imagined himself there under different circumstances than what he'd recently experienced. He was haunted by scenes from high school where he was in the habit of drawing negative attention to himself. In class he always felt incompetent, unable to focus or compete. While the teachers didn't expect him or anyone else to engage in competition, Tijean felt like that was what it was, especially with the other boys. There was no point competing with the girls. They seemed too capable and compliant, so became the butt of derision. Some of their mocks and taunts came back to him. With the girls that often became their only self defense. Tijean always took these malevolent attacks personally. Every criticism became a personal insult, a deliberate attempt to humiliate him. Yet wasn't that what he was doing to them? In his mind these scenes became stuck in replay mode. He would find himself reliving these touchy messes, making endless renditions of his responses. He hated holding these grudges. He was ashamed of how cruel he could feel. Yet the envy took hold, so the attacks continued. He got stuck in the complex web of those peeves to the point that there was no escape, no route out of the emotional miasma.

Now he remembered Miss Mulrain telling him that he took everything too personally. She tried to make him understand that he was experiencing a form of discrimination. He argued that point with her. "Not all discrimination is racism," she told him. Every taunt, every jibe, every mocking comment was a sign of discrimination according to her, whether it be against the girls or against the underachieving. She lumped him in that label, an underachiever. "Until you slough off these grudges you will be incapable of progress." That was her advice.

Finally he admitted to her that he felt different. He couldn't read properly. Every time he finished a line of print he lost his way. The other students seemed to take reading and writing for granted, just something they did as easily as breathing. "That's why I'm here," she told him. "To accommodate your differences." And she did when she guided him through his interview paper.

Despite her kindness, and she was kind - they were all kind, Ms Susan, Mr. Musgrove – Tijean felt humiliated. He was different. He was supposed to accept that he was different.

Tijean thought of his grandfather, the big Jean. He was illiterate, never went to school so never learned to read or write, but like the Grandpa in the story, he could read the sea and sky. Like the Grandpa in the story, he was wise, wise in the ways of the world he inhabited. That world was gone. It no longer existed. Gone was nature in abundance. It was as if nature could no longer give freely so people couldn't just live randomly taking the little they needed to survive like his grandfather had done. People had to get smarter about how they lived. Like the Grandpa in the story at the end telling his grandchild, Tijean could hear his own grandfather saying, "A good education will make you free to choose in life what you will."

Tijean hugged his knees close into his chest. He was feeling the chill of the afternoon as the sun slid lower in the sky. Either the cold or his thoughts brought tears to his eyes. He decided to go indoors. Quietly he opened the door. Inside the children were still asleep in their cots. Tijean stood over Rashid. He looked so vulnerable. Tijean wondered if, as a child, he'd looked like Rashid. Again tears welled in his eyes. At some point, and not that long ago, he'd been a little boy napping in the afternoons. Had his parents stood over him in awe? Tijean guessed they had. Suddenly he missed them.

∞

Most of the animal world inhabits a peaceable kingdom. Not so the Cuban Crow that lives in the West Indies and is native to the Turks and Caicos Islands. On North Caicos it is ubiquitous. Like all crows it disturbs the quiet of its environment with its incessant and very loud cawing. However, unlike any other crow, it imitates another bird, the wild turkey, with a strange 'gobble-gobble' sound. On Sunday morning this avian creature sits in a sapodilla tree outside the window where Susan sleeps. Her slumber is deep and her waking evolves one phase at a time. At first she is barely conscious of remnants from a dream. Her father is performing one of his habitual acts of consideration for the "kitchen staff" as he jovially referred to his wife and youngest daughter. Susan laughs at his joking and watches him leave the room with his empty tea cup. Then she quickly pushes her arm down the sides of the armchair which is still warm from his departing body where she gathers any loose change she finds in her tight fist. This image morphs into a scene from Thanksgiving. Her father is helping in the kitchen by lifting the large bird out of the roasting pan and placing it on the carving board. Susan can smell the strong aroma of cooked turkey. Her consciousness is traveling closer to the surface of wakefulness. The satisfying aroma of roast turkey is replaced by the gnawing sound of a cackling bird. Reality strikes. No pleasant dream. No childhood experience. Only the annoying distraction of the Cuban Crow. Susan moans and curses the bird. Lifting her head she grabs her pillow and pulls it off the bed. Then she collapses and smothers her head with the soft down.

It's no use. The culprit's disturbance penetrates the down feathers covering her ears. Susan flings herself out of bed and flies to the window where she opens the shutters. What a ridiculous sight – a large, sleek, black bird in a tree going "gobble-gobble". If it wasn't so irritating it'd be humourous. "Go away," she calls.

The gluttonous bird stops as if hearing her, but before obeying, it poaches an entire piece of fruit from the sapodilla tree and, holding the fruit in its beak, flies off.

"Damn selfish character," Susan says and closes the shutters. She sees that Ian's side of the bed is empty. He's probably already behind the bar scrambling eggs, cutting back bacon, slicing whole wheat bread and peeling and sectioning oranges. On Sunday he takes pride in offering his guests what his family ate at home in Nova Scotia on the Sabbath before attending the eleven o'clock service at church. He'll be working alone as the islanders who work at the resort religiously attend their local church service. Marcel doesn't work Sundays, either. He's probably not returned from Leila's. On her way to her room Susan checks the gravel driveway where her scooter sits beside a few old bicycles. The space where Marcel parks is vacant. He's the only one at the resort with a car. Ian never saw the necessity of owning one while living on the small island, a state he jokingly refers to as "positively un-American".

Outside the morning sun fully lights the tropical sky, a condition that brings scorching heat to mountainous countries at the same latitude. Here, on the islands, the easterlies moderate the temperature. Susan inhales the salt sprayed air deeply into her chest and fills her bloodstream with oxygen. A full night's sleep leaves her rested and she now understands what happened to her in her past teaching life quite differently from how she felt yesterday. This morning she feels she only wants to be herself. She is better here than she was before having assumed a position of responsibility at a very orderly and highly reputable institution. She need not apologize for the work she does in her professional life. As Ian reminded her she's not to blame for Tijean or any other student's failings. Nor need she apologize for how she lives personally in an informal relationship with Ian.

Remembering her thoughts of her family she vows she will be more attentive to them. Why can't her mother visit more often? Now that Sandra's children are older, her niece and nephew should be encouraged to travel independently, or accompany their grandmother. This is a travel resort and her home, not some asylum keeping her hidden like a criminal. That resolve stops her in her tracks.

Remembering the document she signed Friday night Susan adjusts her thinking. Now what? Will Ian and she have a home after the closing? She's standing in front of Marcel's empty room, the future owner. What will they do? They'll have money. Will she quit teaching? Somehow in all the confusion of Tijean and the euphoria of becoming rich she's failed to grasp the full impact of what Ian's done.

Her room feels stuffy, so Susan opens the shutters before stepping into the shower. The spray from the shower head is half the volume of water she remembers flowing from the showers in Canada where water flowed unrestricted offering not just cleanliness, but also relaxation like a massage. Funny how she's conscious of that difference this morning when most mornings she goes through her cleaning ritual without a thought to its conditions, only to what's ahead in her day. This is living in the present, the here and now, and she knows she's better for it, not just cleaner, but clearer in her mind.

Susan dries herself by patting under her arms and breasts, rubbing her legs and the soles of her feet, wrapping the towel around her shoulders and arms, pulling the ends of it up and down across her broad back in a see-saw motion, tying two corners around her waist, and placing one hand over her lower back and the other over her belly, moving the towel between her legs. She takes a smaller towel and pats her hair dry examining the strands in the mirror to check that the colour did cover all her grey. Then she combs her hair and brushes her teeth before going to her closet where she picks a blue gingham shift to wear, something casual and loose fitting, but presentable.

As she closes the door to her room Susan feels carefree and walks lightly over the sandy pathway to join Ian. When there is a full house at the resort she helps him on Sundays glad to make a contribution to the smooth running of the business. On turning onto the patio she immediately sees Ruth Diamond sitting at the bar and talking with Ian. Ruth's muscular calves hug the stool legs. She always was athletic. The only disquiet Susan feels is how to cover her folly at not meeting the woman yesterday. Susan doesn't want to appear coy, a sign that she hasn't worked things through or must keep something hidden. "Good morning," she calls.

The two turn their heads in her direction. "Good morning, Susan," Ian says. "I trust you had a good night's sleep."

"I did until those damned Cuban Crows woke me up." Susan side-steps through the tables and chairs. "It's Ruth Diamond, isn't it? Ian told me there were guests here from Canada."

Ruth is looking at Susan with her mouth hanging open. "Good heavens," she says. "Susan Borden." She looks from Susan to Ian. "I take it you two know each other?"

Ian laughs. "Only in the biblical sense."

Susan steps around Ruth and joins Ian. "Is that your idea of a Sunday joke?" She turns to Ruth. "This is my home now."

"Well, I'm astounded," Ruth says. Her head moves from Susan to Ian as if she's fitting them together, and deciding that they do indeed belong to one another, nods her chin in approval. "Lucky you, to have ended up here."

"You could say that," Susan says.

"Well, tell me, how long have you been living here?"

Susan recognizes that Ruth Diamond is quick at calculating mentally. The number of years she gives coincides with the length of time since the incident.

"Good for you. I did hear that you'd left the country. So do you work at the resort?"

Susan is piling dishes from the cupboards for serving breakfast. "Only on Sundays," she says. "During the week I teach at the local high school."

Ruth sits more erect. Her posture and tone of voice gain composure. "I'm glad to hear you're still teaching. You're too good a teacher not to be practicing."

Too good, but not good enough, Susan thinks as she returns Ruth's direct gaze. She keeps her smile immobile. Susan must withhold her reaction to this woman who is a guest at Ian's resort for that is what the place becomes when she thinks of how she must control herself, if not for her own sense of proper etiquette, than for Ian. Otherwise she may sneer. Too good a teacher yet not good enough for Ruth Diamond's support when she needed it. How would you define a good teacher? There are many come-backs to her nemesis. Susan feels her smile wan as it dawns on her that she is in the company of a sixty year old woman with the emotional maturity of a thirteen year old adolescent girl. It's as if her former principal and student have merged into one threatening being. This new awareness unsettles Susan's morning resolve as she recognizes she is being manipulated. Ruth Diamond probably thinks she is playing the role of an affirmative administrator, something she's been trained to do. Susan is clinging to her role, too. She will be polite, not misbehave by turning cynical or even juvenile. Her behaviour will pass for conventional good manners.

"And what do you teach?" Ruth asks filling the silence.

"Mostly English. Some Guidance. They still call it that here."

Ruth laughs. "Good for them. Wasn't it a waste of our time, all that redefining and renaming everything? I don't know about you but my brain got tired of learning new acronyms. Why did we put up with it?" She undoes the top button of her shirt and pulls the collar off the back of her neck.

"I mostly ignored it. Too busy teaching." Susan grabs the tray with the napkin holders. "Excuse me. I'm going to set the tables." Turning her back on Ian and Ruth she sashays around the tables dispensing napkins. Her cavalier body language bedevils her critical thoughts about Ruth's comments. Why did she put up with it? Susan can answer that rhetorical question with the obvious – to get ahead, that's why. To remain in an administrative post as a talking head, not a thinking one, certainly not a challenging one. Returning to the other two Susan wears a magnanimous smile as she picks up the containers that hold the cutlery.

Ian gives Susan a look as if to encourage her magnanimity. "Ruth's invited Sam to dinner tonight. I think we can handle an outsider?"

"Of course," Susan says, recognizing that Ian simply means he's not a guest. "Sam's always good company. How do you know Sam Gold?"

"He's my uncle," Ruth says. "And my most notorious relative."

"Oh, really," Susan says, feigning discovery. "Yes, he is an interesting character to have for a relative." She trots away and starts setting the cutlery holders in the middle of the tables beside the napkin holders. The two perforated stainless steel holders match.

George Smitherman and Ted Morrall arrive. "Good morning, duckie," Ted says. "You're a jack-of-all-trades, aren't you? Waitress, night watchman."

"I haven't given up my day job."

"Which is?"

"Teacher at the local high school," Susan says. "Sit anywhere."

"Bully for you. I'd like to hear about that. George, here, is a retired teacher."

"Are you?" Susan says addressing George and wondering if he ever speaks for himself.

George merely nods as he pulls out a chair. He is balding with a ruddy complexion, not from the outdoors, more likely from drink. When seated he gives a wave to Ruth Diamond whom he is facing.

"Good morning. Sleep well?" Ruth's voice is loud.

Again George nods in the affirmative. Ted turns and gives Ruth an equally loud greeting, then sitting, whispers to George. "By God, don't let her join us for breakfast. I need a change of company after last night." Ted has a full head of bushy grey hair on his large head. His hands, too, are large.

George turns his head away from Ruth, and still smiling, waves Arthur and Sharon Copeland over to the table. Rubbing his hands together Arthur greets Susan. "Is it the Sunday special?"

"Sure is," Susan says.

"You guys are in for a treat. Ian makes the best Canadian Sunday breakfast this side of the 49th parallel. Scrambled eggs, back bacon, and whole wheat toast. Fit for a king. Or a queen," Arthur says acknowledging his wife's presence as he pulls out her chair.

"Has she been?" Ted asks. "The Queen?"

"Not recently," Susan says. "Can't land a cruise ship here. So four Sunday specials?"

"Just one slice of bacon and one piece of dry toast for me," Sharon says.

"And to start? Coffee? Juice?" Susan steps aside to let Sharon settle into her seat. The pair of espadrilles she's wearing have laces that tie around her ankles and lower calves like footwear from ancient Rome. Her casual wrap gathers like a toga around her body. Even at this early hour her make-up is applied. She is a sight for male eyes and, by comparison, Susan feels dowdy in her gingham shift. When she gives Ian their order he tweaks her ear, an act that settles her self-esteem. It occurs to Susan that she should be serving Ruth, but she's content drinking coffee until Kate joins her.

"You remember Kate Channing?"

"Of course. So, she's here, too. How is she?"

"Happily retired, like me."

Susan raises her eyebrows at Ian. "They're all retired," she says. "Ted just told me George is a retired teacher."

"The demographics of future guests."

"There's something to be said for that."

A loud outburst of laughter comes from the table. They turn to see Arthur leaning back in his chair thumping the table. George seems to be protesting and Sharon is happily applauding.

"Ted is so entertaining," Ruth says.

As Susan serves juice and coffee Ted is retelling the story of their flight. "They tell you when to nap, when to eat. It's just like in kindergarten." It's the same story he told last night but with a new audience, the social benefit of traveling to different places and meeting friendly strangers. Susan adjusts her judgement. Maybe it isn't Ruth who wears on the nerves, but simply Ted in need of someone else's attention. Leaning over Arthur Susan gets a whiff of a masculine perfume she recognizes. Brut? She notices his shirt and shorts have a pattern showing columns from the Parthenon and Coliseum. So that's how he's matching his wife today? This couple takes joined at the hip one step further to twinned by wardrobe.

Arthur peers up at Susan. She feels his breath on her collar bone. "I smell bacon," he says.

"Won't be long," Susan says. Behind the counter Ian is arranging the orange sections as garnish on four plates. "Arthur is salivating," she says.

"It does smell good," Ruth says.

"I think he's been waiting all week for this meal," Ian says. "Maybe that's why they stayed the extra week."

Ruth turns her head to look at the table of four. "They are a sweet couple."

"Guess how he's matching her this morning?" Susan asks.

Ian peers across to their table. "They're not dressed like identical twins. That's a surprise."

196

"See her espadrilles and toga-like wrap?" Susan says.

Both Ian and Ruth glance surreptitiously at the couple. Turning back to Susan they nod in agreement confirming Sharon's clothes are as described.

"Arthur's outfit is patterned in Roman columns."

Ian smiles and Ruth giggles. "Do they often dress alike?" she asks.

"Always," Susan says.

"I must take notice while I'm here," Ruth says directly to Susan.

Susan picks up the filled plates. Now there's a bond between her and Ruth. Susan hasn't intended to form one, but the sweet couple they're spying upon and innocently poking fun at give them a shared focus for humouring themselves on the human condition. It's the best kind of gossip and the foundation of any casual friendship. Yet she hasn't meant to form a friendship with Ruth Diamond. It seems to have happened spontaneously.

Susan feels Ian's eyes on her as she heads back to the counter. She can second guess his thoughts. He wants her to overcome her past animosities to the two women. Dear Ian. He so wants everyone to be good. Making others feel badly about themselves isn't in his repertoire. That's what makes him such a good host. He can make anyone feel like they belong.

Ruth gives a big wave. "Look who's here," she calls.

Susan turns to see Kate Channing approaching. She stops, frowns, squints, pulls her chin into her neck, then says, "Good God. Is that Susan Borden?"

"The same," Susan says and leans the side of her body against the counter until she's supported above the waist.

Kate is wearing sunglasses on the top of her head. Her hair is pulled back and held in place by the frames. At her scalp dark roots show in contrast to her hennaed hair. A smile lights up her face. "Well, fancy meeting you here."

"You'll never guess," Ruth says. "Susan's a teacher on the island."

"Of children?"

"At the high school."

Kate turns down the corners of her mouth. "Is the island big enough for a high school?"

"Apparently," Ruth says. "Isn't she fortunate? Living in a paradise like this?" Ruth sweeps her forearm across the vista.

"You live here? At the resort?" Kate asks.

"Yes," Susan says turning to Ian. "With my partner." Quietly she adds, "For now."

Kate settles herself on a stool beside Ruth. The ladies are sitting where Susan and Leila sat last night watching Marcel cook. "Partner as in your better half, or partner as in a financial interest?"

"We're man and wife without the formal ceremony or living arrangements," Ian says.

"Les compagnes." Kate leans over the counter. "Something smells good."

"Would you like to sit at a table for breakfast?" Susan asks.

"Can we eat here?" Kate asks looking at Ian.

"If you want," Ian says, then points to the uncooked food in the containers. "Want the Sunday morning special?"

"Why not?" Kate says. She turns to Ruth. "Have you eaten?"

"No, I was waiting for you and I'm starving."

Kate rests her elbows on the counter's edge. "So, Susan, how long have you been here?"

"Since 1996."

"Ever since you left teaching?"

"Yes, I suppose so." Susan wonders at Kate's interpretation. She doesn't say not since you got blackballed or faced the threat of a lawsuit, but simply "since you left teaching". How neutral.

"But she hasn't left teaching, Kate. Susan's teaching here. Isn't that wonderful?"

"What's it like teaching on the island?" Kate asks.

"Very pleasant. It's a highly regulated system following the British model, but given the distance from them, not too officious. Actually it's ideal. Especially since I have all my needs met here so I'm free of other responsibilities like cooking and laundry. Nothing too demanding except my teaching."

"I envy you," Kate says.

Susan looks at Ruth's face with its affirming expression. Could it be that she's genuinely happy for Susan? Or is she relieved that Susan's success gets her off the hook for any blame of failure? Susan's success and happiness frees her from recriminations. She must remind herself of that when the little voice in her head starts talking. There's no need for bitterness. She must stop personalizing the issue. Some events are beyond the personal, even though they affect persons, even ones that impact on her person. That's always been a difficult distinction for Susan to make. It was a lesson her father tried to teach her when she grew emotionally upset over some perceived slight. "Try not to take it personally", he would say, or, "Don't personalize the issue". With her mother and sister he would simply say, "You women are all alike. You take everything too personally". Remembering her father now she recognizes that he treated her differently on this count, too. It was as if he dismissed her sister and mother by passing judgement on their typical female behaviour, but with her he gave advice hoping to teach her to behave more like a man. "I think I'll make some more coffee," Susan says.

"Coffee sounds good," Kate says. "Ah, a fair trade brand."

Susan holds up the package. "Marcel's doing," she says. "He introduced us to ethical products."

"Yes, he would, wouldn't he?"

Susan looks at Kate. "How do you mean?"

"Well, with his brother a volunteer with Médecins Sans Frontiérs."

Susan is scooping the aromatic beans into the grinder, another habit they've adopted at Marcel's insistence. Grind the beans freshly for each pot brewed. "I didn't know he had a brother with Doctors Without Borders," Susan says. As the French teacher, not a subject many students studied without complaint, Kate was often on the defensive so she embraced the culture as its teacher.

"Yes, helping with the tsunami relief in Thailand."

Susan looks over at Ian. "That explains his interest in where Rufus is going."

"Maybe," Ian says.

Typical of Ian, Susan thinks. He doesn't commit himself to ascribe motives for others, unlike the women in the conversation – Kate guessing Marcel chooses fair trade products because he has a brother volunteering in a third world country, she assuming Marcel's interest in working in Thailand so he can see his brother. Susan starts the grinder. Its roaring motor makes a noise so loud it stops the conversation.

When silence returns Kate fills the void. "Actually, Marcel told us a lot about himself yesterday when we arrived. Didn't he, Ruth?"

"He did. A very charming man. Fed up with the treadmill of working for a large corporation in an office in a high rise building. Very intelligent, though. Must come from a successful family, brother a doctor, he's an accountant."

Susan is learning more about Marcel from these two women than she's garnered herself since Marcel started working for Ian two weeks ago. It reminds her of conversations they had at school about students. Ruth was always filling in details about their family background that she'd gleaned from support staff and meeting the parents. Kate always knew about their siblings as she taught most of them in the past. Susan fills the coffee maker with water and starts the machine. Rinsing out the thermos she assures Kate, "Won't be a moment before a fresh pot is brewed."

"Here come the younger crowd," Ian says.

The three women turn to see the Canadian couple with the four Brits, one woman and three men. They shuffle around quietly, then start moving three small tables together. The legs grate across the stone floor. "I think I'll take them some juice," Susan says. "They look like they could use some vitamin C." She hasn't met any of these visitors and decides to have a bit of fun with them. "Good Morning," Susan says holding aloft the pitcher of juice. "I'm Susan, your server for the day."

"Oh," says one of the young woman squinting up at her, then craning her neck to look past her. "Where's Marcel?"

She's got an angular face with straight, thin, brown hair that hangs to her chin.

"Saturday afternoon and all day Sunday are Marcel's days off," Susan says starting to pour. "Who wants juice?" She feels like their unwelcome den mother. Apparently they'd prefer a handsome, younger French man to a dowdy, older woman. And who can blame them?

One of the male Brits of East Indian heritage smooths over their youthful rough edges by making introductions. "I'm Adir," he says. "And this is Kamil." Kamil is a large male. Adir is skinny.

Susan says hello and serves them the first glasses of juice. The young woman who asked after Marcel introduces herself. "Do you want juice, Lizzie?" Susan asks using her given name.

"No thanks," she says in a distinctly upper crust British accent. "Could I have some water?"

"Certainly. Anyone else want water?" Susan looks at the other young woman, the Canadian.

"I'll have juice, please. Are you Canadian?"

"Yes," says Susan.

"I can tell by your accent. I'm Lyn, with one 'n'." Lyn is a buxom young blond.

"Where are you from, Lyn?"

"Toronto. This is Jeff, with a 'j'."

Susan hides her smile and offers Jeff a glass of juice. He is dressed in a short-sleeved shirt and has hairy forearms. She stands beside the other Brit who is taller than the others and not forthcoming.

"Roger," Lizzie says. "Introduce yourself to the waitress."

"Not necessary, Lizzie. You've done it for me." He looks Susan in the eye. "Can I trouble you for a glass of juice and some water?"

"No problem. There's a fresh batch of coffee brewing. I'll bring that, too. Would you all like the Sunday morning special that Ian prepares? Scrambled eggs, back bacon, and whole wheat toast?"

"Is back bacon Canadian bacon?" Lizzie asks.

"All meat, no fat, covered in cornmeal," Susan says not knowing what a young British woman defines as Canadian bacon.

"Sounds better than a full English breakfast," Roger says. "No fried bread. No grease."

They all agree to try the special. "The Full Monty," Susan says and leaves them in stitches.

Susan brushes past Ian on her way to the coffee machine. "Six specials," she says. "Have you met Roger and Lizzie?"

"Yes, when they arrived." Ian relights the gas element on the range.

"And what was your first impression?"

"Members of the upper classes?" Ian smirks at Susan.

After Susan pours the coffee from the pot into the serving thermos she starts making another brew. Then she pours a cup of coffee for Kate and refills Ruth's cup before heading back to the tables. As she's pouring coffee and water she listens to Roger pontificate on BP in Azerbaijan. Four faces watch him attentively while Lizzie stares across the patio over the ocean looking bored. "When BP publicly declared how much oil revenue they'd given to the Angolan dictatorship, they told the company to shut up or get out."

"In other words," Lizzie says, not turning her head, "The problem isn't the oil companies, but corrupt governments."

Susan goes to the other table with four adults and offers more water and coffee all around. Arthur is commiserating with George on life in New York, but Ted disagrees with them both saying how vibrant he finds urban living. "Don't you agree?" he asks. "Could you leave New York, Sharon?"

"Never, but Arthur is forever hopeful. How long have you lived there?"

"Forty years," Ted says. "I never lost my accent, like George."

Susan waits hoping to hear George speak in unaccented English, but Milquetoast doesn't oblige so she rejoins Ian helping him garnish the six plates he's preparing. "I think Roger's an oil man," she says.

Ian guffaws. "Why do you say that?"

"He's talking to them about BP and Chevron and Texaco."

"Ask him if he's in oil," Ian says.

"Why? Do you know what he does?"

"Yes."

"I'm not going to ask him. Tell me."

"He's a head master, Susan."

"Of a private school?"

"No, like a department head."

"He seems awfully young for that."

"It's Lizzie who's in the oil industry." Ian stops what he's doing and looks directly into Susan's eyes. "She's a director of marketing with BP, the second largest oil company in the world, or so she says. How would I know?"

"Get out," Susan says, using a current saying. She looks over to their table. Lizzie appears so self- absorbed, more like a female who's kept and pandered, not a professional working woman. The younger generation aren't always what they seem.

When Susan returns to the group of tables the two young women are gaily showing off their bracelet watches which they purchased at the duty free shop. Susan serves them and then places Roger's plate in front of him. "I hear you're in education?" she says.

"Yes, we're on school break."

"Oh, right. We have different holidays. I teach at the high school on the island."

Roger looks at her full in the face with two unctuous, sleepy eyes that slowly clear with growing disbelief. "I don't mean this as an insult, but don't they pay well?"

Laughing Susan explains.

Adir says that he, too, teaches. "How does one get a job here?"

"You apply. If you're serious I'll bring you the forms. Or come and visit me at the school tomorrow. Then you can decide."

"I teach Maths. Do they need Math teachers? What do you teach?"

Susan pauses before answering Adir. She feels herself sliding into her Guidance role.

"Ah," Roger says. "A teacher with two heads. One for the classroom and one for the community."

Adir seems easily excitable. He starts shaking his head in agreement. "Yes, but all teachers have double heads."

"Careful, Adir," Roger says. "You're painting the portrait of a monster."

Seeing that the other table has finished eating Susan excuses herself from the table of six. "Any plans for the day?" she asks while gathering four dirty plates.

"We're taking them to Provo to visit the conch farm," Arthur says.

Ted stands making room for Susan to reach the table more easily. "Arthur tells us it's the only one in the world and well worth a visit."

Sharon helps Susan place the cutlery on the top plate. "We're staying the day, so don't expect us back until late. We'll eat at a restaurant on Provo."

Arthur rises from his chair and tells the other men what good establishments there are on Provo for dining, elaborating on their favourite, The Grill, which has a magnificent view over Grace Bay.

At the counter Susan scrapes the plates of leftover food and orange rinds before putting them in the dishwasher. She tells Ian of Arthur's plans to go to the conch farm with Ted and George and stay the evening on Provo.

Ian tells her the young people are booked for an all day diving charter that includes a picnic lunch and dinner. "So Kate, Ruth and Sam. Not bad. Counting us, just five for dinner."

Susan is relieved. Cooking for five is no more taxing than a regular family Sunday meal. That leaves the day free. Ruth and Kate make a noise placing cutlery on their empty plates so Susan goes over to them. "Finished?" she asks.

"Yes, thanks." Ruth calls to Ian. "When do you do pancakes and maple syrup?"

Ian is cleaning the pan he used to cook the bacon. The double boiler used for scrambled eggs is soaking in sudsy water. Without raising his head from his task he laughs. "We don't. Marcel does crepes. Don't even ask for maple syrup with them or he'll be insulted. You must express great appreciation for his sauces. He makes a berry sauce for the crepes. But one morning he may serve you French toast with maple syrup. Just don't ask for pancakes. He calls them peasant food. 'Too starchy'," Ian says imitating Marcel's accent.

"Too starchy," Kate says mimicking Ian and laughing.

Susan feels a surge of inner disturbance that she fights to dispel. Is it her imagination or is Kate coming on to Ian? With forced laughter she joins the merriment.

"What are you ladies up to today?" Ian asks.

"Well, we haven't decided," Ruth says. "Maybe snorkeling or going to see the flamingos."

Kate wraps both hands around her empty coffee cup. "What do you recommend, Ian?"

"Susan, here, is the expert on flamingos."

Kate flips her head leading with her chin to direct her gaze away from Ian and on to Susan. "Are you?" she demands.

Closing the door to the dishwasher Susan decides she'll wait for the other table to finish before starting the machine. "Yes. What would you like to know? Flamingo is Latin for flame."

"That makes sense," Ruth says.

"Did you study Latin?" Kate asks.

"I did. Mrs. Cowan taught us Latin and she was one of the best teachers I ever had."

"See how important we teachers are?" Ruth says. "You still remember her."

"So flamingos were around in Roman times?" Kate asks.

"Oh yes. Flamingos are one of the most ancient bird families."

"They remind me of herons," Ruth says. "Are they part of the heron family?"

"Yes, I agree, they are most like herons. But no, they're not the same species."

"Well, how do we get there?" Ruth asks. "We spotted some on a pond from the plane. It can't be far from here."

"It's not," Susan says. "But there are some nearby in a smaller pond. You just have to know what path to take."

"So it's easy to get to?" Kate asks.

"Yes," Susan says and gives them directions.

"Can we walk?" Ruth asks. "I hope we don't get lost."

Ian stops what he's doing and turns to Susan. "Why don't you show them the way?"

Susan is taken aback. Instead of attending a church service on Sunday, Ian's playing minister by inviting her to lead the way for this congregation of two. Follow the path to Flamingo Pond and baptize her soul. His eyes hold her. As soon as she accepts the role Susan feels her struggle come to an end. She is actually happy, radiant with the prospect of an outing with these two women. Her eyes shine with defiant pride. She's in command. She knows the way. She's the experienced guide. She's done serving them. Now she'll lead. This may not be the role Ian is prescribing. He may expect her to lead as an equal, not play one-up-manship, but she allows herself this little indulgence as a tiny bit of revenge.

In her new resplendent role Susan feels an affinity to her earlier duty as big sister. Feeling comfortable in this persona she remembers when she started to think of Sandra as a separate person in her own right, not just someone who did things to her or to whom she did things to or who made her feel a certain way that was unlike any way she felt with any other person. When Susan turned thirteen her mother said, "Unlucky thirteen," because she'd started to menstruate. Doris perpetuated those negative attitudes to a natural bodily function that so typified her generation. Susan harboured the view that menstruation was her monthly "curse" until Sandra started her menses. Then Susan cleared the suffocating prescribed attitudes from the dim haze of fog in her head and recognized a true sister at her side, a little sister with whom she shared a room, only now a person grown bigger and more mature. She, too, bled at monthly intervals. As clear as a tropical day Susan remembers Sandra returning to their room with its twin beds facing north to south along opposite walls. Susan was sitting cross-legged on her mattress doing her homework on a clip board. Sandra had been in the bathroom. Susan looked up when Sandra announced, "I'm bleeding between my legs."

Dropping her clipboard in mid-calculation of an algebra formula, Susan stood and took Sandra's hand. She veered her out of their room and down the hall to their mother. "Mum."

Their mother was putting away clean laundry in drawers. She turned to look at them sensing that this wasn't some ordinary, annoying complaint. Then she stood upright. "What is it?"

"Sandra's started hers," Susan said, still holding her sister's hand.

"Oh, don't worry, dear," Doris said, setting the pile of folded underwear on top of the dresser. "You'll be alright." Then she walked to her closet. "I'll get you a pad and belt."

Susan was waiting for the history lesson on how women used to use rags and how they were lucky to have modern conveniences like a cumbersome pad and an elastic strap with cleats to hold it. Raising her free arm Susan intercepted her mother's advances. "I'll show her," she said.

Doris looked at her eldest daughter with a slight sparkle of amazement. "Why, thank you, Susan." She turned to her youngest. "Is that alright with you, Sandra?"

Despite the strangeness of this new experience Sandra was trusting as she simply nodded and turned out of the room with her big sister. Susan led her to the bathroom and explained the mechanics of wearing the lumpy absorbent pad. She also gave her sister advice about how to prepare herself for public life during her period using proper terms that she felt were kinder than the vocabulary she'd learned with its heavy judgement of burden.

Ruth and Kate return having changed into sensible walking shoes. Together they head down the driveway that leads to the main road along the coast. Susan walks in front with her head down watching her footsteps. Her mind is still enveloped in that moment in her adolescence seminal to pinpointing a developing consciousness. What women do to their own sex. Behind her Susan hears Kate explaining to Ruth that the elderly gay guys have gone to the conch farm with the middle aged Yankee couple. Ruth is laughing at Kate's story telling, repeating her friend's words, "elderly gay guys," and the archaic usage of Yankee. "But I do like George and Ted," Ruth says. "We had such a good time with them last night."

"They are a hoot," Kate says. "So conch is a popular seafood here?" Kate says, throwing the question out to Susan.

"Konk," Susan says over her shoulder correcting Kate's pronunciation of 'ch'.

"Konk," Ruth says, as if highlighting a phonics lesson. "It's pronounced with a hard 'k' at the beginning and at the end of the word."

"Pardon me," Kate says. "How ignorant I am. I've never tasted it. Is it any good?"

Susan is finding this linear conversation difficult. "Yes," she says turning her head to look behind at the striding ladies. No, not quite her sisters in arms, but maybe not the witches she had once made them out to be.

"Watch out," Kate yells.

Susan stops so abruptly she nearly loses her balance. She is at the intersection of the driveway and the road where she feels a gush of wind down the front of her body as a cyclist speeds past her. "Tijean," she says, recognizing the young man pedaling like a racer in the famous Tour de France.

"What?" Kate asks, reaching Susan's side and catching her arm to steady her on her feet.

"No," Susan says, following the cyclist with her anxious eyes knowing it isn't him. "Sorry, I thought it was someone else. Wonder where that guy's going in such a hurry?"

"What was the name you said?" Kate asks.

"Oh, Tijean. His mother works at the resort. She came here from Haiti. But it's not him."

"Where do they get these names? I swear they make them up."

Ruth is standing beside them with her hands on her hips. "I understand there's a big population here from Haiti?"

"Yes," Susan says absently. She is trying to sort out in her mind the confusion of seeing the cyclist. Obviously she confused this near accident with Tijean's flight that she witnessed the other night. Only at the time she didn't know he was in flight. Maybe if she had realized the predicament he was in she could have intervened? But what good could she have done? Rallying her thoughts Susan points to a path across the road. "We can reach the pond by walking along there."

Now the road is empty posing no danger to their crossing.

"So what is conch like?" Once again Kate takes up a position in the rear.

"Mild, sweet," Susan calls, keeping her head focused forward. "Like clams, only bigger pieces."

"I'd probably like it. Funny, I only ever thought of it as being a shell, but of course, it would have to have meat inside."

"The Arawaks, the native Indians, used all its parts. It was an important food source for them."

"My uncle always brought us conch shells when he visited which was rarely, but memorable."

Susan smiles to herself thinking of the personality of her uncle, Sam Gold. "He's a character," she says. "You know conch is a snail like escargots that the French eat."

"You don't say?" Kate says.

"How else did the Arawaks use the conch? Did they put them up to their ear to hear the sea?"

"They carved them into tools. But they also used them as horns. They even held conch blowing contests during their various ceremonies."

"Imagine that," Kate says.

"It's true," Ruth says. "Sam told us all about that."

The women continue in silence aware that talking while walking on a narrow path is more effort than the challenge affords. Eventually they come to a clearing where Susan steps off the path to the narrow gravel shore. The other two women come up behind her and spread out alongside the edge of the wetland. Most of the shoreline is overgrown. Before them a large colony of pink flamingos dot the shallow water.

"Wow," Kate says. "They're so colourful."

"Don't birds always seem brighter in the wild?" Ruth asks.

"I guess these are all males," Kate says. "Where are the females? On their nests?"

"No, male and female are alike in plumage," Susan says. "You can pick out the males, though. They're taller."

"Fascinating," Kate says. "There's a lot of preening happening out there."

Susan has her binoculars to her eyes. "Yes, they spend most of their time during the day preening, more than other waterfowl."

"That's why they're so magnificent," Kate says. "Like self-absorbed people who practice yoga and diet and go to spas." She turns to the other two. "Don't their postures remind you of yoga poses?"

Susan removes her binoculars. Ruth has a small, high-tech pair lifted to her eyes. Kate is squinting. "I suppose. Do you want to look through my binoculars?"

Turning her head to Susan, Kate gives her a wide smile. "Yes, please."

Keeping her arms lifted with her binoculars held in both hands, Ruth pulls away from viewing. "Sorry, Kate. I should have offered you mine."

"You keep yours," Susan says. "This is the only chance you'll get to see them. I can come anytime." To Kate Susan indicates how to use the focus dial between the two expandable lenses.

Kate laughs. "God, I was ready to put them the other way round. Thanks, Susan."

"They're so quiet," Ruth says.

"If we were closer we'd hear them," Susan says. "They make soft vocalizations to each other. Actually, they can get quite noisy. During flight they have a loud honking, like geese do."

"Where are the chicks?" Kate doesn't remove the lenses from her sight while asking this question.

"See further down the pond where the water is very shallow," Susan instructs. The two ladies adjust their sighting. "That's where the creche of young chicks are."

"Oh yes, I see." Kate says. "Those adults are feeding."

"Aren't they remarkable?" Ruth says. "Look how they lower their necks. My, so graceful."

"Such long necks," Kate says.

"Look closely and you'll see them tilt their heads so their bills are hanging upside down," Susan says. "That's how they gather their food."

"There's so many of them," Kate says. "How can they possibly know where their chicks are among that crowd?"

"Actually, it's through vocalizations that parents and chicks recognize each other," Susan says. "It takes three years for a chick to reach sexual maturity."

"That seems a long time in the bird kingdom," Ruth says.

"They don't start breeding, though, for about six years. They are magnificent to watch during breeding. Grand displays, sometimes thousands of them will move in unison, like a gigantic choreographed ballet." Susan watches the women watching the birds to test if she should give them more information. She declines to list the predictable displays that are as recognizable as dance movements – head-flag, wing-salute, twist-preen – as both Ruth and Kate seem content to simply watch.

On their return Susan finds herself at the back of the line. Again she looks down at her feet while walking, not so much to steady her gaze and mark the path, more to retrieve her thoughts. She pictures Tijean barreling along the road at full speed, his head sunk low into his neck and shoulders, his large hands gripping the handle bars, his feet circling in a blur. He had not seen her, his teacher and counselor. Celianne told her yesterday that she woke up thinking he was at sea hunting for treasure having completely forgotten that he'd run away. Tijean is a good diver, in fact proficient at anything he tried that demanded physical expertise, although particularly proud of having passed his levels of certification in diving. Yet there he was at night on land and alone. He seemed way too purposeful for a young romantic playing out the adventure of searching for shipwrecks. Now Susan knows he was playing out another romance. She'd started her work week worrying about him and ended it with everyone sharing the same worry. Again she's plagued by his plight. He's the kind of student who cries out for understanding and guidance, capable in many ways though none in academics. Tijean is aware of the many strikes against him which causes him great resentment. His mother wasn't born on the island, a refugee from a troubled place, and she fears deportation. Yet she does belong here with her family and to return to her roots would only bring hardship. Unlike Toto Tijean shows no pride in his heritage. Toto is not presumptuous in any way. Maybe that's why Tijean lacks much self-respect. He is not well connected to his roots. At heart he's a young man who wants to feel he belongs so he can get on with his life but who is constantly reminded that he doesn't belong on the island or in school. So much about the young man is sad.

After crossing the road Ruth and Kate thank Susan for the outing. They are genuine in their appreciation, having enjoyed the viewing of so many flamingos and learning a bit about their habits. "They give me pleasure, too, whenever I see them," Susan says. She parts company with them at the resort where they plan to lounge and swim. Excusing herself Susan says she has marking to do, work that didn't get done yesterday when she went for that glorious sail.

Before starting into work Susan thinks how Kate Channing found Tijean's name odd and she remembers how Kate used to repeat the names of mostly immigrant students when she was working on class lists in the staff room. Her querying tone challenged their right to be placed in a setting so ordinary as 9A, 10B, 11C or 12D. After a couple of hours bent over her desk Susan stands and stretches, only this time she doesn't check her vital signs for stroke. Instead she decides she needs to have a swim, work the kinks out of her body. While changing she muses on the morning. She must tell Ian the outing was a success. He'll understand her enthusiasm for the flamingos as he's of the belief that being in love connects people to the rest of the species. Susan imagines his response when she tells him how beautiful the birds were, how content the women were just to watch them preening and feeding. He'll smile, acknowledging her gesture of kindness. He won't say, "See, I told you they were decent women." Since he's not the kind of person to gloat he won't say, "Aren't you glad you stopped sulking?" He's not the kind to lecture, either. She knows his personal philosophy as well as she knows his physical body. A person makes their own loveless world that can confuse and frighten. There are so many lost souls. Isn't it wonderful they made a loving world for each other? Gone is her confusion from yesterday, from the past. Now she is in a parallel universe with his. They are comfortable in a harmonious space, a space that now includes some wealth, giving them financial security.

Susan's actions seem hypnotic while in this exclusive state. Seeing Ian laughing with Kate Channing who is lounging like a poster girl for a tourist brochure shatters her euphoria. Unlike a mature woman over fifty she feels aroused. Is she jealous? No, once again she is threatened. "Damn, damn, damn," she says under her breath. These highs and lows won't do. They wring her out emotionally. She is reacting like her teenage students. Has she been in their company too long? Are those young girls her role models? "Get a grip," she tells herself as she raises her hand returning Ian's greeting from across the patio. Who is Kate Channing but a divorced, middle-aged, retired teacher? So what if she's flirting with Ian? Who doesn't?

He's an attractive man. Susan can feel flattered that he's hers. To Hell with Kate Channing. Where will she be at the end of her holiday? Back in the city and Susan will be here in this paradise. Not an asylum, but a destination, more a sanctuary. Her love den. Only they're selling the love den so she won't be here. Where will she be? That thought so unsettles her she loses control of her dive and does a belly flop. Feeling embarrassed by the splash she's caused, Susan resurfaces only to dive deeper to the bottom of the pool where she swims holding her breath for as long as she can. Like a whale she breaks through the water giving a blow and cavorts in an undecided pattern of crawl, butterfly and backstroke. They need to talk. What other plans does Ian have?

When she pulls herself out of the pool Susan is breathing heavily from the exertion of the swim. She pats her exposed skin dry with the towel. Kate is still lounging on the chair. Ian is still standing beside her giving her his full attention, something he often does with guests. Maybe that's part of the problem. Maybe the problem is this manner of living together which isn't exactly just the two of them under one roof. There are always other people. The more people around the more distracted they are, and therefore, less able to give each other their full attention. Yet until now Susan has not demanded Ian's full attention. Or, at least, she's never been jealous of a guest's attention.

What is this crazy threat? Of course, Kate will have a very different perspective on Ian than Susan does. Not only is she the same height as he is and able to stand shoulder to shoulder, eye to eye, (except now when sitting and looking up to him) she only knows him as the host, the owner of a holiday resort, a tenuous position from her point of view. Susan holds the permanent position. She knows the Ian of bold decisions, of risk taking, of hard work. She knows the man of gentle countenance. His charm is widespread, his affection individual. This consciousness should reassure her.

Back in her room her bed beckons. Maybe she needs to get horizontal? As soon as she flops on top of the bed she relents to the comfort of the mattress underneath her. Beds are like nests, practically a separate abode from the bedroom, a burrowing space that offers great comfort. Only it's a mistake to lie down. She's aware she'll fall asleep if she stays prone so she rolls off the mattress remembering the time when she was a child of nine and she fell out of bed and fractured her wrist.

Susan stands bolt upright. A hairline fracture. Of course, why hadn't she remembered that before? Now it all comes flooding back to her – the shock of waking, of lying on the floor, of crying aloud, of her sister staring down at her, of her parents running into the room, of being bundled into the car and taken to emergency. "Just a hairline fracture," the doctor said when the family was called into the office where he displayed an X-ray of her forearm and hand. The bluish picture defining her bones both fascinated and repulsed her. That was her arm, but it was inside her body. They couldn't do much for her. It didn't require a cast like a broken bone. With some amusement they agreed to put Susan's arm in a sling so she'd remember to keep it immobile.

Now Susan remembers herself as a nine year old child with her arm in a sling. Like her former student, Jessica, she, too, suffered a hairline fracture. Only in her family it was practically a joke. Of course Susan hadn't been pushed by a teasing boy like Jessica had. Some nightmare had scared Susan out of her nighttime nest. It's her awareness that her injury was the same as Jessica's that stuns Susan. She'd been told by others at the time of the incident at school that an injury like a hairline fracture is nothing serious and didn't take an act of violence to inflict. It seemed cold comfort then, but now she feels vindicated. She sustained a similar injury simply by falling out of bed.

Why hasn't she remembered that childhood incident earlier? Why didn't anyone in her family remind her of it when the same injury happened to Susan's student? Slowly Susan lowers her backside onto the side of the bed engrossed in contemplation. She mustn't have told either her mother or Sandra the exact nature of her student's injury. After all, they were still grieving the recent death of Andrew Borden, husband and father. She must have made a casual, general reference to the injury. Susan can now picture herself saying something dismissive like, "A student in my class got hurt." Maybe she had to simply clarify that the accident happened in her class, not outside on the street or in the hall to explain why the parents were threatening a lawsuit against her, the school and the Board.

Now outside her room there's a pounding of running feet and a sharp wrapping on her door. Who could possibly be in such a hurry to reach her? Without rushing Susan rises and opens the door to Ian. "Oh, it's you."

Huffing and puffing he leans his outstretched hand against the door frame. "I couldn't find you."

Puzzled Susan waits for him to explain.

Dropping his arm Ian exhales. "You weren't at the pool?"

"Well, I was."

"Sorry," he says. "I mean. Only I saw you dive to the bottom, but then you didn't come up."

"You mean you didn't see me come up?"

"No," he says more as a confession than in agreement. "I guess I was worried about you. Anyway, glad you're safe."

Clutching each elbow in opposite palms Susan holds her arms against her body. "Ian, do you think maybe you were so preoccupied, or engrossed in your conversation, you didn't realize I'd had a swim, got out of the water, and returned to my room without you noticing?"

Like a confused child caught out by his mother, Ian stares at her quizzically. Then his eyes brighten. "You're not jealous?"

Throwing open her arms Susan shakes her head. "Who me? No."

"Susan?"

Gesturing to the wicker two-seater outside she invites him to sit. "Actually, we do need to talk."

"Yes," Ian says as he drops his body to the narrow seat. "We never seem to get time to ourselves." Fanning his fingers at her he invites Susan to join him.

"When you knocked now, I'd just come to a realization."

"What's that?"

"I had a hairline fracture on my wrist when I was a child." It's obvious from his facial expression that Ian finds her news irrelevant. This isn't what he had in mind for a talk. "Don't you see? That's what my former student suffered."

"The one whose parents sued?"

"Yes."

"And your point is?"

"My family thought it was a big joke."

Laughing, Ian picks up her arm by her wrist and examines it. "Your family's normal."

"Are they?" Susan looks at her dangling wrist. "I can't even remember which one it was. Left or right? There's no scar."

"Not too serious, then?"

Fortified by Ian's judgement, Susan relaxes. "That's my point. It's not so serious. The fall out was way more serious than the injury. That was easy to treat, but the other hurt." Sighing she immediately abandons her easy pose. "Not like Tijean. The problem with Tijean is serious."

"Oh, Susan. Do you always have to have some trouble in mind to keep you worrying?"

"I'm not like that, am I?"

"Sometimes. You can be something of a worry wort."

Wrapping her hand around his palm she settles their arms between their bodies. "What about this other business? Do you have some plans for our future?"

Ian shakes his head. "No, I wouldn't do that, make plans without you. Like I said, this business with Marcel came up suddenly. I suspect he thinks prices are just going to continue to rise so he needed to get in sooner rather than later, and as you know, I'm finding the whole business too much. Ain't getting any younger."

"I still haven't digested it. How rich you are."

"We are, my dear." Squeezing her hand Ian communicates his reassurance and sincerity. "I do hope, though, that you will quit your teaching job? Then we really can make plans."

"I'll speak to Carl on Monday. I don't have the foggiest notion how to go about retiring."

"That'a girl. I hoped you wouldn't say that you feel you owed it to the students to stay until you turn sixty-five."

"Not bloody likely. The young professionals are quite capable of carrying on without me." Susan releases her grip on his hand. "But that said, there is still Monday morning ahead of me and I have marking to finish."

Rising Ian says, "I'll leave you to it then."

When settled back in her room Susan pulls another class list from her file folder. She commits to the task knowing it is the last set of marking she has to do, maybe ever. That thought puts a smile on her working face. By the time she records the last student's grade on the list she is stifling a yawn, although she is not really tired, merely bored by duty. Instead of going to her comfortable bed again, Susan thrusts her feet into her flip-flops. Time to get ready to help Ian with the evening meal. For one day a week she's the sous chef. He'll already have the pot roast simmering, his Sunday supper special, not a meal that appeals to most of their guests. When here they want to experience the island cuisine. Do Ruth and Kate know what's on the menu? Probably not, but old Sam Gold will. He likes Ian's pot roast, declaring it the best beef meal on the island.

Indeed, Dr. Sam Gold announces his arrival with reference to Ian's cooking. "I can smell the roast."

Susan looks up from setting the table. "Hello, Sam. Yes, Ian has it simmering in the crock pot." He is a hearty looking elder with tanned skin deeply wrinkled from too many years spent outdoors in the tropical sun. Masses of age spots deepen the colour of his tan. In his younger years he was a muscular man and his physical outline still presents a sturdy bearing.

Brushing a kiss on Susan's forehead Sam looks over her head. "So where's that niece of mine?"

"Changing for dinner. They spent the afternoon around the pool."

Sam lowers the left side of his mouth in disapproval. "She's brought her butch friend."

"Kate is Ruth's colleague." Susan knows better than to rise to Sam's bait. He can be blunt and obstreperous. "And mine," she adds.

Sam pauses, stilling himself to digest Susan's words. "Your colleague?"

In a facial gesture of acknowledgment Susan raises her eyebrows until her forehead shows wrinkles. "Yes. I, too, taught at Randolph Street High. Ruth was my principal."

Throwing back his head Sam roars with laughter.

Ian comes on the scene. "Welcome, Sam. I see you're already enjoying yourself."

"By golly, I am." Sam places his knuckles on his hips and stares at Susan. "Poor you," he says.

Ian glances from Sam to Susan. "And what, pray tell, is the cause for this sympathy?"

"I just told Sam that I taught under Ruth at Randolph Street High."

Smiling Ian puckers his lips and says to Sam, "It's been a homecoming for the three ladies."

"Not quite," Susan says.

"Tell me, how long did you serve under her as principal?" Sam asks.

"Less than a year," Susan says.

"Yes, I remember the year you came was the year she got her promotion. Having her as your boss would be enough reason to leave any job. That one's just like my sister." Sam is shaking his head.

Ian, too, shakes his head. "I'm sure you're being too harsh, Sam."

"Me?" Sam asks. "Don't say I didn't warn you. I learned to keep my distance. Not that she isn't competent. By God, if those women are anything, they're competent." Sam raises his chin in Ian's direction. "Which is why I invited her here to serve as my executor."

Again Ian laughs. "Are you planning on dying?"

"Not just yet," Sam says.

"You're a funny one, Sam," Ian says. "I thought a person simply had to name an executor in their written will. No need to invite them in person to visit you while you're still alive. Doesn't the executor's work start after you've passed away."

"That's right," Sam says. "But I want Ruth to know all the details of my will, especially what I'm worth. In fact, I want to see the look on her face when my lawyer tells her. But that'll have to wait until tomorrow." Sam's eyes bulge leeringly in anticipation of the unfolding of a family drama he's choreographed. As his protuberances relax he softens his gaze on Susan. "I'm sorry, my dear. I forgot my gift to you. I come empty-handed. Mea culpe."

"Don't apologize, Sam. You can give it to me another time," Susan says with the dignity of a hostess taking control of a situation that's only slightly embarrassing. After all, Sam does have a well founded reputation for being a tight-ass.

"Here they are," Ian says.

Susan settles her gaze on Ian after catching a glimpse of Ruth and Kate. His calm movement toward them confirms their presence as honoured guests. That niggling sense of disloyalty returns to brush aside Susan's own sense of confidence. As the women come closer Susan studies them. Kate has grown into an Amazon. It seems the relaxing day spent in the tropics has agreed with her. Her skin is shining with a new tan; her hair is full of body; her eyes glisten an extravagant blue; her smile reveals rosy gums; her height impresses its superiority to the two attending males. She wears a long, fringed, cotton skirt with a black tank top and a knitted cotton sweater over her shoulders knotted through the sleeves in the European fashion. Ruth looks less dramatic beside her colleague, definitely not her butch. She wears a fitted skirt with a flared hemline that ends just below her knees. Her mighty thighs curve to a narrower but still thick set of ankles. Her outfit offsets her upper body by emphasizing her narrow shoulders and small bust. Her face glows, the effect, too, of a relaxing day. Her countenance does not change when greeting her uncle and introducing him to Kate. She expresses not so much false courtesy as defense against the possibility of a bungled social encounter, the bungling, of course, by her uncle. Ruth is setting the tone as Ruth so often does. There'll be no nonsense here. Of course, Uncle Sam isn't one of her minions.

"So you're another one of these early retirees," Sam snorts not hiding the contempt he feels.

"Happily so," Kate says seemingly unaware that she's been slandered.

"Don't know how anyone can get rich when you have to support so many pensioners." Sam pulls his upper body away from the physical presence of the two women and thrusts his hands in his side pockets.

"The object, Uncle, isn't to make any one person rich," Ruth says maintaining her decorum.

"Do I detect a note of envy?" Kate asks.

"Just ignore him," Ruth says. "He doesn't have a social conscience."

"Envy?" Sam sputters. "I'm self-made. Was always self-employed."

"And proudly so, I take it?" Kate presses her will to Sam not intending the question to be rhetorical. Since Sam stays silent in the unfamiliar pose of not having a quick answer, Kate continues. "I think our pension scheme is the hallmark of financial democracy. We're a force to be reckoned with. We hold power on the stock exchange. No, we're not self-made like Conrad Black or even some family dynasty like the Weston's. What we are is a group of public servants who gave our time and talent to others and, instead of being shunted off to pasture at the end of our working life, we're lucky enough to receive a small, but secure, living allowance guaranteed until the end of our days."

"Holy Mother of Joseph," Sam says. "I've only just been introduced to you and now you're lecturing me. You're like all the other women in my family. If you're not ignoring me, you're telling me off."

"We know," Ruth says. "And you came here to get away from all that."

"Best decision I ever made."

Susan sees Ian has his chin tucked into his neck. Knowing how much he hates squabbles, she musters enough courage to resume her hostess role. "Will you join us at the bar?" she asks.

"Let me get you a drink," Ian says raising his head and establishing a less formal tone.

Kate isn't letting Sam off lightly. "So I understand you were a vet?"

"I like animals," Sam says. "You can trust them." He shows some remnants of polite society by standing aside to allow Kate to pass in front of him on her way to the bar.

"Except pit bulls," she says. "And alligators in Florida. And grizzly bears in Alaska."

"It's not the animals that's the problem in those parts," Sam says. "The problem is with the people. Population explosion. Too many tourists. Even here."

Susan registers Sam's speech which is like a native Canadian although he's lived most of his adult life as an expat amid a medley of nationalities. Yet he still retains his old accent and semantics.

Ian turns to face the two visitors. "Present company excepted," he says.

"What's that?" Sam asks.

Susan senses Sam is, despite his heartiness, experiencing the decline that comes with age. "We appreciate our guests, but we don't really want more people here. Most people on this island come because they like it underpopulated." She smiles at the two women.

"I caught onto that right away," Kate says.

"So when you return home and recommend this place to others," Ian says. "Warn them. We don't want the wrong kind of visitors."

"Looking for gambling casinos," Susan says. "But then, those types don't come here."

"Thank God for that," Sam says. "Don't much like gamblers."

"No," Ruth says taking what's become her usual stool. "You're more of a risk taker. Like playing the stock market Mother tells me."

"That's the only honest gambling there is," Sam says. He leans his weight against the side of the stool before riding the seat. "Never much liked cards, either."

"No, I don't much like cards either." Susan again recalls the argument with her mother over cards. "Yet, once, as a child, I found myself arguing in favour of playing them. A neighbour wanted my mother to play cards with her. What I wanted was for her to get out of the house, something my mother rarely did, except for shopping." In the ensuing silence Susan thinks oftentimes an argument isn't in the specifics. More often it's in the gestalt. That's why it proves difficult to analyze the details after having an argument. Probably Sam doesn't really care that a group of people collect a pension. Or gamble. He may simply want to prove to the women in his family that his life has value, and not just in the decisions he's made about how and where to live it, but in the financial success he's earned. Of course, he doesn't understand that others will not admire him simply for being wealthy.

Across the bar Ian is pouring drinks. The conversation babbles over the mundane like flight plans and time zones. It's as if everyone wants to begin again only in a more familiar pattern of proper etiquette that governs the newly introduced and recently reacquainted. Then Kate threatens to once again disrupt the social ambiance by honing in on the personal. "You have large hands," she says. "Like a surgeon." She is staring at Sam's deeply veined and liver-spotted hands that are wrapped around his old-fashioned glass as if he's trying to stop it from sliding off the counter.

"A doctor's hands," Susan says, although she immediately realizes it's a dumb comment. The insinuation is that he's a medical surgeon whereas he's a veterinarian, an animal surgeon. Susan decides to join Ian behind the bar, but he motions her away. He doesn't expect her to help him pour drinks so she pulls a stool around the end of the bar where she gains a perspective on the guests.

Sam looks down at his own hands. "I did do surgery, but mostly on small animals. You don't get many big animals on this island. A few donkeys."

"Oh, we haven't seen a donkey." Ruth sounds as excitable as a child.

"You will," Ian says.

Susan gives Ian a smile in recognition of his eternal optimism. "Or possibly a goat," she says.

"B'bookie," Sam says. "I can tell you about B'bookie."

"Is that a goat?" Kate asks.

"Yes," Sam says with the soft, low tone of a storyteller about to begin his tale. "Once upon a time was a very good time, Monkey chew tobacco and he spit white lime."

"Why, Uncle Sam, this is a side of you I'm not familiar with. But where's the goat? So far, you've only introduced a monkey."

"This is how the oral tradition begins," Sam says.

"Like the Anansi stories," Kate says.

"Yes, Anansi the spider. There's also B'rabbie the rabbit."

"Remember in the early nineties when all the schools were ordering Anansi books?"

"Yes, Ruth, I do," Susan says. "I got them for my students from the Caribbean. We read those tales about the tricks the spider plays, and often dramatized them."

"The art of storytelling is making a swift comeback on the islands here," Sam says. "But the storyteller has to also be a musician." Sam starts beating a rhythm on the counter top with his large hands that sound a hollow noise. "They play a goatskin drum to accompany their tales."

"They're like our fox and hare stories," Susan says. "The fox always trying to outwit the rabbit and failing."

More quietly Sam continues to beat, but with his fingertips. "They tell cautionary tales."

"We saw them at the Queen's jubilee celebrations," Ian says. "Remember, Susan?"

"I do."

"They celebrated Queen Elizabeth's jubilee on the Turks and Caicos?" Kate sounds only mildly incredulous.

"The Queen is revered here," Sam says. "Remember we are governed by the Brits."

"And use American dollars," Ruth says. She doesn't hide her disdain.

"Uncle Sam's bucks," Sam says.

"What a wit you are," Ian says, raising his glass to his male visitor.

"The best of both worlds, British governance and the almighty dollar," Sam says, returning the toast. "We made a lot of improvements during 2002, the year of the Queen's Jubilee, mostly to attract more tourists. Like the raised thatched gazebo or viewing platform and telescopes at Flamingo Pond."

Ruth and Kate look at each other quizzically. "We didn't see either of those," Ruth says.

When both women turn to Susan, she shrugs. "You have to go to Flamingo Pond via Whitby. It's a much bigger pond than what we saw today," she says. "It's the one you saw from the plane."

"Still, we do get the odd birder staying here," Ian says. "Or lister, as the Brits call them, come to see the pink flamingos."

"I'll take you two ladies there tomorrow after our meeting with my lawyer," Sam says. "We can have a picnic lunch."

"That sounds fine by me," Kate says. Raising her drink she downs the contents.

"Another?" Ian asks.

While the others proffer their glasses for refills Susan declines another drink. In this exclusionary status she becomes vague and turns her attention to the distant nebula. There is a silence to the approaching night like a theatrical backdrop. She realizes she often becomes vague when the light fades and the tropics experience a dramatic transition. The harsh electric lights glare and people turn their attention to each other. It is always like this with company at the resort in the evening. Tonight is no different, except for her. Susan experiences an internal turmoil. It feels like her blood is fizzing through her veins and arteries. When she was a young, single woman, she often found herself in company with unequal numbers of men and women out socializing, sometimes at bars or in living rooms in each others' homes or apartments. The early days were marked by dinner parties which friends gave to introduce their single acquaintances. Sometimes married couples hosted these affairs in the aftermath of their recent union before other pressing matters impinged on their time like starting families. Over the years these events dwindled as did the number of eligible men. The memory of these men is no retreat for Susan. A retreat conjures someplace warm and comfy, but somehow Susan never found that with any of her amorous adventures. Finally, she was compelled to admit that all her experiences with these men were delusional. She just never felt connected, so in mid-life she gave up the whole complicated pursuit and lived a solitary, but contented life, as a spinster as Doris called it in her unalterable vocabulary. There was one man whom her mother quite liked and Susan made the mistake of prolonging their relationship to suit her family's expectations. Martin Duncan was his name, a man of small stature with scant chin and bare scalp having gone prematurely bald. He had small hands and long fingers that typed at a voracious speed. He worked as a journalist for the Telegram, a local paper that shut down its printing presses before computers became the standard tool of the trade. Those same hands played nicely on her skin and Susan craved his touch when they parted, but not in a dreamy way, not like a girl desiring attention, but as a thirty something woman full of carnal lust that went unsatisfied for most of her womanly years. Sometimes she read articles written by him in national magazines. He'd moved out west shortly after they split and found work in a prairie town which is all she ever knew about him. Now she stares at the dark silence and wonders how he fared personally. Did he marry? Have children? Is he even still living? His unknown existence fills her with a queasy miasma of loss. It's not that she wishes circumstances were different between them. It's more a hollowness relating to her own life. She feels a dreamlike definition to her past existence that was so undefined, that looms now as a troubled time. It's only been a decade since she escaped that confusion, a decade of living here, on this island, in this tropical silence where she's been comfortable in her adult self.

"Susan?"

Susan turns her head slowly to engage Ian's eyes. "Yes?"

"You're a million miles away."

"Sorry." Susan returns to the conscious world of expectant company who are engaged in a conversation about the members of the royal family like some die-hard nineteenth century monarchists. Sam is being his usual louche self; Ruth, the perennial administrator, is making proclamations; Kate is adding spice with salacious revelations; and Ian appears mildly bemused. Susan wonders how she has found herself in present company? Given the rule of six degrees of separation the likelihood is there, yet she can't help but think the gathering miraculous: an aging uncle of a former boss friend to a mutual colleague at the place run by her partner. Who are these people really? Lover. Acquaintance. Associate. Neighbour. These words are tags, limited like inanimate objects. While in the real sense they are part of her being, not simply people in her world, but sensibilities, part and parcel of her emotional awareness. It is through them she makes sense of the world, her world. That personal revelation practically brings her to tears, and she hates being sentimental, yet realizes these glistening eyes of hers are outwardly expressing her love. God, she loves life. Bring it all on – her would-be enemies, her aging fellow citizen, her knight-in-shining-armour. That she could go on like this forever, drinking Pimm's surrounded by the night's silence in the company of others.

The conversation slips and slides, backtracks and detours, hovers and finally hones in on the nature of Haitian immigrants. In many ways it seems they are no different here than in other North American countries: some bring their voodoo culture, some bring musical talents or more tradeable skills like journalism, some bring broken families usually fatherless, and the women – well, the women carry many burdens. Ruth is telling a story Susan remembers hearing about the mother of one of Ruth's students, a troubled black youth. He was the woman's only child. She'd lost all her daughters in the early term of her pregnancies. "Her husband accused her of killing them in her womb."

"What we know simply as miscarriages," Kate says bitterly.

Susan turns her attention to Kate wondering why her tone is so acrid. Her face is contorted in a sneer as she listens to Ruth describe how the woman had to flee her husband and country with her infant son in fear of being jailed for infanticide or simply killed by her husband, or worse, by a mob.

"She's from a country that has little, if any, sophisticated medical knowledge," Ian says.

"Yes," Ruth says shaking her head, not in affirmation, but at the horror of her accounting.

"Not to mention they're superstitions," Sam says.

"My husband left me because I kept miscarrying," Kate says.

Susan's eyes haven't left Kate's face, and she senses now that the others are also staring in disbelief at Kate's personal revelation, although Susan isn't surprised as she's half-expecting such a sentence to drop from Kate's lips. All that pent-up bitterness has to have a brutal source. The seconds of silence stretch before them like a ticking bomb. Is there more? But Susan knows Kate isn't being accusatory. She is speaking from the heart, a heart that hurts.

Finally her friend leans her head close to Kate. "Surely he didn't say that?" Ruth asks. "He didn't actually say that he was leaving you because you had too many miscarriages, did he?"

"Not in so many words," Kate says. Again she finishes her drink. "But I know he never understood. I know he blamed me for the miscarriages. He made me feel like a failure." Kate twirls the empty glass on the counter. "And I guess I was."

"God, men," Ruth says.

"Here we go again," Sam says. "It's all our fault."

"Don't blame us for the way some men behave," Ian says.

"I'm not really," Ruth says. "Sorry, I know I shouldn't generalize. It's just so aggravating how some men get away with what they do."

Susan wants to explain to present company how Ian is different, but knows her defense will sound weak. She hears old Sam's stomach rumbling, and uses its noisy interruption as a segue. "Shall we eat?"

Sam smacks his lips. "Wait 'till you taste Ian's pot roast, Ruth. Just like my mother used to cook it." He sniffs the air in an obvious gesture meant to compliment the cook.

Susan makes the connection. That would be Ruth's grandmother. Ian also claims his pot roast is just like his grandmother cooked it. Home cooking as comfort food, she thinks. This association sends Susan's mind to home, not hers but Ian's home, a place she can only imagine as she's never been there. Neither has Ian since he left, yet he continues to pay homage to his roots with his Sunday cooking. He's never said he misses his family, never admitted to homesickness. She suspects his acceptance of his self-imposed exile is a veneer and sometimes wonders if it will crack to reveal a depth of sadness and loss like the feelings that threaten her, feelings revealed this weekend by the presence of Kate and Ruth. The past comes to haunt Susan who smooths her personal unrest with work, as she suspects Ian does. The resort demands his attention twenty-four/seven. Now she helps him serve the pot roast. He carves the meat and she spoons the vegetables and broth. They still haven't discussed what they'll do when she quits teaching. She's the only white face left on staff. Many second generation immigrants have returned to the islands after getting an education to teach or nurse or govern. Will Ian and she stay on the island into their old age like Sam? Or will they make other long term plans? Probably they'll travel. Of ourse, they'll go home for a visit. Maybe she'll finally get to see where he was raised. That thought pleases her with its connection to a younger Ian - the child, the adolescent, the teenager, the adult. Something to look forward to - gaining insight into his personal history.

Silence falls as everyone takes a few mouthfuls and then the compliments begin. Ruth agrees with Sam that the pot roast is just how she remembers her grandmother making it. "I can't remember the last time I ate pot roast," Kate says.

"Ian made one at Christmas," Sam says.

Kate laughs. "What about turkey?" she asks.

"Oh, I made that, too, for the family. I cooked the pot roast for Sunday supper when friends joined us."

"How's Gregory?" Sam asks.

"Greg's fine. He's doing well," Ian says.

"Who's Gregory?" Kate asks.

"My son," Ian says. "He came for a visit over Christmas."

"Led us in singing carols," Sam says. "He's got a good voice, your son."

Ruth stops her soup spoon in midair, en route from the bowl to her mouth, and looks at her uncle. "You sang Christmas carols?"

Sam peers at her over his spoon laden with chunks of meat and vegetables. "Yes," he says.

Ruth shakes her head. "You have mellowed."

Sam grunts as he chews, then swallows. "I quite enjoyed myself."

Ruth turns her attention to Ian. "You have a son?"

"Yes. He's in his first year at Dartmouth."

Kate rests her back against the chair and looks directly at Ian. "Any more children?"

"Just the one boy," Ian says.

As Kate leans over her bowl to resume eating she flicks her eyes across to Susan. "So you're a stepmother?"

"Hah, hah," Sam says. "The wicked stepmother."

"I've hardly played a role in mothering him," Susan says.

"His own mother dotes on him," Ian says. "He's remained number one in her affections."

Again Kate rests against the back of her chair. "She never remarried?"

"Yes," Ian says. "Yes, she did, but that didn't seem to change her relationship with Greg."

"So the stepfather gets to play second fiddle to your son?" Kate asks.

"I guess you could say that," Ian says. "I've never met the man."

Kate cocks her head at Ian. "That must feel odd?"

Ruth wipes her mouth with her napkin. "Is that why you came here, Ian?"

Swallowing a morsel of food down her windpipe Susan starts coughing. Reaching across her place setting Ian lifts her glass of water to her mouth. Susan takes it and swallows. "Sorry," she says.

"No," Ian says. "I originally came here with my wife and son. He was just a toddler. You may be surprised to learn that I, too, used to teach."

"Did you?" Kate asks.

"So why did you quit teaching?" Ruth asks. She turns to Sam in an aside. "Obviously it wasn't for the same reasons that you came?"

"We all have our reasons," Sam says.

Susan remains frozen in her gesture of drinking from her glass of water. Her eyes flit from Ian to the speaking company. She's never heard him publicly admit that he used to teach. By the time she arrived on the island it was old news. Her mind is a buzz of defensive excuses she could give on behalf of Ian's quitting teaching, but it seems Sam successfully scuttles Ruth's prying question.

"That Dubois fellow you've got working for you?"

Turning his attention to Sam, Ian nods. "Marcel?"

"What do you know about him?"

"He's an accountant, from France," Ruth says to her uncle. "And his brother's a doctor."

"And he's handsome and charming. So gentle," Kate says.

"Hah," Sam retorts. "You don't know much then."

Without even apologizing for having interrupted the question originally directed to Ian, the two female guests roll their eyes at each other. "Tell me. What's the scoop?" Ruth asks.

"You'll be interested to learn he comes from a very wealthy family."

Giving an insinuating nod to Kate, Ruth says, "Does he?"

"You two don't stand a chance," Sam says. "Besides, hasn't that Sarton woman got her clutches on him?"

Since Sam is looking at Susan she feels compelled to defend her friend. "They have met."

"We have recently learned something about his riches," Ian says diplomatically.

"Okay, I don't get it," Kate says. "If he's an accountant from a wealthy family why is he working here?" She turns to Ian. "Not to insult you, but, if I was rich, I wouldn't be standing behind a counter."

"He's learning the trade," Ian says simply.

Feeling the need to elaborate Susan says, "Before coming here he worked for Club Med on Provo."

"Isn't that the one for adults only?" Kate asks.

"Yes," Susan says.

Turning to Ruth, Kate says, "That's the place I originally suggested."

"You don't want to go there," Sam says. "It's for the younger crowd. All rah, rah."

"Thanks, dear Uncle Sam," Ruth says.

Ignoring his niece, Sam turns his attention back to Ian. "So what's he up to, this French man? Is he here for business prospects? Does he want to get into the tourist trade?"

"Something like that," Ian says.

"I'd like to talk to him," Sam says.

"Oh, now I get it," Ruth says. "You want to make an investment?"

"Maybe," Sam says, pushing out his lower lip. "If he can show me a healthy business plan."

"I wonder how his family became rich?" Kate asks.

"Apparently some distant ancestor owned coffee plantations." During the lull that follows her stark comment

Susan remembers the discussion her students had in class after Tijean disappeared about the history of Haiti's poverty.

Swiveling her head on her neck Kate eyes the adults around the table. "I guess that'd do it."

Ever the rational businessman Sam holds Kate's gaze. "That depends," he says.

"On what?"

"On where the plantations were? If Cuba, they're gone. Now under communism. If Haiti, they were lost centuries ago during the uprising. If Jamaica and in the mountains, then the family still prospers."

"I see," Kate says.

So does Susan. It dawns on her that this money Marcel brings to them is earned on the backs of others. His ancestral wealth that's paying for the resort comes from not just privilege, but from siphoning the resources off far away islands. How different from being an absentee landlord? Looking at Ian she sees that he's engaged in business talk. He accused her of being too serious and maybe she is.

By the end of their meal they are joined by returning guests. George, Ted, Arthur and Sharon tell them about their visit to the conch farm and lovely meal at a restaurant on Provo that included conch sushi. "Never had that before," Arthur says. He turns to his wife in a gesture of confirmation. "We've been to many sushi bars in New York, but never been served what we ate tonight."

"It was a real gastronomic treat," Sharon says.

Before long they are joined by the younger guests full of anecdotes about their diving adventures. They gleam against the quiet night, their bodies energized by their earlier physical activity. Lyn and Jeff compare the dive to ones they've taken off the coast of Florida and rank the diving here superior. Lizzie and Roger remain sanguine. They've dived all over the world – the Seychelles, the Philippines, Australia. For Adir and Kamil diving is a new experience and they're like adventurous boys back from a treasure hunt.

Later Marcel appears. Everyone stops their multiple conversations to greet him. He claims their attention with the latest island news. "The missing teenager, Tijean Williams." Marcel's eyes come to rest on Susan.

"Yes, the boy's a student of mine," Susan says, acutely aware that Kate and Ruth have followed Marcel's gaze to rest on her. She has to remind herself she's not to blame.

"The one who vanished. Poof," Marcel gestures as if he's performing a disappearing act. "And no one has seen since."

"We heard about him," Kamil says. "From the taxi driver."

"His father's a taxi driver," Marcel says. "Maybe it was him."

Kamil casts a glance at his mate. "No, it wasn't his father driving the taxi."

"Doesn't his mother work for you, Ian?" Sam asks.

"Yes, she does. She's originally from Haiti," Ian says.

The entire company turn their attention to them. All fifteen pairs of eyes fall on her and Ian. She wants to shout it's not her fault Tijean ran away. "I can't imagine he's gone far." She recalls saying the same thing to Guy, but he wasn't convinced. He seemed deeply worried about his son's whereabouts, as if they lived in the slums of New York or London or Rio where he could be the victim of gun violence, instead of here, on these safe islands where most people know one another.

"He's a diver," Marcel says turning to the guests. "Initially he ran off with them. Now they think he's boarded a plane to Canada."

"To Toronto?" Susan asks.

"Yes," Marcel says.

"Where do they keep their boat?" Roger asks.

Like a ping pong ball the focus of the conversation changes with each player's hit bouncing along lightly, sometimes high, sometimes low. Connect and keep the ball in play.

"Sandy Point," Sam says. "At the marina."

"But they're not there now," Marcel says. "They're gone, too."

Sam snorts. "With their deep-sea treasure," he says. "They've pulled anchor and left with all they stole from the bottom of the sea." His baritone voice holds his audience. Even the most educated and sophisticated among them could believe his tale given his captivating delivery.

"They pulled anchor tonight," Roger says. "We saw them pass us when we were coming into harbour."

Lizzie looks askance at her husband. "We did?"

"You didn't see them, darling," Roger says, without returning eye contact. "You were busy at that moment with our diving guide."

"Ships passing in the night," Jeff says.

Roger does turn his attention to the young Canadian man. "Right, old boy. You were standing on deck with me at the time." Now he turns his head to address the assembled guests. "It was our instructor who recognized the vessel."

"Like a pirate ship," Lyn says.

Her husband, Jeff, is the only one to laugh out loud.

"Why do they think he ran away?" Sam asks.

"That's the question?" Marcel asks assuming the role of the detective on the case. He could be Maigret, that French connoisseur of crime. Only, unlike that police investigator created by the writer George Simenon in many slim volumes including 'Maigret Has Doubts', Marcel exudes confidence. He is a polymath: a chef, an accountant, an investigator showing off his analytical skills.

"It's a long story," Susan says. "Something to do with Tijean wanting to dive and his parents wanting him to get a decent education."

"Yes," Marcel says firmly as if he's only just succeeded in communicating the real intent of his message. "Yes, I heard that, too. That's why they think he went on the dive boat." Marcel raises his arm in an 'ahoy' gesture while turning in Lizzie's direction.

"Oh, please, Marcel," Susan says. "That's how rumours start." As if on cue, the company spill apart into smaller groups to gossip and speculate like tabloid journalists. Susan feels Ian's hand on her forearm. She sighs feeling the warmth of his gesture relax her nerves. "I wonder if he has family there."

"Where?" Ian says.

"Toronto?"

"Have to ask his parents," Ian says. Nudging her, he adds, "Aren't you just the little detective."

"Ruth Rendell or Barbara Vine? Sorry, she's a writer. I need a detective, say Kate Fansler."

"You mean to say, 'They're writers'. Hah," Ian says exuberantly. "I caught you. An error in agreement. And you the grammar expert."

Indulging Ian, Susan simply smiles. "Maybe now I can help."

"What do you mean?"

"I mean if we go to Toronto," she says, holding his eyes in her quizzical gaze. "I could look for him."

"Tijean?" In answer to her affirmative shrug, he tells her she's not the boy's mother. "So stop worrying. He's no longer your problem."

Susan inhales deeply through her nostrils. The night air always smells sweeter than during the day, as if the calm sea has given over its saline spray to the pungency of plants that flower on land. He's right. She's not his mother. Yet what could even his mother do? It's not her fault, either. These things happen in all families. The attentive conversation between their guests serve as a backdrop, like the undercurrent of a tsunami tidal front. During this lull Susan visits earlier thoughts that she wants to share with Ian. "Will we grow old here?"

Ian chuckles. "We'll grow old together, but hopefully, not here," he says looking directly at her.

"Where then?" she asks. Susan leans her upper body closer to his.

"Home," he says simply.

Where his hand still holds her arm Susan lays her free hand over it. "You mean you're not going to be like Sam Gold and remain in exile?"

"No," he says.

Susan tightens her clutch on his hand. "You're ahead of me since I only started thinking about what we might do this afternoon."

Moving his free hand to the side of her head, Ian lifts her hair behind her ear. "Do you really want to go to Toronto?"

Susan shrugs, feeling a tingle down her spine from his touch behind her ear. "Just to visit," she says. "I only got to the part where we decide whether or not to stay on here, at the resort. I guess I'm at the branch of the Y."

Ian furrows his brow, making his eyes appear small. "We can do better than spend the rest of our lives here."

"We can? You always give the appearance of loving it here."

"I do, for now. Just not forever."

"Home?" Susan asks. "What do you mean by home, then? Nova Scotia?"

"Yes, Nova Scotia. Canada."

Susan takes a turn chuckling. "So when we're suffering from aching bones we'll return to the cold. Is that what you're thinking?"

"Just for the summer."

Marcel interrupts them by placing his two hands on their table and leaning his body weight onto his arms. "I want to thank you two for introducing me to Leila."

Susan lets her eyes travel slowly up Marcel's arms. Black hairs cover the back of his hands and his forearms. "You're welcome," she says languidly.

"I'm glad you two hit it off so quickly," Ian says.

Marcel puckers his lips. "We did." He nods in the affirmative and leaves.

Susan collapses into giggles. "A repeat of us?"

Ian gives her a quick kiss. "They could be."

Behind Susan the lull ends. She turns around to see the table where George and Ted sit explode into raucous laughter, guessing their conversation no longer dwells on any of the problems on the island, or around the world. Their conversation's turned from the gossip of the place to entertainment, something Ted seems particularly gifted at doing. A feeling of nostalgia swamps her, only it's a strange kind of nostalgia that already yearns for all that's now before her. It's as if she's projected herself into her future life where she knows she'll look back upon her time at the resort and feel sentimental about her days here with Ian. In silence they regard the others. An intimacy bonds them. With this confidence restored Susan feels bold enough to ask Ian what he thinks of Kate and Ruth. "They're not really my type," he says.

Susan laughs quietly. "No, I mean," she says, then stops to wonder why she's so curious about his feelings toward two women who are virtual strangers. Now they are living in close proximity, but by the end of the week the two will leave and Ian and she will probably never see them again. Unless they bump into one another in Toronto. Why compare herself to them? They have the company of women. She has a future with Ian. So, in the end, it won't matter what he thinks of them, or what they think of him, or what they think of her, or even, what she thinks of them. She doesn't need to get sucked into that pathetic desire to be liked, nor does she need to do the liking. They've come together like those two ships in the night, passing, not colliding. In the end, there's virtue in accomplishing that much between people. She can feel content that she's faced her old enemies and stared them down.

Yet there's a new yearning in her to right wrongs. Susan keeps returning to the problem with Tijean, and she won't feel content until she helps him settle. Despite what Ian says, she'll find him in the city, if that's where he is, and remind him that he's missed on this island where he belongs. That'll give her a purpose outside teaching. She still has a role to play as counselor on these islands. She can still do some good.

∽

When Tijean found himself alone one day at his aunt's house he retrieved from his back-pack the scrap piece of paper with Jake's contact information. The multi-folded sheet was a discarded print-out from the airline showing Jake's itinerary in coloured print that held Tijean's attention.

He skimmed the details in red listing Jake's flight number and in blue showing the departing and arrival terminals with times. The information on checked baggage allowance was in black print. These words conjured up an image of Jake with his trunk and Samsonite cases, a picture that made Tijean smile in memory of the deep sea diver. Turning over the paper he found the phone number beginning with the 416 area code. When a woman answered Tijean remembered that this was an office number of a friend of Jake's as he hadn't known where he'd be living. "I'm looking for Jake Kearney."

"Yes, he's here."

There was a brief pause before Jake came on the line. He sounded different over the phone than in real life, but when Jake heard who was phoning, his tone enlivened and became familiar. Jake said he'd caught him at a good time and asked Tijean if he would like to visit him that morning. Of course, Tijean agreed to go, and took down details on how to find Jake in the centre of the city. Later, when Tijean rode the bus along Spadina Avenue, he peered out the grimy window in fascination. This part of the city was even busier than where his aunt lived. Mostly the pedestrians were older than he was, but younger than the adults in his life. He guessed they must be students who came from all over the world. There were many Asian faces in the crowd. He couldn't imagine what life was like for them. The buildings, too, were mixed: huge, old brick houses the size of mansions; tall, newer apartment blocks with no balconies; windowless, institutional buildings that sat on entire blocks of land. Finally he came to his stop and got off. The building he entered must have been a hundred years old. It felt colder inside than out and he ran up the stairs trying to warm up. The echo his pounding feet made on the bare stairs made him self conscious so he stopped running and carefully took large steps.

Inside the door Tijean pushed open was an office where a woman stood in front of a green, metal filing cabinet. She was no taller than it. Her hair was totally grey and cut in a bob. She wore layers: a burgundy sweater coat over a patterned vest over a black turtle neck. Without smiling at him she said, "You must be Tijean? I'll get Jake."

Within seconds she returned with Jake in tow. His limp was more profound than on their flight, but he smiled apparently in no pain. "Hello, Tijean. You've met Terri."

Terri answered, saying her full name, "Terri Barlow," and extending her hand to shake. Then she turned her back on the men and resumed her work.

"Come in, come in," Jake said, gesturing the way.

Tijean nodded and followed. "You haven't had your hip operation yet?"

"No, but I've been for pre-op tests." Pulling out a chair Jake indicated where Tijean might sit. Then Jake eased himself into the swivel chair in front of the computer. He started chuckling. "While there I put my hospital gown on wrong. They're a puzzle. I couldn't find anything to tie it with. Then I noticed there were three holes, so I put one over my head and my arms through the other two. That left my ass in the breeze unless I clenched one tail of the gown over it, which I did and emerged to be informed I had to go back and do it right. I wondered aloud what 'right' meant and the nurse said I shouldn't put my head through the armhole. I said there were three armholes and I only have two arms. Then she showed me what I'd done wrong."

Imagining Jake in a confused position with a green regulation gown covering only half his body Tijean laughed aloud.

"I bet they get that all the time," Jake said, more out of good humour than self defense. He hit the keyboard. "I have to get another computer. I intended to wait for blu-ray. They're too expensive for now. Someone recommended an Acer. They're cheap, but I don't know how reliable."

"I don't know about computers," Tijean said.

"You don't? I thought everyone your age did."

"I never paid much attention to them in class." Tijean didn't say that they didn't own one at home on the island or at his aunt's place.

"Don't you haunt internet cafes?" Jake asked, as if reading Tijean's mind.

Tijean nodded.

Jake seemed to take a moment to seriously consider Tijean's response before brightening. "So, do you want to see some sex and violence on the reef?"

Tijean laughed with Jake. "Fish mating?"

"Look, when the coral spawns," Jake said, letting the preamble dangle in enticement. Quickly he typed an entry code.

"Hey, you know how to type?" Tijean said, showing surprise that a man in his sixties had such a useful, technical skill.

"I went to high school in Quebec where they taught typing. Then my family moved to Ontario where the kids studied Latin instead, which I couldn't take because by then I was too far behind. Too bad. It would have proven useful to me later as a biology student."

That reference got Tijean thinking for a fleeting moment about his old high school. What would the students be doing now? Maybe sitting in front of computer terminals typing or searching the internet.

"During this editing and video analysis process I discovered that some of my tapes were going off. I have found ways around that and am transferring the tapes to other media. That was a bit of intense sweat."

Tijean watched the screen as Jake moved through the menu. Finally he clicked Play. There followed a show of vivid colour with creatures from the deep. Tijean was immediately transported to the bottom of the ocean.

"Better than Hollywood, eh?" Jake clicked on a file titled birostris.

On screen a school of manta rays swam in formation as if performing a dance for the camera. Tijean got excited, but Jake shushed him. He was to simply watch the graceful aquatic creatures move. Their open filtering mouths gave their bodies a heavy shape that belied their fluid performance. Their bulging eyes seemed to look directly into the camera like performers making contact with the audience. Their undersides brushed overhead revealing rows of gills that could have inspired the design of a pick-up truck's grill. Their wide flippers undulated in rhythmic waves like the long arms of a ballet dancer. Then they started performing back-flips, sometimes in unison. These movements kept Tijean fixated. As soon as the film ended he felt he had permission to speak. "Those back-flips were great, especially those they did in pairs."

Jake smiled. "Did you notice how the one on the inside would exit? Just like a dog roll in a fight." He stepped aside as if performing the exit strategy. "So, do you want to have some lunch?"

Tijean looked at the bottom right hand corner of the screen. He was surprised to see that it was already past noon. "Sure."

"There are lots of Chinese and Vietnamese restaurants on Spadina just south of here."

Tijean followed Jake as he hobbled out of the building. When they reached the street Tijean didn't know whether he should offer Jake his arm. It seemed an absurd gesture toward a physically strong man. Instead he kept to the man's slow pace, patiently walking in step. As if their altered manner of being together compelled them to become more personal Jake asked Tijean if he had a girlfriend back home. "Yes, Carolyn," Tijean said. Saying her name conjured an image of her in his mind as she was that last day, small in his arms when he kissed her goodbye, only the size of a girl really. "But I don't know if she'll wait for me."

"Ah," Jake said. "I suppose that depends on the nature of your love."

Tijean felt embarrassed. "I never declared my love. Just asked her to wait."

"Well, if you're important to her, she'll wait. Desire can endure. But, I'm a biologist and biology rewards patience. Here we are." Tijean held open the door. "My treat," Jake said as they entered.

∞

The bird songs of robins and sparrows sound a chirpy conversation. Are they white throated? On second thought,

Susan doubts it because what she remembers from their little throats is a long, lonely call at the end of the day. Maybe they're song sparrows? Are there cardinals in their midst? Could those lovely, bright-red finches with their burnt-orange beaks be singing, too? The backdrop to the birds' melody is a washboard noise of cars. Ron, Sandra's husband, warned them yesterday that they'd hear the rush hour traffic very early. "It used to be we'd hear it at 6 a.m. Now it starts before 5."

Lifting her head to peer over Ian's shoulder Susan sees the digital display on the clock in Kit's room where they've been sleeping since landing in Canada two days earlier. It shows 4:43. Who could be driving to work at this hour? Poor souls, Susan thinks as she collapses onto the warm bed. Too early for her to rise, although later she will to say goodbye to her niece who came for a Sunday meal just to see her aunt. Chrissie, as her father calls her, is getting up with him as he'll drive her back to the university campus where she's in the middle of writing exams. Such was her eagerness to see her aunt she made time when time is most valuable to her. Cautiously Susan closes her eyes. She doesn't want to oversleep and miss the girl's departure.

Waking from inside a dream Susan thinks she's in the old house in Mimico with her family. For seconds she's transported to that interior with its familiar walls and wood trim. She could be decades younger it feels so real and comforting. Yes, a strong sense of comfort holds her to that place and time before she comes fully awake and realizes she's in her sister's house lying in her nephew's double bed beside Ian who's breathing is regular with the pattern of sound sleep. There's the sound of water rushing through the plumbing in the house. Someone is taking a shower. Glancing at the clock again she sees the time now is 6:43. Not wanting to wake Ian she carefully folds back the blankets and rises. On tiptoes she goes to Kit's desk to retrieve her robe from the back of the chair. Then she goes to the door which she quietly opens and, peeking down the hall, sees that the bathroom door is closed.

Ron is in the kitchen making coffee. "Good Morning," Susan says on her way through the room to the back door where there's a two-piece bathroom. The narrow window in this tiny room is open letting in the morning chill, as well as more bird chatter which includes the distinct notes of the white-throated sparrow, another "good morning" greeting. Here the traffic noise is louder. Ron and Sandra's house is in the middle of a residential area that sits on a rise above Mimico Creek, though its proximity to that slip stream doesn't mean it's in the same neighbourhood where Susan lived with her family. This house is miles away from the one in her dream and situated in a more up-scale part of the west end of the city, but south of them is a thoroughfare which holds The Queensway and The Gardiner Expressway, multi-roads with multi-lanes bringing vehicles to the downtown core.

On her return to the kitchen Ron asks if she's ready for a "cuppa"?

"Please," she says, accepting his offer and his lingo, a youthful attitude Susan ascribes to his work as a salesman in a leading drug firm. He's wearing a heavy terry bathrobe, solid red in colour, that's open at the neck revealing some salt and pepper hairs sprouting from his broad chest. His legs and feet are bare - no shoes, no hair - but there's a stubble of whisker growth on his dimpled chin. Last night, before retiring to bed, Ian said he could understand why Ron is successful at his job. "He's like the perennial college football player. Youthful. A team player. Reliable."

"But now he plays golf," Susan said.

"He has to, doesn't he? Isn't that part of the role?"

In his role as coffee maker Ron excuses himself to take a cup upstairs to Sandra in bed. How wonderfully spoiled her sister is. From upstairs comes the sound of the bathroom door opening, then Ron greeting his daughter before two bedroom doors open. A hush follows. Outside the kitchen window the forsythia bush is bursting into yellow, inside a window planter holds yellow and purple pansies which Sandra says she'll transplant to the garden in a couple of weeks, as soon as the threat of night frost passes. All this reassures Susan with its familiarity. Initially she'd felt like a stranger arriving on their doorstep, the foreign visitor. Other times on her return she'd stayed with their mother. Only Doris recently sold the family home cashing in on the rise in real estate prices, much like Ian did on the island with the resort. Now Doris lives at St. Hilda's where her older sister also has an apartment. Today Susan and Ian will visit her mother and aunt after they pick up their newly purchased car.

Upstairs the shower starts again, a flow of water through pipes muffled by interior walls. The busy activity of a household beginning the morning, Susan thinks and realizes it's been decades since she experienced such domesticity. In Mimico the morning started early with their father in the shower. Then she would rush into the bathroom to beat Sandra. After his departure the room was humid and she could smell the shaving cream he used. Another muffled sound wafts downstairs. It's an electric powered hair dryer, probably Christine blowing her hair dry, puffing and shaping it into a flattering style. She is a stylish young woman, unlike her brother who cares little for his appearance.

Taking another sip of coffee Susan checks the time lit up on the microwave panel. Later she'll take Ian a cup of coffee. No point disturbing him yet as the car dealership isn't even phoning them until 10 a.m. to arrange delivery. There's another digital display of time on the panel of the

BOSE radio. Pushing the soft, black, on/off button on top, Susan watches the time display whirl through a chronological series of numbers, settle on a station location, then return to the exact hour and minutes. Clear notes of music surround her. Examining the multiple buttons arranged on top Susan finds a rectangular series for tuning the station and setting the volume. She holds the button with the reverse arrow for volume. A series of numbers counting backwards fill the front display panel. Ah, Susan thinks, that's what those numbers indicate – the volume level. She's unused to so many digital gadgets.

The plumbing rattles when Ron's shower ends. Within minutes the bathroom door opens, then the bedroom door, then the bedroom door and the bathroom door again. Must be Sandra who's taking a shower. Listening to the progress of her relatives' morning rituals Susan ponders the reverse order to their family. Doris waited until the household was hers before using the bathroom to shower. Christine must be keen to get back to campus, or nervous about her exam. Sandra may not be in a hurry since the school where she teaches is close by, but still, she has to get up and get going. As her sister explained when showing them to Kit's room when they arrived, their house renovation a decade earlier included a two-piece master ensuite and a two-piece ground floor bathroom leaving them with just one shower to share. "So we all have to take turns."

Susan hears her niece bounding down the stairs. "Good Morning, Christine."

"Auntie Susan. You're awake." Wrapping her arms behind Susan's neck Christine gives her a long hug.

"I'm not too sure I'd call it awake," Susan says patting Christine's back with her free hand and trying not to spill her coffee in the other. Against her chest Susan feels the soft flesh of her niece's ample bosom, a physical asset that Sandra ascribes to the Whitney genes, not the Borden's. A fresh smell of herbal conditioner spills off her silky soft, reddish blond hair.

As quickly as the hug is given it ends and Christine charges to the refrigerator. "Did you get some breakfast?"

"No thanks. I'm not ready to eat." Susan watches Christine take out a small yogurt container, pull off the foil top, rifle through the cutlery drawer for a spoon and dig into the dairy product. "I just wanted to be up to say goodbye. And thank you for interrupting your studies to visit."

"Oh," Christine moans. "I wish I could visit longer."

"Maybe you could visit us down east this summer when we get settled?"

A clang of metal hitting metal sounds as Christine drops the spoon in the sink. Before throwing the empty container in the waste bin, she turns to her father who's just entered the room. "Another good reason to buy me a car."

Rolling his eyes at Susan Ron walks to the sink with his dirty coffee mug. "What reason is that?"

"So I can visit Auntie Susan and Uncle Ian."

Ron smirks. "Or you could travel with us. We plan on going east to visit them."

"But I have to work and save money."

"So you can't go to see them when they're settled on the east coast?"

"Dad!"

Turning away from his daughter's exasperation, Ron addresses Susan. "There are many reasons to get Chrissie a car, but visiting you isn't one of them."

Excitement replaces exasperation. "Really Dad? You are thinking of getting me a car?"

"Whoa! I didn't say that."

With a banana in one hand and a coffee in a traveling mug in her other Christine gives her aunt another hug, this one a loose gesture. "I think we can work on this idea." Freeing her hold, Christine winks at Susan. "In the car."

"Don't you have to study?" Ron asks. "Last minute cramming."

Remembering how Christine could always read while sitting in the passenger seat Susan looks from father to daughter imagining how their drive together will unfold. After locating his keys Ron offers to carry his daughter's binder to the car. Susan watches from the back door as they pile into Ron's Camry, then goes to the side window to watch the car back out of the driveway. With them gone a fearsome loneliness unsettles Susan. This is what she's missed and her sister takes it with such a cavalier attitude that she doesn't even come to wave goodbye.

When Sandra does appear downstairs she takes the mug and spoon out of the sink and puts them in the dishwasher. "I have to warn you, our mother is the youngest resident at St. Hilda's."

Susan watches her sister cleaning up after her husband and grown daughter wondering why those two didn't perform this simple, domestic act? Once a mother, always a mother. So, their own mother is the youngest one admitted to a facility caring for the elderly. Why doesn't this surprise her? There's always been a side to Doris' nature that's elderly. Susan imagines that her mother was one of those children who seemed like a little old lady right from the get-go. At six she was probably sensible and helpful staying at home instead of roaming the streets and countryside, while her elder sister was more likely to be the gad-about spending her time out of doors. Their Auntie Dot is also something of a gadfly and Susan wonders how their mother is coping with their aunt's persistent interference. Yet maybe that's exactly what Doris needs, someone to take charge and direct her day. Susan resembles their Auntie Dot in physical appearance while Sandra is more like their mother. In fact, her sister's aged exactly as their mother with a hint of jowls under her jaw line, a thickening around her middle until there's no waistline, and a reduced height from rounded shoulders.

"You'll notice that right away in their dining room." Sandra has a box of cereal in her hand that she offers to Susan by gesture before taking out one bowl. "Help yourself to anything when Ian gets up." Going to the refrigerator Sandra continues her explanation. "It's a lovely dining room, by the way. All the facilities there are quite nice. The food is cheap, too. They pay for their lunch. Breakfast and dinner are included with the monthly fees, but the dining room is open to guests for lunch. Actually, anyone can go there for lunch, like at a restaurant." Now she's chewing so stops talking.

"I'm glad she was able to keep some of her furniture. Having what's familiar around her must have helped her adjust."

Sandra shakes her head. "She had no trouble adjusting. After years of refusing to even consider moving, there she is in a perfect set-up. Aunty Dot to keep her company. Lots of activities to keep her busy. What more could you ask for?"

"And she can afford it," Susan says, thinking that she should offer to pay for something besides a cheap lunch. "This is a great 'cuppa' coffee Ron made," she says, using her brother-in-law's lingo.

"Yes, fair trade," Sandra says. "Remember how I used to shop on Roncesvalles for it? Now you can purchase it anywhere. Even the grocery store, although I do still like to shop at that specialty store."

"Well it's certainly better than anything you get in a vacuum packed tin," Susan says, thinking how she hasn't intended to start a political discussion about where and how coffee is produced or where and how to shop. It's just the "cuppa" is an aromatic brew of flavourful beans, not a stew steeped in dishwater.

Rising from the table Sandra says she has to get going. "Still have some prep to do before the day begins. You got everything you need?"

"I think so."

"Just treat the place as your own. You've got a key, right?"

Remembering that Ian took the key and directions from Ron Susan nods in the affirmative.

"Good luck with your new car," Sandra says.

"Tonight we want to take you two out to dinner. Our treat for having us stay here."

"I think I can handle that," Sandra says, then enters the downstairs bathroom to brush her teeth.

Soon sounds of departure reach Susan from outside – the garage door opening, the engine starting up, the Saturn backing down the single lane driveway, the gunning of the accelerator as Sandra drives away. Filling another mug with coffee Susan goes upstairs.

Pushing the door with the toe of her slippered foot Susan enters the bedroom. "Wakey, wakey," she says in a sing-song voice.

"Umm," Ian moans. "Has everyone gone?"

"Yes," Susan answers. "And this morning you're in luck. You get coffee served in bed. Now it's your turn to be spoiled." After all this is the man who's spent over a decade rising early to serve paying guests.

"Ah, yes." Rolling over and propping himself against the pillows he extends his right arm. "What about breakfast? Do I get breakfast in bed, too?"

"Anything you want."

After taking a sip Ian exhales. "They do good coffee in this joint. How about some of that left-over rhubarb and strawberry pie?"

"For breakfast?"

"Sure. Why not? Perfect morning food. A healthy serving of fruit."

"Hardly. Well, Sandra did say to help ourselves." Thinking to spoil him Susan peers down at Ian with a flirtatious look. "But no ice cream."

Shaking his head and shoulders Ian mocks the self-importance of a cock. "Definitely not à la mode," he says.

His perfect high school French opens some synapse in Susan's brain. There's Kate Channing again. Go away, Susan tells her thoughts as she retreats from the bedroom eager to perform a task in the kitchen. When she returns with the slice of pie warmed for 25 seconds in the microwave Susan bends down to study the bottom shelves of her nephew's bookcase. "I think Kit has a Perly's here somewhere."

"Come again?"

"A street map for Toronto."

Angling his head in the direction of the computer on the desk Ian mumbles through a mouthful of pastry. "Search the internet."

Her hand alights on a coiled binding. "Here it is," she says, pulling a maroon book off the shelf. Then she goes to her suitcase and opens a zipped pocket on the outside. Feeling a corner of the desired piece of paper Susan pulls it free and stuffs it inside the Perly's guide. There's a mess of coloured paper clips in a holder. "One of these will do the trick," she says hoping the bright pink will catch Ian's attention and not the slip of paper. "What was the address of St. Hilda's?"

"800 Vaughan Road."

Opening the guide to the back of the street index Susan finds the street and the coordinates. "Ah, I see what Sandra means at Eglington and Dufferin. Vaughan enters that intersection on the diagonal and ends there."

"Oh, how exciting," Ian says. "You mean we're going to a place in this city that isn't a square block?" On circling the city in the airplane Ian commented on the monotonous grid below and since landing kept up his tirade against the boring layout of the streets.

Returning to the index Susan searches for the street that Celianne wrote down as the place where Tijean is staying with his aunt, her younger sister who came to Canada as an au pere and got landed immigrant status. Now she runs a daycare from her house. At first it seems the streets could be far away from each other as they're separated by ten pages, but in fact they are adjacent pages and Kitchener Avenue is only five short blocks west. Straightening her cramped legs Susan rises with the Perly's secure in her hand. "I know where we can park," she says. "There's a school parking lot right off Dufferin just south of Eglington."

"But won't it be full of teachers' cars?"

"No, it closed as a regular school. The last I remember it was being used for adult programmes."

Ian stretches. "Time for a shower," he says, kicking off the sheets.

While the water is running the phone rings. Susan answers. It's Queensway Volkswagon asking for Mr. Ian Cameron. "Can I take a message?" she asks.

"His car's ready for him."

"I think he's expecting a pick-up." Over the line she hears the salesman shuffling papers. When he confirms the request he asks for the address. "197 Humbervale. Do you know where that is?"

"Yes. Off Royal York Road?"

"That's right."

"We'll have a car there at 10:30."

Doing a mental calculation Susan figures that will give them enough time to finalize the sales agreement, then drive to St. Hilda's for an early lunch. Repeatedly on the phone her mother told her to arrive on time for the reservation as the service is slow. Susan isn't sure if the problem implied is that they'll have to wait awhile for lunch to be served thereby wilting with hunger before being fed or that their tardiness could result in them not being served at all. Either way Doris seemed very concerned that they not be late.

Later, just as Susan begins a hunt for her outdoor shoes, the doorbell rings. When she opens the door she feels she's in a time warp and it's 1985. The man standing before her looks exactly like Neil Diamond did two decades earlier. Susan remembers seeing him at a concert with Robbie Robertson accompanying on guitar and for a fleeting moment she wonders how they look now, if they, too, have aged the way she and her sister have? Probably, but as musical icons they have the advantage of remaining forever young. Telling the Neil Diamond double they'll be there in a minute she closes the door and calls upstairs to Ian.

It's a fifteen minute drive to the Volkswagon dealership and in less than an hour they're back on Royal York Road, only driving north this time instead of south. Inside the Passat the smell of newness so dominates the interior air Susan wonders if there's even a mite of dust anywhere. Instinctively she wipes the grey coloured dashboard with her finger. It comes up clean.

"Pretty nice, eh?" Ian asks.

Nodding she affirms his judgment. "Do you feel comfortable behind the wheel?"

"Surprisingly, yes," Ian says. "It's like riding a bicycle. It all comes back. Although I can't say I've ever driven in so much traffic. Glad it's not rush hour."

"Yes. Otherwise you wouldn't be clocking 30. You'd be at a standstill."

"I'd hate that." Without turning his head away from the road he smiles at her. "Aren't we lucky to have lived and worked on the island?"

"Fortunate, indeed," Susan says. "And lucky to have sold the resort for so much money."

"Ron couldn't believe the price when I told him."

"You told Ron?"

"Sure." Ian's demeanor changes. "Why, is it a secret from the family?"

"I haven't told Sandra." Shaking her head Susan adds, "Anyway, it doesn't matter." Looking down at the Perly's that's open on her lap Susan traces the route north along Royal York. Except for the dip over Mimico Creek it's a straight line to Eglington. The traffic on that avenue moves until they reach the intersection at Keele Street where they wait for two light changes before advancing. "Where have all the people come from?" Susan asks after glancing at the time. At this pace they won't make it to St. Hilda's by noon.

"I'd say from the Caribbean."

Looking out the window Susan understands Ian's meaning. There are many black faces, but also some Asian and Indonesian: mothers walking along the street pushing strollers; a father holding the hand of two toddlers; other men gathered in groups talking and laughing together; store owners standing inside the entrance to tiny shops; young men driving cars. The accelerated sound of an unmuffled motor passes them on the inside. "That's suppose to be the bus lane," Susan says.

Indicating with his head Ian draws her attention to a road sign. "Only during rush hour," he says.

Ahead is a winding trail of red tail lights going uphill. "Guess it's too late to change lanes," Susan says as she peers at a row of headlights reflected in the side mirror. Like a ship's navigator going through a narrow canal Susan keeps one finger on the road indicated on the map while watching the slow progress of traffic. At Caledonia the bottle neck clears and they speed past the northern boundary of Prospect Cemetery, through the green lights at Ronald and Harvie Avenues before coming to a standstill at a T-junction west of Dufferin. Crowds of shoppers cross the road.

With a sigh of boredom Ian drops his skull against the headrest. He turns his eyes on Susan. "Are we nearly there?"

"Yes, but we need to get into the right lane to turn." The clock on the dashboard indicates 11:52, another minute gone. At exactly twelve noon Ian shuts off the motor in the parking lot. Susan is first out the passenger door striding fast onto the street with Ian trailing. He catches up to her when they reach the long ramp leading to the entrance causing them to double back half the distance they've covered on the sidewalk. Inside the first set of doors they buzz the receptionist to let them through the second set of glass doors. There they get directions taking them through another set of doors and down a long hallway past a solarium, a greenhouse, a library, a tuck shop. They know they're at the restaurant when they reach a sandwich board listing the day's specials. Just inside the door Susan finds her mother and aunt sitting at the second table. In a flurry of greeting she bends to kiss her mother's cheek, then her aunt's. Ian says hello to Doris and gets introduced to Auntie Dot who directs him to sit beside her.

"We usually like to sit near the window but we didn't want to miss you," Auntie Dot says.

"Oh," Susan says, straining her neck to look across the dining room. "There's an empty table."

"Don't worry. We're settled now," Doris says.

"How was the traffic?" Dot asks, and without waiting for an answer, piles other questions onto the conversational stack. "Doris says you bought a new car. What did you get? Or have you picked it up yet? Did you come by TTC?"

"We drove in Ian's new Passat," Susan says, giving Ian a smirk as if to confirm the earlier warning given by Sandra about the character who is their Auntie Dot. In Susan's private acknowledgment she feels she's hiding something. In their girlhood on visits to their aunt she was always saying to her nieces, "What are two laughing at?", or, "What are you smirking about?" "Sly as a fox," their father said about his sister-in-law after every visit.

The waitress hands two mimeographed menus to Ian and Susan. "This is my eldest daughter, Susan," Doris says to the young lady in uniform.

Raising her eyes to the tag pinned on her chest pocket Susan reads her name. "Hello, Melissa," she says, recognizing that this waitress is probably well acquainted with Sandra and her family.

"And this is Ian," Auntie Dot says, finishing the round of introductions. "They're from the Turks & Caicos."

"So I've heard," Melissa says. "The usual?" she asks, directing her gaze on Doris.

"What's the soup today?" Dorothy asks with an imperiousness that only a senior resident could attain, or an elder sister vying for attention.

"Beef barley." Melissa looks directly at Ian. "It's very good."

"I'm sure it is," Ian says.

"All the food here's good," Doris says.

"Shall I give you a few moments to decide?"

With the grand gesture of a theatre actress making an aside, Dorothy leans towards Ian. "I hope this isn't too early for you to lunch. We have to eat now because they serve dinner here at 5:30, and that's the second sitting. Some of the residents eat a simple lunch in their room. Or they don't eat at all. Just a little snack and dinner at 4:30. My Harold and I used to dine at 7. That was after the children left home. It was very civilized dining with my husband after years of serving the children an early meal before their father arrived home. I still haven't gotten used to this schedule." As if to give closure to her soliloquy Dorothy returns to her upright posture and pats the cloth napkin on her lap.

Ian's mouth is open, jaw slack, eyebrows raised. Definitely too much information.

"I'll have the usual," Doris says perfunctorily. She's used to Dorothy's manner – the elder sister who married well, lived in a tony enclave, gave unsolicited advice.

"What's that, Mother?"

"Soup and a half sandwich. Salmon on white bread. They serve it with a few vegetable sticks."

"Sounds perfect," Susan says. "But can I have mine on brown?"

"We have pumpernickel or rye."

"Oh, pumpernickel," Susan says. "I haven't eaten pumpernickel bread in years."

"I'll have today's special," Dorothy says. "Quiche and roquefort dressing for my side salad."

"That sounds good," Ian says. "I'll have the same."

"Oh, a man who eats quiche," Dorothy exclaims. "I couldn't serve Harold quiche. He hated it."

As soon as Melissa leaves a short lady with large brown, sparkling eyes stands between Doris and Dorothy. "You've got guests," she says. "How lovely."

"Sarah, this is Doris' eldest daughter, Susan," Dorothy says.

"Nice to meet you," Sarah says. Her whole body posture takes on a gesture of genuine interest, relaxed and bent toward the table. "I've heard so much about you. And you must be Ian?"

"I am."

"Are you staying long?"

"No," Susan says with an air of apology. What kind of a daughter comes from afar for only an hour or two? Yet Sarah's warmth dispels guilt. "We're preparing for a road trip to the east coast."

"But first we have to go to Niagara Falls," Ian says. "I've never been."

"Well, that's wonderful," Sarah says. "One of the natural wonders of the world. I'll leave you to your lunch and visit. So nice to have met you both."

"She's Jewish," Dorothy says as soon as Sarah's gone. "They accept them here. You know, we have interfaith services, but on Sunday the Anglican minister holds a regular service in the chapel."

"We're interdenominational," Doris says in support of her sister's claim.

"I see," Ian says.

"Is that him, the man in the collar there?" Susan asks. "His face looks familiar."

"Yes," Dorothy says. "You probably know him from his political days. He was a city councilor. From the west end. I don't think Mimico, though. More the area where Sandra lives."

"Right," Susan says, recognizing that once again Auntie Dot's got a dig in about the working class neighbourhood where they grew up. Isn't she proud of Susan and Sandra leaving all that behind? And now Doris, too, under her instigation.

"Is it a nice car, your Passat?" Doris asks Ian, then turns to Dorothy before he can answer her. "They never had a car on the island, you know?"

"I remember you telling me," Dorothy says to her sister before turning her gaze on her niece. "Your mother did worry about you driving around those roads on a scooter."

Moped, Susan thinks, but says, "They're very popular in Europe."

"Can't blame them on those narrow roads. Wouldn't do here. But I couldn't believe the number of them in Rome, Doris."

"I wouldn't know about that," Doris says.

"No, you wouldn't," Dorothy says then leans again toward Ian. "She's never traveled to Europe. Can you imagine? I tried to get her to come with me on a tour. Very easy on a tour. They do all the work. But she wouldn't come, would you?"

"Don't want to."

"So you've retired from teaching, Susan? How does that feel?"

"Quite liberating, actually."

"I bet. Aren't you lucky. Congratulations."

"Thank you, Auntie Dot," Susan says, trying to sound polite. She's not used to her aunt being generous in spirit. "The principal at the school had a niece who was homesick so he found a replacement for me in short order."

"Is that so?" Auntie Dot says with the intent of a lead-in question.

Susan feels comfortable explaining. "Like many of the students on the island they have to travel away from home to continue their education. She went to Teacher's College in Britain, then got a job there teaching, but didn't like it. Some horrible school in the east end of London with mostly delinquents in her class, so returning to work under her uncle was a god send."

"You know my Patrick's in London," Dorothy says.

"Yes," Susan says. "Sandra told me. He's doing well?"

"Very. The company pays him a cost of living bonus, so they're able to send the children to public schools. So expensive, but worth every penny."

"Yes, I'm sure," Susan says. Auntie Dot's done it again. Why does it always feel like one-up manship when conversing with her?

Doris smiles as Melissa sets down her lunch. "Now we order tea so it comes as soon as we're finished eating."

On cue the tea arrives as Doris chews her last bite of celery. There are two waitresses now, one to clear away the dirty plates and Melissa who's serving them tea. "Eating celery at the end of a meal is very good for digestion," Doris says. "You'll come and see my room after tea, won't you?"

"Yes, of course," Ian and Susan say in unison.

"Later this afternoon we have a concert," Doris says.

"It's just the local school children," Dorothy says.

"They come every month. A grade six class. I enjoyed their performance last time."

"Oh, I admit they're very sweet, but we also have regular concerts by real professionals. Why last week we heard an all women's choir singing Haydn. Now that was a treat."

"It was long, though."

"Oh really, Doris." Dorothy turns away from her sister. "Do you two want dessert?"

"No, tea's fine," Susan says. "We're taking Sandra and Ron out to dinner tonight. Plus, it seems we spent the weekend eating."

When finished drinking his tea Ian insists on paying the bill. "My treat," he says.

"Thank you," Dorothy says. "I bet you got a pretty penny for your place in the Caribbean?"

"A Frenchman bought it," Doris says with the tone of criticism relegated to a guilty party.

"He worked at Club Med before coming to work for me," Ian says. "Getting experience."

"Oh, right," Dorothy says with enlightenment. "There's a Club Med on the Turks & Caicos. We never went there. They don't allow children."

How the guilt spreads, Susan thinks. Her cousins took annual holidays at resorts like Club Med with Auntie Dot, something Doris' family never experienced. The privilege of the rich to enjoy such vacations, or purchase a resort like Marcel has. Is it envy that makes her mother sound critical of someone with the bucks to purchase a resort? Susan doubts that's the case. Envy is an emotion her aunt has, not her mother. So what makes her critical of the buyer? Is it greed? Susan thinks not. Again, greed is more an adjective to attach to Dorothy, not Doris. Maybe it's her mother's puritanical streak? More to do with the dubious nature of how the wealthy get rich. Susan can't help shaking her head in silent affirmation. It isn't guile that makes her mother spot on with her attitude. More artlessness.

In the hallway outside the restaurant they turn left to the second lobby which is at the opposite end of the building complex from the one where Ian and Susan entered. Here they wait for the elevator. When it reaches the lobby floor Ian steps aside and holds the door while an elderly man using a walker exits. An attendant nurse advises him that he needn't worry about the doors closing as they're programmed for safety reasons not to shut until after a timed interval. Then they rise to the fifth floor on the south east tower where Doris has a room with a window facing west. She says she likes to get the afternoon sun and watch the evening sunsets. The bed she kept is a single one from the girls' room. The other furniture is the teak set from the rec room and a tall dresser that her husband used in the master bedroom at the house. "It belonged to his father," Doris says of the piece. Then she shows them her kitchenette where she can boil the kettle for a cup of tea or make a light breakfast or lunch if she doesn't feel like going downstairs to the dining room.

Ian examines the family photos on the wall and the old wedding portraits on the top of the dresser while Doris explains whose weddings they depict. The integrity of the room is a portal to her life. It's all there in compact – the comfort of an ordinary life lived in relative peace and domesticity. When they bid the two older women farewell Susan doesn't feel guilty about leaving her mother behind as she feared she might before her visit. Instead she feels a sense of relief.

On the elevator going down Susan and Ian find themselves alone. Sharing her relief at how she finds her mother so well settled only starts them giggling. Nudging Ian Susan tells him to stop.

"It's hunky-dory, isn't it?" Ian says.

"Dory as in a craft on the east coast?" Susan says trying to regain her composure.

"I don't know about that," Ian says. In a sobering gesture he shakes his head.

"Well, at least we don't have to worry about my mother. She seems perfectly settled."

"Did she know what she was getting herself into coming to live with her big sister?"

"Auntie Dot's always been like that. At least Mom doesn't have to share a room with her, like Sandra and I did growing up."

The slow elevator stops and they return to the car via the route that takes them to the exit with the ramp. Before clamping the seat belt over her shoulder Susan picks up the street guide from the carpeted floorboard. "I have a confession to make," she says.

Stopping his hand holding the ignition key Ian asks, "What?"

Pulling the colourful paper clip out of the book Susan shows him the loose sheet with the name Camilla Saintus at the top. "This is an address nearby."

"Who's this you want to visit?" Ian asks, squinting to read the name.

"Tijean's aunt. Celianne's younger sister."

"I don't know, Susan," Ian says, shaking his head. "A third set of grown up sisters? Might be too much for me in one day."

Extruding her lips in a pursed gesture Susan calls his argument. "You don't mind, then?"

"Why would I mind? Although you must think I would, otherwise you wouldn't have hidden this from me?"

"Hidden from you?"

"Hidden from me."

"I suppose I thought you might think it was none of my business."

"It isn't," Ian says, starting the car. "Where to?"

Susan gives him directions to drive west along Eglington as far as Harvie Avenue where they turn south at the lights and drive past an elementary school where the street takes a turn before continuing down a steep hill. At the bottom is Kitchener. "This is it," Susan says.

Turning right Ian parks on the street under a budding tree, a welcome bit of shade in a neighbourhood chock a block full of small houses with tiny gardens and few mature trees. Susan guesses it's the house with the fenced front yard full of toys for toddlers. They open and close the latch on the front gate and walk the short sidewalk to the porch in an eerie silence. Where are the children? That question gets answered with their knock which rouses a female voice calling to a child heard scurrying to grapple with the lock that the woman unbolts letting the door open a smidgen. A short chain holds it in place. The vision of visitors is bright in the child's eyes. The woman looks at them with suspicion. "Hi, I'm Susan Borden and this is Ian Cameron. We know your sister, Celianne, on North Caicos in the Turks & Caicos."

The child is breathing noisily, maybe suffering from asthma. The woman remains stoic.

"Are you Camilla?"

"Yes," the woman says slowly.

"I was wondering if Tijean Williams is here?"

"Tijean?" the young boy repeats happily. "Car."

"He out driving with my son. You the one Celianne work for?"

"Did," Ian says.

"And I used to teach Tijean," Susan says.

"That right?"

"When do you expect them back?" Susan asks.

"Come," the child says, making his bright eyes bigger.

"Rashid, he like Tijean," Camilla says. "All the children. They like Tijean."

"So will he be back shortly?"

"Maybe."

Since there's no encouragement forthcoming, let alone an invitation to wait, Susan says they'll hang around awhile and check back a little later. When the door closes on them Ian asks, "Now what'll we do?"

"Let's just go for a walk," Susan suggests. She knows from the open space indicated on the page in the Perly's that Harvie Avenue borders Prospect Cemetery and Kitchener Avenue passes through it. When they are back on the street Susan gazes between the houses.

"What are you looking at?" Ian asks. "Don't you trust her? Do you think Tijean's hiding in the backyard?"

"No, I was just wondering how their backyard is situated. It seems unlikely a Haitian would pick a house to live in that's beside a cemetery."

"What cemetery?"

"Prospect Cemetery," Susan says, leading him along the sidewalk past the neighbour's house.

"Maybe she doesn't practice Voodooism," Ian says.

"The gods must be hungry for the dead here, too. Baron Samedi in his black clothes."

"I'll keep an eye out for that white top hat of his on a skull."

"My protector."

"There is a cemetery," Ian says matter-of-factly as they approach the wrought iron fence.

"I wasn't joking, but no, we aren't here looking for dead spirits like Baron Samedi."

"Haven't we had enough of cemeteries for one visit?"

"We're just going for a stroll, not a visit." Yesterday Sandra took them to their father's grave at Park Lawn Cemetery where the week prior she and Doris had placed fresh flowers on decoration day.

"So we're going to walk here?"

"Why not? You'll find this cemetery to be very park-like," Susan says.

Indeed the grounds are like an arboretum with a wide variety of trees and bushes: short magnolia trees shedding their fat white and purple petals onto the grass; brilliant forsythia bushes bursting with the yellow of sunshine; ancient crabapple trees spreading twisted branches full of dark pink buds; tall gingko trees competing for light; an odd specimen with full blossoms. Amid this luxury they discuss their itinerary for the next day when they plan on visiting the Niagara region making them feel like a newly married couple organizing a honeymoon. After circling the grounds walking uphill they find themselves at the northern limits of the cemetery that border Eglington Avenue. Here there's a small amphitheater sunk shallowly into the earth with a wide stone arc of inscribed headstones which they explore reading names and particulars aloud to each other. When they return to continue their walk along the road Susan tells Ian of a mystery writer who learned to read in this cemetery. "Gail Bowen," Susan says. "She was part of a writers panel we had at our high school. My students really liked her because she read a passage about characters their age so they could relate. Then she told us her grandmother brought her here, to Prospect Cemetery, at the age of three. Marvelous, don't you think?"

"Precocious," Ian says.

"That, too."

Ian again steps off the road to read a headstone. "These are the same dates my grandfather lived and died," he says. "They both served in the war."

Drawn by his solitary remembrance Susan joins Ian and stands silently beside him. How history lives through generations: grandmothers caring and teaching; grandfathers fighting and liberating – still pervasively present.

The road bends and they walk the return leg along the ledge of the hill. When down they leave through the tall gates just as a very old Mercedes Benz speeds along the street, then squeals to a stop leaving an echo that is the lingering roar of a badly muffled motor as well as a trail of exhaust fumes from stinky diesel fuel. The body is painted blue but hardly recognizable as a colour because of age and rust. They watch two young men get out of the car. Both Ian and Susan recognize the one as Tijean.

By the time they reach the house at the end of the street the two men are in the front yard where the children are now playing. The toddler who greeted them at the door is showing off to Tijean trying to pull wheelies on his plastic tricycle. Tijean is so engrossed in this mayhem he doesn't notice the couple on the sidewalk until Camilla announces that he has visitors. Since he is wearing sunglasses with very dark lenses his eyes reveal nothing of his response to their surprise visit, but his grin is wide. "Hey, Miss Susan, what you doing here?"

"Come to say hello." None of the adults move. Not wanting to join the front yard playground activity Susan holds her ground. "We, too, have left the island," she says.

At that news Tijean nods, then saunters the few steps it takes to reach the gate where he extends his arm to shake Ian's hand.

More quietly now Susan says, "Your mother gave me your aunt's address and since we were in the neighbourhood we thought we'd pay a visit."

"Susan's mother's at St. Hilda's," Ian says. "The towers on Dufferin."

"Is my Mom coming?" Tijean asks.

"Not that I know," Susan says.

Tijean laughs. "I waiting for her come drag me home by the ears." He bends down to pat Rashid who's followed him to the gate. "Show us how you can ride that trike," he says.

"She wasn't surprised that you ran away," Susan says. "Only disappointed. Your Dad, too. He was very upset. As were my students. You had everyone in an uproar."

"Ah, Miss Susan. You exaggerate. I the one in an uproar."

Now Ian laughs. "I suppose you were upset. Leaving suddenly like that?"

Shifting his weight from one foot to the other Tijean sways. There's a rainbow shimmer coming off his hair from the sunlight giving colour to his black curls and a glint off his dark lenses reflecting the parked car making it appear more distant than it is. Appearances conceal the truth.

Taking a different tack from Ian, Susan asks, "You remember Ms Mulrain?"

Tijean smiles when he says yes.

"She's engaged to Mr. Musgrove."

"Yeah? The principal? Man, that wild."

"Quite natural given they're in the same profession and working together."

"He so big and she so little," Tijean says.

"That's true," Ian says.

"They asked me to say hello," Susan says. "If I found you."

Tijean turns coy and shy not knowing how to respond. Then he straightens and challenges them. "So how you know I here?"

"As I said, your mother gave me your aunt's address."

"She betray me."

"When your mother learned I was coming to Toronto she told me about her sister so I asked for her address. I took my chances. I figured you had to go somewhere." Susan feels like she's talking too fast now, trying to cover up for the confidences extended her. "But I'm surprised to find you in this land-locked city and not on the coast or on a boat on the ocean."

Tijean just nods, whether in agreement or not is unclear.

Behind them the excitement of play continues with shrieks from the children, commands from Camilla and shouts of encouragement and challenge from the other young man who, turning his back on the toddlers, saunters over where they're standing at the gate. Tijean introduces his cousin, Sherlock.

"How long have you lived here?" Susan asks.

"All my life."

No mystery in that, Susan thinks. Bluntly put, he was born in Canada. Here she is trying not to embarrass Tijean's cousin with a smart remark about the literary or historical significance of his name, and instead she commits the usual white imperialist faux pas of assuming he's a foreigner. Trying to retrieve her credentials as a bona fide sincere lady, Susan takes a different tack with Tijean. "You must find the city quite a change from the islands?"

This sends Sherlock into hysterics. He's shaking and laughing while pointing at his cousin. "Tell them," he says repeatedly.

"Tell them what?" Tijean asks indignantly.

"You know, Man. Tell them what you think when you first arrive." Not waiting for his cousin to speak, Sherlock fills them in on the details of how Tijean thought the earth was going to cave in on them when riding the subway for the first time, how he assumed there was a carnival going on because of the crowds of people, how he asked if there were any birds as he couldn't imagine them flying around all the obstacles in the sky. "Man, you don't have nothin' on that island," he concludes.

"Only tourists," Ian says. "Some of them come for the birds."

"Is that right?" Now it is Sherlock's turn to be gullible. "Tourists come just because you got birds?"

"Yes," Tijean says, not registering that Ian is playing with his cousin's sense of incredulity.

"Huge flocks of pink flamingos," Ian says.

"Those the tall ones on long stilts for legs?"

"They migrate to the ponds we have."

"Where they come from?"

"Canada."

Sherlock is speechless, staring at Ian. "I ain't never seen no flamingos here."

"We passed some on a lawn a few blocks from here."

"Hey," Sherlock says finally twigging. "You pulling my leg, Man. Them birds are fake. They're just lawn ornaments. There ain't no flamingos. I knew they aren't real birds."

Susan holds Tijean's gaze while they smile at Sherlock's expense. They're in agreement. Let the Canadian boy believe there's no such animal.

Since they're not going to be invited inside Susan decides to pursue her course on the street. "Do you remember the last paper you wrote for me on the interview with the people at the Marine Centre?"

Tijean simply nods.

"I talked to Ms Mulrain about it."

"She helped me."

"Yes, I know," Susan says. "We think with some accommodations you could enroll in their program."

Tijean shakes his head. "You think so, Miss Susan?"

"Yes, you could study diving. We've also spoken to your parents. Well, actually, Mr. Musgrove has, and they now understand that that's what you want to do."

"Do they?"

"Please think about it, Tijean. You could go back. You could finish high school"

"Maybe."

"I know this isn't any of my business," Ian says. "And I don't want to scare you off, but don't you need a visa or something for landed immigrant status if you want to stay?"

"Yeah, I know that."

"There's as much a future for you on the island as here," Ian says.

Susan recognizes advice coming from Ian carries more weight than from her and she silently blesses him. "If you return no one will be angry at you."

"Maybe not."

"You're such a gifted diver," Susan says. "Sometimes it's best to do what you know and are good at. There's a future in diving. The oceans are the next frontier." Sensing she's carrying her argument beyond the pale Susan stops herself from expanding on that theory.

During this three-way conversation Sherlock is silent, but paying attention. "You really that good a diver?"

Cocking his head at his cousin, Tijean gives a diagonal nod in the affirmative.

"You tell my Dad," Sherlock says. "His brother a diver."

"He is?" Tijean hasn't altered the angle of his head, but the message of his body language changes from cocksure challenge to querying curiosity.

Now Sherlock is fidgeting. He's doing some little dance changing his weight from one foot to another. "Yeah, I'm sure of it. Our uncle came this past winter. He live down east. I hear him telling my Dad about it. I remember 'cause he say it too bad I not a diver. But hey, I'm not even a good swimmer. They close the pool at our high school so we no longer get to swim there."

"You don't have swimming classes?" Susan asks.

Sherlock shakes his head in reply.

"I heard about those cost cutting measures," she says.

At the sound of a child's scream Sherlock leaves them to mitigate a fight.

"I sold the resort, you know." Ian says.

"Hey, my Mom still work there, though?"

"Yes, she works for the new owner, Marcel Dubois."

"The guy from Club Med?"

"That's the one. He has some big plans. I know he'd help you out."

"Ah, you guys," Tijean says while careening as if he's been thrown a punch knocking him off-balance. The movement sends him facing the intersection. "That your car?" he asks, spotting the shiny new Passat.

"Yes, want to have a look at it?"

"Sure," Tijean says. Opening the gate he follows Ian up the street.

Lagging behind Susan wonders at the incentive that draws Tijean away from the sanctuary of his aunt's place. While Ian shows off the vehicle she plots. In her purse are business cards from the resort that Marcel had printed in bulk. Before they leave she hands one to Tijean with her sister's phone number jotted down on the back. Her parting words from the open window in the car door are, "Please phone your mother." In response Tijean waves and she returns his wave while rolling up the window with the automatic push button. "Do you think he'll listen to us?" Susan asks, keeping her eyes on the sidewalk where he stands.

"No."

Susan faces Ian. "That's encouraging."

"My opinion. Too little too late."

"I hope you're wrong. He still seems receptive to me."

"Where to now?"

"I guess you don't want to go downtown?"

"You guessed right. How about another walk? It's too nice to go indoors."

"What about that pedestrian bridge across the mouth of the Humber River? Sandra said it is used in commercials."

"Sounds perfect. How do we get there?"

Rooting on the floor at her feet Susan finds the street guide and gives directions. They travel south to the lake and park beside the shoreline at the foot of Windermere Avenue. Spanning the river is a steel arch bridge serving as a key link between the old boundaries of the city of Toronto and the former borough of Etobicoke. The arches themselves are slender tubular ribs inclined inwards. They rise high above the walkers and cyclists giving those who use the bridge a sense of a heavenly, modern roof. At the centre Ian and Susan stop to gaze at the hangers and abutments that are part of the unique structural features. Then they lean over the railing to watch the river flowing below and the city scape along the horizon. Starting from west to east Susan points out well known landmarks: the recently renovated Palais Royale, the private Boulevard Club, the public buildings at the Exhibition and Ontario Places, and the prominent CN Tower.

"It's beautiful, from a distance," Ian says. "This could almost be the ocean. It's so vast."

Tugging at his arm Susan suggests they continue their walk. At the end of the bridge they find a garden of boulders which they explore and an information kiosk on the history of an earlier wharf as well as maps showing the waterfront trail. Before long their steps become methodical, and instead of seeing the landscape, their thoughts turn to other affairs. Ian wonders about her parting words to Tijean as well as her knowledge of where to find him. "I got the address from Celianne."

"But if his mother knows where he is why hasn't she spoken to him?"

"He swore Camilla to secrecy. He thought his parents didn't know his whereabouts."

"I think you blew that cover."

Resenting his criticism as disloyalty Susan turns defensive. "I thought I could help."

"Of course you did," Ian says, trying to assuage her guilt. "Why shouldn't his parents know where he is?"

"Do you think he'll listen to what I said?"

"Let him mull it over. Maybe it'll sink in."

"I should let Celianne and Guy know we saw him."

"That's probably a good idea. We could phone the resort. Talk to Marcel. Leave a message."

"Yes, let's. Do you think we should visit Tijean again?"

"No, definitely not. I think we should leave it in their hands. Otherwise you'll appear interfering. He's still a rebellious youth."

"I just wish I'd done more."

"Susan, you did what you could." Ian takes her hand. "Do you think you're under some sort of obligation to save the young man?"

DONNA WOOTTON

"I suppose it seems that way with all my inquiries."

"Yes, it does. What harm can come to him here? He's making his own choices. He's not the first kid not doing what his parents want him to do."

"Or what his teachers think he could do. It seems such a waste."

"You're being defensive."

"Of course I am. We all feel like we failed him."

"Nothing good or true can come from a posture of defense."

Susan ponders this truism. It's not one she's heard before, yet it seems valid, not in a Freudian or modern sense. More like down east good sense, or even Biblical in nature.

After nearly an hour of walking they find themselves on another span bridge only this one is much smaller than the Gateway Bridge. Checking an outdoor trail map they learn they are at the mouth of Mimico Creek. "We could walk back to Sandra and Ron's," Susan says.

"You go ahead," Ian says, not disguising the irony in his voice. "I'll go back and get the car."

Laughing with the enjoyment of simply being in each other's company they do an about turn and return along the shore of Humber Bay to where they parked the car. At the house on Humbervale Ian easily opens the side door with the key he's been given and, once inside, goes upstairs to retrieve his laptop. Setting it up on the kitchen table he

306

explains that he wants to check his messages before phoning just in case Marcel has emailed him. "Hey, there's a message here for you," Ian says turning the screen around to face her. "It's from 'Geek Philosopher'."

Susan reads, *"Big greeting for one Auntie Susan. Did you know it was me from the messenger sender address?"* Yes, she thinks. As if she's acquainted with any other philosopher but her nephew, Kit. *"Sorry I can only interface with you via email and not in person like my sibling did, but your timing's off. My nose is usually buried in a book these days. That, or randomly searching the internet for useful knowledge that I can squeeze out of my monitor like toothpaste in little dabs of cleansing pertinence. Do you know how much junk there is stored under the guise of information? Don't get me started on the highway of facts available to the masses of users. Do you know that 'geeks' or 'nerds' are now popular because everyone thinks they're worth millions, or potential billionaires? No one gives a nickel for a philosopher. Hence my new nomenclature. It's just my feeble attempt at becoming more popular. NO, I don't have a girlfriend. YES, I do have lots of friends who are girls. Tell my mother that. She doesn't understand, even though she teaches high school. But enough about me. What about you? Back in Canada, eh? Are you, like, moving here permanently? Dad says Ian sold the resort for BIG Bucks. So, should I open a Philosopher's Resort? This email's going on too long. Ciao!"*

"You have to read this," Susan says, turning the screen around to face Ian. "It's priceless." As Ian reads and chuckles Susan conjures a picture of Kit in her mind as a "Geek

Philosopher". She sees an image of her nephew with his
undeveloped post-adolescent body who doesn't even shave
yet sitting in front of a computer terminal littered in post-it
notes while beautiful girls look over his shoulder at a screen
showing dollar signs. "Any other messages?" she asks.

"No," Ian says. Rising from the table he pulls out his cell
phone and hits a key on the pad that automatically dials
the long distance number of the resort. By his side Susan
prompts him to pass along a message to Celianne and to give
her greetings to Marcel, then she leaves him to his business-
like conversation. Picking up a section of the weekend paper
she starts leafing through the articles until her eye catches
one on "birth dearth". She can't help but marvel at how
journalists invent such bon mots. As she reads Susan feels
a kinship with these women who never had children. Like
her they value their independence and aren't housewife
types. Mostly they're professionals: a lawyer, an accountant,
a CEO, a judge, an editor, an entrepreneur. No teachers
or principals, or educators of any sort listed. This dearth
sets Susan wondering. Rationally she knows there are many
women in education who aren't mothers, yet can't help
speculating if it's a profession with a higher than average
incidence of mothers. Another reason the article gives for
these women not having children is that they "couldn't find
daddy material that they liked". To Susan it sounds like a
defensive way of saying they never fell in love, or aren't

romantically inclined. Yet on some level she knows she fits in with the bunch described. Lately, though, she's been feeling she missed motherhood because she lacks courage. Compared to her sister. Compared to Celianne. They are women who took the risk. Her lucky sister reaps the rewards while poor Celianne faces disappointment. Maybe that's why she never experienced motherhood. She lacked courage, feared disappointment. All the other reasons listed are posturing. The underlying reason comes down to guts.

Isn't that what she's trying to make up in her character? Some lack of maternal instinct like a personal flaw. Not only has she had occasion to abandon her family and profession, she's rejected the continuity of descendants. Like any other human she's lived in the ruins of previous generations, but unlike her parents or sister or even Ian, she's missed something as important as bearing children. Her defection. Her ultimate act of defection.

The "birth dearth" article continues to talk about the impact of this phenomenon on the population in the city. Immigrants are now in a majority. Other areas of the country are depopulating. Anglo Saxon Canada, the white population, is dwindling. This spells cultural suicide. Yet it's not just happening here. The journalist cites Russia as an example of a country whose population is in free-fall, as well as Japan and all of Europe. So she's not an aberration. She's part of a trend.

A picture of the plight of immigrants runs through her mind as she recalls the visit to Camilla Saintus' house with its front yard turned over to a playground, no beauty of a garden in sight. In her head Susan hears the screams and cries of children in need of attention. Yet neither Camilla nor Celianne have increased the human population above the replacement level. Even the poor want smaller families.

Ian is still talking on the telephone. Turning the page Susan finds in the newspaper another article that catches her attention from the accompanying picture. It shows an owner of a tattoo salon fixing an implant into the wrist of a customer. This device allows the wearer to open the door to his car without having to search for his keys. A boon to anyone who's forgetful and looses things easily. Why aren't they showing the implant on the arms of the elderly, those poor souls who need reminders? Susan can't help but react cynically. Yet that's not really what this article is saying. They aren't selling convenience. No, they're bonding to their cars. She feels she could slip into her mother's generation. What will they think of next?

Before long Sandra arrives home and enters the kitchen in a whirlwind as illustrated on the weather network. She's full of stories that Susan recognizes as familiar from her former days on the job: who did what; who said what; what's expected of her making all time-lines impossible to fulfill.

To calm the disturbance Susan makes a pot of tea and listens empathetically. Through all this Ian continues to talk on the telephone. Finally Sandra exhausts her litany. Susan seizes the opportunity and rushes in with her own disturbing agenda. "Do you know I only have one memory from my childhood of going to hospital?"

"Did you go to hospital?" Sandra warms her hands on the china cup. "I don't think I went as a child. Been there lots of times as an adult."

"Do you remember when I fell out of bed?"

"Oh yeah," Sandra says. Both her face and her voice light up in recognition. "Did you break your arm, or something?"

"Hairline fracture on my wrist."

"Oh, is that all. I recall a great disturbance in the middle of the night. At least, it was dark out at the time, whatever hour it was."

"I'm glad you remember," Susan says. "I was hoping I hadn't imagined it all."

"So what do you do to treat a hairline fracture? Were you in a cast?"

"Not a plaster one. I think it was more like an elastic wrap to immobilize my wrist. I know I didn't have to go back to hospital. The doctor removed it in his office."

"Remember Christine broke her forearm falling off her bicycle in the driveway?"

"She had a cast. I remember autographing it."

"So did every kid in the neighbourhood." Sandra sips her tea, then sets the cup in its saucer. "Is Ian conducting business over the telephone?"

"Yes, with Marcel." Raising her eyes to the clock on the wall Susan notes the minute hand. "So far, he's been talking for forty-seven minutes. I wonder what that'll cost him on his cell phone bill?"

"He could have used our line. We have a special rate."

The sisters shrug at one another in recognition that it's not their problem. Looking down at her wrist Sandra notes the time. "Ron will be home soon." Then she holds Susan's gaze. "So how was our dear Mother?"

"In fine form. I can't tell you how relieved I am that she's so settled there."

"You're relieved? Let me tell you how I feel."

"I was beginning to feel guilty about you shouldering the burden of her care." Susan lifts her shoulders in a gesture of freedom. "Now I have nothing to worry about."

Sandra laughs. "No, I suppose you don't. What about Auntie Dot? How was she?"

"Her usual self. Ian wondered if Doris knew what she was getting herself into, living on top of her sister like that."

"Let me tell you. Mom is so proud that she can pay her own way. It's like she's finally arrived. Auntie Dot's attitude is water off a duck's back." Gulping the dregs from the bottom of the cup Sandra reaches for the pot and pours herself more tea. "So what else did you two do today?"

"Actually, we walked a lot. Explored the waterfront. Crossed the bridge you told us about at the mouth of the Humber River."

"Nice, isn't it?"

"Very attractive. We also walked through Prospect Cemetery."

Not hiding her disdain Sandra wrinkles her nose. "Why did you go there?"

"It's not far from St. Hilda's."

"Yeah, but. Didn't you get enough of cemeteries when we went to Park Lawn to visit Dad's grave? Who's buried there?"

"No one we know. I just wanted to visit someone who lives nearby."

"Oh," Sandra says without any sense of confirmation. "Tell me. I can't guess who you'd know who lives around there?"

"No, you don't know them. We were at the house of a sister of someone who used to work for Ian and who's the mother of a former student of mine."

"I see."

Probably you don't, Susan thinks, but says, "I did leave them your phone number in case they need to contact me."

313

"That's fine."

"Sorry, I suppose I should have asked you first."

Shaking her head Sandra dismisses her sister's doubts. "No, really, I don't mind."

"It's just that her son ran away from the island and I was hoping to convince him to return home, but I doubt he will now."

"Why? Does he want to stay here?"

"I think so. He was a difficult student. But, he could've stayed and been a diver. By the way, I got an email from Kit. He asked me to tell you that he doesn't have a girlfriend, yet."

"Silly boy," Sandra says. "He's too serious."

"I disagree. His email was anything but serious."

"Really? How do you mean?"

"Kit has a great sense of humour, Sandra. I'm sure someday some girl will fall for him. She'll have to be the type who likes 'geeks'."

"Kit's not a 'geek'. Maybe a 'nerd'. He's so studious."

"What's the difference?"

"Well, 'Geeks' grew up on cartoons in the age of computers. They've never known a world without tv's and monitors. 'Nerds' are, you know, nerds! We had them in high school. They didn't fit in. Couldn't dance. Didn't party. Always studying."

"According to Kit, 'geeks' are popular because they're potentially rich."

"Yeah, right," Sandra says sarcastically. "A few programmers from Silicone Valley cashed in before the Nasdaq collapsed and now every 'geek' is a potential multi-millionaire."

"Nothing's changed," Susan says. "Everyone wants to be a millionaire. I remember kids talking about getting rich in high school. Big plans."

"Only now they want to be multi-millionaires, or billionaires. Everyone's a millionaire nowadays. Even you."

"That wasn't intentional," Susan says almost defensively. "Sheer luck. Unlike poor Tijean's parents. They work hard. Have one son. He's their future. And what does he do? He runs away."

"God, I'm grateful for the children I have."

"Yes, you can be proud of them. I'm so glad I got to see Christine."

"You never know what they'll get up to, or what will happen to them when they're gone."

Susan studies her sister's countenance. Talk of the fate of grown children has taken her thoughts somewhere miles away from here. It's a private moment and Susan's grateful to be sharing it with her. This is the intimacy she's missed being distant so much of the time. Together they hold the silence until they hear a car turn off its engine in the driveway.

"That'll be Ron," Sandra says.

No sooner is Ron inside the house before Ian's off the phone. Then they're both outside, gone to look at the new car discussing on the way stats that mostly men comprehend, stuff about engines and tires. Through the exterior walls the low sound of their muffled voices is heard continuing the banter. Going to the side window Susan peers at them huddled together over the open hood. Wondering what they find so interesting, so absorbing, so factual that they can instantly meet on mutual terms Susan slides one window pane open and puts her nose to the screen. On the spring breeze Ian's voice carries like birdsong – crisp and sharp. He's telling Ron that the Passat is designed for thermal flying and is equipped with flaps and ailerons for control and landing. As Susan examines the arctic blue silver body of the vehicle she considers telling Ian he's delusional. After all, he's purchased a car, not an airplane. Using the, as Ian describes it, "4-function remote key FOB", he unlocks the door, and opening the driver's side, invites Ron to take a seat. While Ron sits and plays with the steering wheel like a youngster with his favourite toy, Ian describes the anti-theft alarm system, the in-dash push-start ignition, and the multifunction trip computer. This is the candy. The two men start programming the trip itinerary. Suddenly it hits Susan that since returning here much of their focus has centered on the purchase of this vehicle. Then, like an igniting spark plug, it strikes her that much of what life off the island is is about cars.

~

On the day of the funeral Tijean hopped a bus at the corner of Eglington Avenue that took him east to the subway stop. There he rode the escalator from the underground bus bay to street level where he was to meet Terri. The layout above ground confused Tijean. Funny how he could find his way around marine life at the bottom of the ocean, but become completely disoriented by traffic at an intersection. The directions she'd given him finally made sense and, as he started to make his way to the meeting spot, he heard a car honk. Turning he saw Terri peering at him over the steering wheel of her red Subaru. More honking came from the cars behind as he quickly got into the passenger side. He realized he was smiling in embarrassment when Terri snarled into the rear view mirror at the blocked cars, "Hold your horses."

"Hi," he said simply. Should he call her Professor Barlow? He didn't know how to address her.

"Good Morning," Terri said, "and despite what we're doing, it is a good morning. Thank God the rain's stopped." She wheeled the car onto the on ramp to the Allen Expressway.

What Tijean thought was that it didn't matter if it rained for a funeral, but he wasn't the driver, didn't even have his driver's license, so he wasn't thinking in terms of road conditions. The atmosphere in the car seemed oppressive. When Terri had phoned his aunt's house to tell him of Jake's death she was full of anger and resentment, anger against the medical establishment for "their cock-up", and resentment that Jake had "succumbed to such an inglorious demise". In anticipating this ride with her Tijean had felt a creeping sense of shame, afraid he might expose himself as unintelligent and uneducated, fearful that he wouldn't understand her. She used such big words. Yet he did catch on to her meaning, mostly through her tone. That anger and resentment that he'd sensed over the phone was still lingering at the edges of her voice as she filled him in on the details. The hip operation had gone as expected. Jake had had the best surgeon in the business, a highly reputed specialist. The problems came with the hospital stay. Jake was recovering well from the implant, but had picked up a nasty germ.

"You'd think we would have learned from SARS," Terri said, "to keep our hospitals clean. But they're abominable. Full of bugs, and not just the ones you can see with the naked eye. Ones only visible through a microscope. They're more dangerous. He spent the first weekend after the surgery in emergency. There's another death trap. Our emergency wards. They never did give him a proper bed. Then, of course, they released him too early. They're always doing that. So he was right back inside. Sorry, God I'm making it sound like he was incarcerated. He may as well have been. Sent to prison or hell. Oh, by the way, his parents are Catholic. Be prepared for rituals."

By this point Tijean's head was spinning from Terri's driving as she was weaving in and out of traffic changing lanes at an alarming speed. Also from her conversation, "SARS?" "Incarcerated," he understood. His mind was like that, full of meaningful words that he could never retrieve to use in his own conversation, but understood when others spoke them. He asked again where they were going?

"Port Hope," Terri said. "It's an hour's drive east of here. At least, that's what all the radio ads say. 'Come to Port Hope. Only an hour's drive east of Toronto.' Sure, on a clear day, free of traffic and no obstructing construction. Maybe we'll be lucky this morning and make it in an hour. I hope so. I want to stop first at Jake's parents' house to drop off his stuff. His sister said she'd wait there for us, then show us to the church. By the way, I have a case for you. He left you his diving gear."

"He did?" Tijean pictured the case he'd carried for Jake and imagined the contents, what he'd seen him wear in those videos.

"He never had any children. He claims his sister's kids aren't interested in what he did, although he did try to teach one of them to dive. That proved a disaster from what I gather. Too bad. But there you have it. You're his surrogate son."

"Surrogate?" Tijean asked. Suddenly Tijean felt the pang of loss. He'd been shocked by the news, and somewhat confused by events with Terri directing his response offering to take him with her to the funeral out of town.

"You know, substitute."

Substitute, Tijean thought. Like replacement. He replaced the son Jake never had, but Jake couldn't replace Tijean's father. Tijean still had a father living on the island. His father was alive and well, but not supportive. Gone was the adult male who supported him as a diver. The grief Tijean felt was made more intense by a longing to see Jake again, to hear him, to laugh with him. If only he'd gone diving with him. Just once. That would have been an experience. He would have liked that. They both would have. "What about the videos? What will happen to them?" Tijean asked.

"Someone at CBC is turning them into a documentary."

Hearing that comforted Tijean. He would get to see Jake again, if only on film. For the next hour Terri chattered. Tijean was amazed at her energy. She could drive at top speed and think and talk at the same time. He wanted to turn on the radio or plug in a CD, hear some music. That's what he did when driving with Sherlock. They listened.

They didn't talk much, at least, didn't have conversations. Of course, they talked in their mutually understood lingo. Tijean felt restless and exhausted by the time they arrived at the turn off on the highway. "Welcome," he read.

"That's the village north of town," Terri said, "not a greeting."

"They have villages here?" Tijean asked.

"Sure. Villages, towns, cities," Terri said. "I guess this is the first time you've left the city?"

Tijean simply shook his head in the affirmative as he looked around at the landscape. They'd first traveled past houses and factories, then acres and acres of fields. Somehow the road into town made sense now. The empty land was dotted with small buildings serving various purposes: residences, storage sheds, meeting halls. Then they passed a shopping mall with gas stations positioned kitty corner. Beyond that a cemetery. Tijean wondered if that was where Jake would be buried.

"Here," Terri said, thrusting a piece of paper into his lap. "Tell me where I turn."

Tijean picked up the note. There were scribbles with arrows. "Turn left at Bruton Street," he said, unsure if he was pronouncing the street name correctly.

"Yes," Terri said. "I remember. At the corner with the car repair shop called Trotters."

They wound their way through side streets until they came to the house indicated on Baldwin Street. No sooner were they parked on the street out front of a tall, three storied house, than a woman appeared to greet them. "You must be Terri," she called across the grass.

Tijean got out of the car and stood beside the trunk that Terri had opened by a lever on the door. The woman introduced herself to him as "Leanne." She didn't look at all like Jake. She had dark hair with grey streaks and was fine boned, taller than Terri. Gathering his composure he offered to carry the bags into the house.

"Such gallantry," Leanne said, leading them up the wooden stairs to the porch and inside the house. "Just leave them in the hall. We'll sort them out later. We're used to having Jake's cases littering our houses."

It smelled different inside this house than any other he'd entered. It was an old smell, years of accumulation. Terri had told him on the drive that the Kearneys lived in an historic house. Within minutes they were back outside following Leanne to the church. Inside a Father Quinn conducted the service in severe tones and those gathered sang the hymns in subdued voices. It was unlike anything Tijean had witnessed. He was used to more frolicking tones, even at a funeral. Afterwards he followed Terri into the basement where sandwiches and tea were served at long tables by elderly people. This, too, struck Tijean as odd. The few men, for they were greatly outnumbered by the aged women, didn't seem to mind pouring tea. There was one other black face in the crowd. He thought she might talk to him, but she kept her distance while others were kind and friendly in a gentle manner asking him if he had known Jake in the Caribbean.

"Sit with us."

Tijean looked into the blue eyes of Leanne. That was where she resembled Jake. He stared into their pools of colour wondering how she could have dark hair and blue eyes. In the confusion at the serving tables he had lost Terri so he sat down at the seat being proffered. Leanne introduced Tijean to her parents. "Pleased to meet you, Mr. and Mrs. Kearney," Tijean said. This introduction embarrassed him. All of a sudden he felt he didn't have a right to be at the table, that he didn't belong among this crowd. What if they found out about the diving gear? Would they resent him having Jake's stuff? Wouldn't they want what belonged to their son? Tijean was beset by torments that no one could answer. They were old, these parents who had outlived their son. What would they do with Jake's equipment? Store it away? With that thought Tijean realized he was closer to Jake in a way that even his parents couldn't understand. For the short time he'd known Jake, Tijean had become connected in a lasting friendship of mutual interest. Forever, when diving, he would remember Jake. With that recognition Tijean settled into the spindly wooden chair and listened to the stories the Kearneys told about their son, stories that were mostly recollections from the past. Jake as a boy. The Jake they knew.

∽

On their road trip Susan never remembered her dreams. She slept soundly exhausted from the sightseeing, but now, waking in Ian's childhood bedroom, she holds the images from a bizarre dream. She's standing at a long, kitchen counter in a narrow room with a wall of glass opposite through which she sees a Volkswagon Beetle traveling towards her over the top of a hill where it's gaining serious speed and height. When it lands its rounded body shakes then crashes through the house narrowly missing her before plunging into the basement. After peering below she grabs the phone but can't make a connection when she pushes the three emergency numbers. "Help," she calls to the outside through the shattered glass whereupon help immediately arrives. Then she wakes, and keeping the dream in her conscious mind, ponders the picture of the car she's imagined. It's a retro model like the one Ian wanted to buy to remind him of the first car he owned, but recognizing it as an unpractical vehicle for their road trip, he settled on the Passat. Tomorrow they'll be back in the car to drive to Halifax to pick up Graham from university. Susan wonders if Ian will buy his son a car like the one he once owned.

He's hinted at it jokingly. She's not saying anything, but thinks it's a mistake to start treating the boy like the spoiled offspring of a millionaire. A conscious image floats through her mind of Ian throwing the keys of a Volkswagon Beetle to Graham saying, "Son, here's the keys to your car, just like the one I had when I was your age." Only Ian worked and saved to buy that car. He's told her all about the odd jobs he did to earn the money.

Peering across Ian's shoulder Susan sees that the time is only 4:23. Way too early to rise. She lets her head flop back onto the pillow. The next image she has is of bright light, a blaze as strong as sunshine in the Caribbean, and for a moment, she is transported there enjoying all the accompanying sensations: tropical air, brilliant seas, warm sand. Only when she opens her eyes she sees that the light is coming through a gap in the curtains and concludes it's sunrise. Checking the time again she notes that it is now 7:12. Satisfied that she's enjoyed nearly three more hours of sleep she gets up to close the curtains thinking to make the room darker for Ian whose slumbering is as still as a newborn baby's. On tiptoes she feels her way around the bed so as not to bump into any obstacles. When she reaches the window she's tempted to peak outside where the rising sun glows a filament orange as bright as an electrical burner turned on to the highest temperature. Its intensity causes momentary blindness. Blinking Susan lowers her sight to the shiny, oil painted window ledge which comes into focus with the picture of a small beetle's carcass. A ladybug, she thinks while remembering those lovely little books with that red insect's insignia on the spine, books that she bought for her niece. They helped her learn to read in stages of complexity all serialized numerically and alphabetically. When doom sayers predict the end of the world with only rodents and insects do they imagine such pretty creatures? Or are they picturing tarantulas? Something outside the window grabs her attention the way only flying things can. Susan follows the flight pattern of a fat bumblebee. The sun catches its bold yellow and black striped markings as it hovers outside the screen making so much noise she wonders if it'll wake Ian's slumber. Its wings are buzzing so fast they're a blur. What's it doing up here, she wonders. Just then it drops, and pushing her nose against the window, Susan peers below, but the fat insect disappears.

Now she can look at the scene outside knowing to avoid the pull of the direct rays of the burning sunlight. The sight swamps her with sentimentality – dawn over the ocean. How she's missed this view while traveling across the country. Along the shoreline there's a skittering movement of long-legged birds. Later she'll have to unpack her binoculars to identify them. To think that this is the same body of salt water that laps the shores of the Caribbean. Gone is the turquoise. No wonder all those earlier explorers got confused by the world's immense bodies of water. Like Christopher Columbus looking for a shipping route to avoid land travel only to discover ocean after ocean. Into her head comes a remembrance combining Columbus, the Caribbean and birds. The Indians thought the explorer was the biggest parrot they'd ever seen when he arrived on the islands dressed in a plumed cap and a red cape.

Back in bed Susan fits into Ian's warm body remembering their time at the Chateau Frotenac in Quebec where they made love like a couple on a honeymoon. Definitely more romantic than their stay in Niagara where, despite the hype, they felt it was not the real thing. Sure Ian was awed by the Falls and they kept getting caught up in the natural wonder of the spectacle – the roar, the spray – the monumental size. Yet romance didn't follow. It took a tug at history to do that for them – old buildings, a restored harbour – French cuisine. As Susan snuggles deeper into the warmth of Ian's body she experiences a sense of being in a real place. All their traveling has stilled her sense of yearning. This is Ian's childhood home, but she feels right at home, too, in a place that's like a magnet of familiarity. When they arrived late yesterday afternoon Ian's parents, George and Marjorie, rushed outside to greet them at the car. Now as Susan relives that moment she remembers that his parents didn't even notice the car. All the attention was on them, the arriving couple. After embracing Ian, Marjorie kept patting her son as if to prove to herself that he was real. George shook Ian's hand, then as if regaining some deep connection, clasped his son in a bear hug. Later Ian's sister, Heather, came for a cup of tea. Since she works as a real estate agent she offered to show them properties, just in case they could be encouraged to stay permanently. Heather wanted to know all about Susan's sister, Sandra, saying she missed that experience as she only had two older brothers. "And all they did was tease me," Heather complained. "It was terrible growing up with Ian and Roy. They were merciless."

"Now, Heather," Marjorie said. "You know they only loved you."

"Right. We were always putting on shows," Heather said, directing her story to Susan. "We didn't even have a t.v. in those days. Unlike other families we were late getting one, so we had to entertain ourselves. Ian and Roy would lure me into staging talent shows getting me to sing and dance, which I've always been good at. Their performances were awful, but they were the judges, so they'd give themselves first and second place, leaving me in third, and I'd break down crying."

"Heather still sings in the church choir," Marjorie said.

"It's a wonder I have enough confidence to do even that after my upbringing."

"So I take it you no longer dance?" Ian asked.

"Oh, shut up," Heather said dismissively and laughed. "You still can't admit I was always better than either one of you."

"I danced with Heather at Gary's wedding," George said, "And she's a fine dancer."

"Well, you're amazing, Dad," Heather said. "You wouldn't believe how strong Dad still is. He had me twirling around that dance floor so fast I was out of breath after two minutes."

Susan remembers she kept looking from one family member to another absorbed in their tales trying to imagine a younger Ian, but when George mentioned Gary's wedding she held her breath. They'd been invited to the wedding of Ian's nephew, Roy's eldest son. Roy was so insulted that she and Ian didn't make plans to travel to attend the wedding that he hasn't spoken to them since that day. Susan has never been able to understand such family rifts. Auntie Dot's family is always engaged in similar bouts of in-fighting. Despite the dissimilarity between her and her sister, Susan's family never holds grudges. Now she ponders why that is, why some families feud and others don't. It always seems to Susan that the reason or cause of a disagreement proves too trivial to turn into so hostile an act as estrangement. If families can't get along, how can the world expect peace between nations? A bit of a leap in thinking she realizes, but

Susan recognizes she draws analogies on that scope. Often she sees patterns where there are only tenuous connections. As a result of this brotherly quarrel she never has met Roy and his family. Most of Ian's relatives traveled to his resort in the early days, years before Susan arrived. No one came in the last ten years, except Graham who traveled alone between his parents' homes.

Ian stirs, and suddenly realizing Susan's beneath him, grunts. "Oh, it's you," he says.

"You were expecting someone else?"

Laughing, Ian rolls back onto his side. "You're hogging the bed."

"No, I'm snuggling up to you."

Lifting the quilt Ian sits on the edge of the bed. "Boy, I slept soundly."

Retreating from Ian Susan lies flat on her back. Then she raises her shoulders and shimmies herself upright until the back of her skull rests against the headboard. Curious about the bed cover she pulls the quilt closer and examines the squares and stitching. "Did your mother make this?"

"My grandmother did."

Turning to Ian Susan stares at the back of his head where a whorl of hair reveals a bare patch. "How old is it then?"

Unable to make direct eye contact Ian turns his head over his shoulder in acknowledgment of her presence. "Older than me. Probably seventy years, at least."

"Look at the condition it's in. My God, it'll last for a hundred years."

"Probably. Century old quilts aren't that uncommon in this household."

"I don't believe it." Yet she does because while she's holding it in her hands wondering if she shouldn't be touching such antiquity and imparting the oils from her skin into the material she feels the firmness of the thick fabric. It's strong, like his father who's still a desirable dance partner. "Your father's mother, or your mother's?"

"My father's. All this furniture, too, comes from my father's side of the family."

Susan looks around the room noting features she missed last night when falling into bed simply grateful that she wasn't in another hotel room. The furniture is heavy and dark, not a rich darkness like exotic wood, but a matted finish with stained, off-white knobs for drawer pulls. There's no fancy work to the carpentry, simply sawed with the corners rounded. Lumber cut from the surrounding woods, she suspects. Then hewn into posts and boards before assembly.

"Time for breakfast," Ian says, rising.

Despite the comfort she feels being in Ian's family home, Susan decides to put on yesterday's clothes rather than wrap a housecoat over her nightie. In the kitchen Marjorie is making coffee in a stainless steel percolator. She rests the top with the glass bulb in the centre on the counter beside a round, plastic lid while scooping ground beans out of an economy sized tin. "Oh dear," she says fussing. "I was hoping to have the coffee ready for you when you got out of bed."

"Relax, Mom," Ian says, giving his mother a peck on the top of the head. "You don't need to wait on us. What can I do to help?"

"Your father's getting the eggs."

Susan looks around the room wondering where George is hiding before realizing that he's in the hen-house gathering freshly laid eggs.

Opening the refrigerator door, Ian squats to stare at the shelves.

"The bacon's in the larder," Marjorie says. "So's the butter."

While Ian disappears into the pantry at the back of the house Susan studies the table wondering what she can do to help set four places. An oilcloth decorated in a floral print covers the table. In the middle is a small Lazy Susan with a painted porcelain set of salt and pepper shakers, off-white cloth napkins in a matching holder, a glass spooner stacked with cutlery, a full sugar bowl and an empty creamer. She's not supposed to take an inanimate object personally, but she wonders how this revolving tray got its name. To her offer of help Marjorie commands her to sit down. "Did you sleep well?" she asks while returning the coffee tin to the cupboard under the counter.

"Yes, thank you. Uninterrupted. I feel totally refreshed."

Marjorie takes four plates out of a top cupboard and puts them into the oven to warm. Her soft, white hair sits flat on the top of her small head. Using her tiny right foot she pushes the stepping stool she's used to reach the cupboards out of the way in an alternating step/slide rhythm, then hastily returns to the sink where she wipes the soles of her slippers on the braided rag mat which isn't a recognizable pattern because the folded material disguises the original cloth. There's one just like it by the back door only it has a reddish hue. The one in front of the kitchen sink is blue. Susan's only seen such mats in craft shops in rural Ontario. There they fetch a high price as anything that's handmade does. Here, she suspects, they're a dime a dozen, made from worn out clothing or bedding, not crafted into colourful patterns that can be matched to a stylish interior décor. Watching Marjorie's white head bobbing around the room makes Susan feel guilty for simply sitting, but she knows she'd be in everybody's way if she added herself to the mix. It strikes her that Marjorie's hair is the softest thing about the woman. Everything else is tough, including her manner. "Ian said his grandmother made the quilt on our bed."

"Yes. She was handy with the needle. Could stitch together any pattern, that woman, from all sorts of scrap material." From the drawer under the stove Marjorie removes an iron frying pan. Her forearms are tanned from working outside in the spring planting the garden. The tight wrinkles on her face give her complexion a weather-beaten appearance that's hearty, not aging and slack like her own mother's, but then Doris' complexion always was pasty. Both Doris and Auntie Dot have blotchy skin.

Trotting beside Ian is the dog, Heddy. She's an old, black lab with a bum hip. Slowly she makes her way from the back larder to the table where Susan is sitting.

"Hey," Ian says, lifting the fry pan by its handle. "Are you still using this heavy, old thing?"

"Well, why wouldn't I? Nothing wrong with it. Cast iron doesn't wear out. You still remember how to cook the bacon, don'tcha?"

"Sure, Mom. I know how to cook bacon." Ian regards his mother with a knowing look as if to say some lessons taught are never forgotten.

Heddy nuzzles Susan's lap. She scratches the bitch behind the ears. "Good Morning," Susan says in the soft tones reserved for friendly pets and nursing babies.

George enters through the back door beside the pantry holding the handle of a basket over his forearm. "Shoo her away if she's bothering you."

"Not at all," Susan says, looking directly into the wolf blue eyes of Ian's father. The resemblance between the two men is unmistakable. They have the same lanky, tall build. Susan feels kindly towards Ian's father recognizing that some day in the future a version of him will be at her side. Having such a person to accompany her into old age is a pleasant thought.

Lifting the linen tea towel he shows the eggs to Susan. "Can't get them fresher than this, eh?"

Touching a shell lightly Susan feels the warmth. She agrees, then turns back to the nuzzling dog. "And what about you? What do you get?"

"She's been fed already," George says. "Last night's leftovers. Not that she eats much these days. Mostly she sleeps." He laughs. "Like me. We both need our naps."

Before long the smell and crackle of bacon fill the air. George is lathering butter onto the toast before stacking it with the rest inside the oven. Reaching across Susan Marjorie places two opened jars of homemade preserves, one strawberry and the other blackcurrant. "Do you want juice?" she asks.

"Yes, please," Susan says and watches the efficiency of Ian's mother as she opens the top freezer door, pulls out a small can which she empties into a plastic jug before filling it with water from the small tap to the right of the faucet, the one that's connected to the drinking water. With a wooden spoon she stirs the liquid around and around until there's a vortex making the juice lap precariously close to the rim. "I can pour," Susan offers.

"One egg, or two?" Ian asks.

Susan's the only one who asks for one. It seems the others are hungry. She sips her glass of juice which is watery, totally unlike the freshly squeezed variety.

"What do you take in your coffee?" Marjorie asks, setting a mug in front of Susan.

"Just cream."

Marjorie lifts the empty creamer from the centre of the table and goes to the fridge with it. Returning with the small, china jug full she tells Susan the cream comes from their neighbour's dairy farm. "We don't keep cows any longer. Too much work for us. Just the chickens and the vegetable patch for our own use. They grow a few crops on our fields that we let out. That's how it is nowadays when the sons don't stay on the farm."

There's no malice in the tone of her voice, just a simple statement of fact. Whether or not she thinks it's better for her sons to be gone than stay is moot. Despite her harshness Susan feels kindly toward her. She's totally accepting, in a way that harbours strength of character, no conflicting ego in her. Susan sips the coffee from the lip of the thick mug. It's the consistency and taste of dishwater. What is it about beans from economy sized tins? It's as if the brew missed the flavour and captured only some oily residue. Even the aroma is telltale, less richness than from a strongly roasted brew. Somehow Susan doesn't mind the weakness of the drinks. This morning she doesn't feel at all fussy like she would if she was paying for service. In company that nourishes there's a contagion of friendliness.

After breakfast Susan is able to help with the washing up since Ian's parents don't own a built-in dishwasher. In fact, there's no big appliances under the kitchen counter, only a fifty year old Sunbeam mixer sitting on top. Taking the clean tea towel that Marjorie hands her from a linen drawer Susan decides not to comment on the embroidery along the edge suspecting that it, too, could be nearing one hundred years of service. How things used to last. Not like disposable items on the market nowadays.

Marjorie isn't satisfied having her prodigal son home. She wants to know when Graham, her youngest grandson, is coming.

"We're picking him up tomorrow," Ian says.

"Well, I know that. But when are you bringing him here for a visit?"

"I'll arrange something with him tomorrow."

"Do it when you're on the road," George says. "I find it's always easier to arrange things with him, like family visits, when he's in the car."

"Is that right?" Ian asks. "Did I tell you what he said when I told him I sold the resort?"

"Oh, he must have been pleased you were coming home," Marjorie says.

"Actually the resort was my home," Ian says.

"You know what I mean."

"Yes, I'm afraid I do," Ian says. "Anyway, Graham couldn't believe I'd sold it to a Frenchman."

"Didn't Graham meet him at Christmas?" George asks.

"No, he wasn't working for me then."

"Well how long has he been working for ya?"

"Just since January," Ian says. "Anyway, like I was saying. I told him who I'd sold it to and he asks me if Marcel's French. Then he wants to know how he's going to succeed because Graham thought my success had everything to do with my being friendly to the guests and, according to Graham, the French aren't friendly."

"I don't know about the French French," Marjorie says. "But the Quebec French are. At least, the ones who come here are. And so are the French in New Brunswick."

"Why doesn't he think the French are friendly?" George asks. "Are there students on campus from France, maybe?"

"No, no. Nothing like that," Ian says. "He's got this idea from something he read in a novel by Douglas Coupland."

"Is that one of them comic book writers?" Marjorie asks.

"That was a graphic novel he was reading, Dear," George says. Turning to Susan to include her in the family conversation, he explains, "His Grandma told him off for still reading picture books." Then George turns back to his wife. "You'll be lucky if he wants to come back and visit after the razing you gave him last time he stayed here."

"How was I to know they make picture books for grown-ups," Marjorie says. "No wonder their teachers say the young don't read no more. So, what kind of books does this writer you're saying he reads writes?"

"They're just like novels, but for his generation."

"Actually," Susan says. "Douglas Coupland wrote Generation X."

"That so?" Marjorie says hesitantly.

"It was in some book about nerds that Graham read a passage about the French employees at Microsoft who couldn't write user-friendly software because they're so rude," Ian says.

Suddenly the shrill sound of the phone ringing interrupts Ian's chuckling leaving all of them mute and immobilized. Marjorie is the first to stir. "Now who can that be at this hour in the morning?"

Out of consideration the other three remain silent while Marjorie answers it. Then she turns to Susan holding the ear-piece that's linked by a cord to the phone. "It's your sister."

Within the backdrop of silence Susan's thoughts rush from concern for her mother to members of Sandra's family in less than a second before taking hold of the receiver. "Hello, Sandra." Her sister's familiar voice arrives over the long distance with news that holds Susan's attention while calming her fears about the safety of their immediate family.

"What is it?" Ian asks when she says "goodbye".

In her hand Susan continues to hold the plastic receiver that rests upright on the kitchen wall.

She raises her eyes to hold Ian's before answering. "Tijean's gone home."

As Ian approaches Susan he first takes her hand away from the receiver before embracing her around the shoulders. "Is that all? I was starting to worry."

Behind the couple comes the sound of chair legs scraping the linoleum floor. "Sit down," Marjorie says. When Ian has Susan seated she asks, "Is it family?"

"No, Mom. Someone Susan used to teach and the son of someone who worked for me. He left the island. Ran away from home. Went to his relatives in Toronto. In fact, we visited him. Just briefly."

"Ah, so you're talking about a boy," Marjorie says.

Susan nods in the affirmative. "His aunt phoned Sandra." Covering Ian's hand that is still resting on her shoulder Susan looks up at him. "Remember I left the number?"

"Ah, right," Ian says. "Well that's good news?"

The pause that follows extends into what seems an eternity. There's such a muddle of images in Susan's head that she can't find the words to explain all the details. "He's diving," she says.

"That's even better news," Ian says.

"Yes, it is. And it gets better. He's working with divers at the Marine Centre."

Once again Marjorie's clucking around her like a mother hen dismissing the ingratitude of grown sons as one of the prices to be paid for raising children, at least male children. "A daughter is a daughter for the rest of her life. A son is a son until he takes a wife." Her shaking moves from her hands stubbornly holding the coffee pot to her head. It's as if her stubbornness mimics the early stages of Parkinson's in any part of her body attempting free movement. "Or until he runs away from home. Can I pour you another cup of coffee, dear?"

Before she consents Susan squeezes Ian's hand. Marjorie is, of course, referring to her own son, now the prodigal son. Ian slips his hand free and joins her at the table. Together they sip cautiously from their full mugs of coffee that have practically reached the boiling temperature. At the stove Marjorie lifts the heavy frying pan. It's shaking in her grasp and Susan registers that the woman is full of energy. In her head the kitchen scene is playing in slow motion. Susan's mouth feels unresponsive to her thoughts as if she's lost some connection between her mind and her motor ability. Then George is by his wife's side taking the fry pan out of her hands and indicating that she should put the old coffee tin on the counter where he pours the liquid grease from the morning's meal. Marjorie replaces the tin to the back of the range where it's handy for their use in frying foods. The domestic mime registers in Susan's brain as totally ironic. They're a couple in their eighties living independently in their own home following a lifestyle of economy by eating and using left-over fat. That defies all rules of modern medicine for good health and longevity. How lucky they are. They still have each other, their health, their home, family and friends. Such peace and harmony. But for how long will this ideal state last? Tomorrow Susan and Ian will leave to get Graham in Dartmouth. Already they come and go freely assuming the older couple will manage in their absence. She asks Ian about their plans for leaving.

"We won't be picking up Graham until early afternoon. He is a night owl. Besides, he wants to sleep in after all the studying for exams. He won't be ready until at least 2 o'clock."

"What time should we leave, then?" Suddenly the wave of sickness returns, but subsides as quickly as it arrived.

"Probably early. I thought you might like a tour of Halifax?"

"Yes, may as well as I've never been there before."

George supports their plan, saying it's a port worth visiting and she should get to know the east.

Suddenly the lingering odour of fat mixed with the weak aroma of coffee turns Susan's stomach and she flees upstairs to the bathroom just in time to retch into the toilet bowl. Soon Ian is at her side with her guest towel and face cloth wiping and drying her mouth. He then offers her a glass of water for gargling. After cleansing the insides of her mouth of their putrid smell Susan spits, then lifts her pale face that's reflected in the mirror below Ian's forehead which is wrinkled in concern.

"Do you want to lie down?"

Mutely she consents to his nursing.

"I thought you were looking pale after breakfast," he says.

"Sorry, I don't know what's the matter with me," Susan says as she crawls on all four with Ian's support to the bedroom.

"No need to apologize. Probably some bug you picked up during our travels."

At the side of the bed Susan stands weakly as Ian helps her up and into bed. When her head hits the pillow her mind races in dizzying swirls. It feels like she's on a roller coaster ride, instead of lying still in a horizontal position. Within seconds she is sound asleep.

The calmness that comes with waking reassures Susan that she is well again, if not full of vim and vigour, at least stable in her stomach. Remembering the drive to the farm yesterday along Highway 366, a collector highway as coded in brown on the provincial map, reminds her of how she felt before falling asleep. More undulating than any two-dimensional map could portray, they traveled its twists and dips at a speed that left her stomach behind on the top of crests of small hills. Ian was enjoying himself immensely, and while steering the wheel like some racing car driver, regaled her with stories of learning to drive on the very roads they were traveling. For her, that half hour drive was the best part of their road trip. Hearing about his past made her feel like his trusted soul-mate. Love is unstable, but trust and confidence endure. Unless betrayed. But she doesn't want to think about that. Perish the thought. What a nice saying. She'll use it to hold her optimism.

Rolling onto her back she lets her eyes wander around the darkened room while her mind wanders to decades earlier when Ian slept in this very room with his brother. Isn't this what she wanted, to open the door onto his personal history? Meet his parents? They have the entire summer ahead of them, here, in this Maritime province, close to his immediate family, as well as to his extended family, some of whom he pointed out to her on the drive here – farms, villages and towns full of Camerons. The romancing Camerons.

There's a creaking on the stairs. Someone come to check up on her. Ian pokes his head through the door. "Ah, you're awake."

"Just."

"Do you want some supper?"

"Is it that late?"

Entering Ian comes and sits beside her causing the mattress to cave in the middle. "No big lobster dinner for you tonight. Maybe you could stomach a fish chowder? The milky kind."

"I'll try," she says. "Do I have time to shower and dress."

"Of course," Ian says. Before rising he feels her forehead. "At least you don't have a fever."

Like an indelible imprint the touch of Ian's hand on her skin leaves a lasting feeling that comforts her with its reassurance. She's fine. In every sense she's fine – well, in good health – loved, by him - secure, for now. Stretching widely Susan casts the slumber from her joints and, as if the oxygen she delivers her body renews her mind's consciousness, thinks that all that really matters is how anyone feels. These moments of feeling good about herself are treasures that make life worthwhile. How fleeting they are. Too rare. Life should be more full of this goodness. Finally, how people feel in relationships is what makes for well being.

In the shower she carries this exuberance too far and knocks her elbow against the tiled wall hitting her funny bone which doesn't make her laugh, only wince. The bathtub in the small room is narrow, barely wide enough for a body to soak, but she doesn't imagine that either Marjorie or George spend much time soaking in the tub. They're not the kind to indulge themselves. While drying her body Susan peers over the top of the frilly sheers that cover only the bottom half of the small window. Outside Ian is playing with Heddy, throwing a stick a short distance then squatting to take it from her mouth and pat her broad neck. Briefly she wonders if he'll want a dog, but of course, that would be impractical if they're to live here only part of the year. Then she realizes he'll propose they transport the animal on a plane back to the Turks & Caicos.

Downstairs she passes through the parlour which is what George and Marjorie call the room that holds a two-seater couch with a crocheted throw flung over the back, a chair with a matching Naugahyde footstool and the t.v. that's on mute. The weather channel shows a map of the Maritimes for the next day. Apparently the good weather is not going to last. Hurricane season has started and a system is moving up from Florida. Susan watches the swirling blue with ominous green cells indicating wind and rain. George enters the room. "I don't know about driving to Halifax tomorrow," she says.

"Maybe it'll all be over by noon."

"I hope you're right."

"Could be the weather channel's got it wrong." Going over to the window George pushes aside the sheers. "Though the wind's changing. Not a good sign."

Taking a place beside him, Susan, too, peers out the window. There's only grass that's blowing as the view from the parlour is across a field that borders the shoreline, the same view as from upstairs. Ian's old bedroom is above the parlour. "I guess you're used to forecasting the weather."

"Yes, done a lot of cloud-watching in my day. We farmers always keep one eye on the sky. Weren't always right, mind you. Sometimes just a lot of wishful thinking. Wanting rain after planting. Wanting sun after the seeds sprout. Then complaining when it doesn't happen. You can tell when the weather's changing, though."

"So we are going to get rain?"

"Probably a storm. Won't be a good day for driving," he says, "or diving."

Last night they'd met a neighbour whose grandson was also a student at Dartmouth. He was proud of the boy who was a diver helping a research team. "You mean your neighbour's grandson?"

"Oh," George says, nodding his head. "I don't know too much about him. I know the boy was always bright in school. Got good grades. Liked to study the tidal flats when he was here visiting."

"I see." Susan watches George slowly pick up the remote and push the off button. Picturing Tijean in a wet-suit and pulling on a big helmet before pushing off backwards from a Zodiac she wonders how he would feel diving off the coast of Nova Scotia as compared to the Caribbean. "I guess the water's cold this time of year up here. Cold and murky."

"Only murky in the harbour. Still, dark at the depths they dive. They lower them fancy lights down to penetrate the dark."

"I guess you can't hear much, as well. Only yourself breathing in and out."

"You have to be a certain kind of person to like diving."

"I even find recreational diving claustrophobic. I can't imagine what it's like to go deep sea diving."

"Damned expensive sport. No, not everyone can do it. Ha," George says as if he's just struck gold. "That's what they get paid for."

"Right," Susan says, imagining Tijean back on North Caicos making his family proud, proving to them finally that the work of a diver has value. Will that make him feel good about himself, and about the choices he's made? She hopes so. She truly hopes that returning there will satisfy Tijean's family and foster in him a sense of worthiness. She speculates on what made him change his mind about going home. She knows she played a small role. There's a whiff of toasted bread coming from the kitchen. "I think I should offer to help," Susan says, getting up and heading for the kitchen.

"Don'tcha worry about that," Marjorie says to Susan's offer. "Sit yourself down. Dad, you want to call Ian in. Maybe tie up Heddy. We don't need her smoochin' around the table tonight."

Taking the seat indicated to her against the wall Susan finds herself hemmed in. She figures Ian's mother places her there so she can't comfortably get in and out thereby rendering her unable to be of any help. As a guest she gets served, no offers of help accepted. It's a question of honour with Marjorie. The painted wooden chair feels sticky underneath Susan. There must be ninety percent humidity in the atmosphere from the cooking vapours inside the house and the sea air outside. In front of her Marjorie places a stack of toast. It's thickly sliced, homemade white bread with butter dripping down the crusts.

"Help yourself."

Susan does help herself. Without waiting for the men she picks a piece of toast off the top of the pile and bites into it. "I hadn't realized how hungry I am."

"Of course you are. You haven't eaten since breakfast." Marjorie wipes her hands on her apron. "Do ya want some ginger ale? It's Canada Dry, the best. We don't buy the cheap stuff."

"The generic brands," Susan says.

"Don't know about that." Marjorie sets a glass in front of Susan. "I always give the children ginger ale to settle their stomachs. It's room temperature. Most of the fizz gone out of it so it won't make you burp."

Susan smiles. She feels like one of Marjorie's children. When Ian comes inside he goes directly to the sink to wash his hands. Like a farm hand, Susan thinks, only she knows it's because he's been playing with the dog. He helps his mother with serving the soup and brings Susan a bowl, then gets his own. Sitting kiddie corner to her Susan recognizes a new mood in him. He seems more happy at this moment than he's ever been since she's known him. Not the carefree happiness from his island days. There's more firmness in him. He's full of rectitude, happy to be home despite what he's said about having a home on the islands. While she was sleeping he phoned Marcel to check how things were going and to pass on what they knew about Tijean.

George starts reminiscing about the stories he's heard about the island. "Remember what happened when Heather went to visit you at your resort?"

"You mean the nighttime visitor?"

George starts laughing. "That gave her a scare. No wonder she never went back."

"What happened?" Susan asks.

Putting his soup spoon down on the saucer Ian retells the whole story. "I'd put her up in my office. All the guest rooms were booked. She decided to keep the door open to catch the night breeze, zephyr. Anyway, a strange noise wakes her up in the middle of the night and she thinks she's having a nightmare because she sees a beast beside her bed."

George is still laughing. "A donkey."

"It'd wandered in."

"Only, she thought it must be Ian playing a joke." George can hardly say the sentence he's laughing so hard.

"The least she could have done was do me the honour of calling me 'Don Quixote'."

"On a donkey you'd be Sancho Panzez," Susan says.

"Please," Ian says, dragging the vowel sound.

"Who are they?" Marjorie asks. "More characters on the island?"

"From the classics," George says. "You know, Marjorie. Don Quixote and the windmills?"

"Oh, that guy. He's not a real person, though, is he?"

"No," Ian says. "A fictional character."

"So what did she do? Scream?" Susan asks.

"No, no," George says, protesting.

"She started yelling at me. 'Ian, get out of that costume and get back into your own bed.' From my bed I hear her yelling my name so I get up and come into the room. Then she thinks she's seeing double. So she jumps out of bed and starts pulling at the donkey's ears."

At this, George slaps the table.

"Of course the donkey brays which scares her so much she jumps on top of the bed and starts yelling at me to get the thing out of her room."

"Did he go?"

"Of course not. They're stubborn animals you know."

"What did you do?" Before he can answer Susan interrupts her own question. "Why haven't I heard this story before?"

"I don't know. I never told it to you?"

"No. But tell me now. How did you get it out of your office?"

"I didn't. I gave up my bed to Heather. Which, by the way, I'd offered to her in the first place but she'd insisted she didn't want me put out. Anyway, after that experience she went willingly into my bedroom and I slept on the couch. In the morning, the donkey was gone."

With that conclusion all four silently finish their soup while happy tears dry in their eyes. "Then there were the beer cans," George says.

Curiosity piques Susan. She looks at Ian.

"Didn't I ever tell you about the beer cans?"

"No." Susan begins to wonder if she's missed Ian's best stories and all along she thought she'd heard them all innumerable times.

"Well, Heather brought me some cases of beer, Keith's Ale, made right here in Halifax, since it was my favourite and, of course, not available on North Caicos. So I put some in the propane fridge, stored some under the bar and put an extra case in the shed at the back of the resort. A mistake. It had no ventilation and faced south. After a few days they heated up and exploded covering everything I had in storage in a smelly foam of sticky beer."

"Heather said it stunk to high heaven."

"Know what it's like to walk into Saunders?"

"That's the local pub," George says by way of clarification to Susan.

"It's where she works."

Looking at Marjorie Susan guesses that she doesn't mean what she's implying, but Susan can't figure out who "she" is.

"Where who works?" Ian asks, holding his animated features on his face while having his story interrupted.

"You know? Her."

"Now, Marjorie. That's all water under the bridge."

"Still, just warning ya."

"Sounds like you enjoyed yourselves on the island," George says, attempting to recover the spirit of levity that the retelling of old stories gives.

"Yes, I wish you'd come for a visit."

"But aren'tcha settling here?"

"Only over the summer, Mom. We'll go back to the Caribbean during the winter months. You could visit us there. Take a holiday."

"Oh, we haven't taken a holiday since our honeymoon."

"Never was easy leaving the farm."

"You can now, though, since you've given up the livestock and rented the fields. Now that you're retired, too. Funny, eh?" Ian says, turning to Susan. "I retire the same year my Dad does."

"Ah, you young folks. You have it easy," George says. "We can, Marjorie. We can take a trip next winter, if you want?"

"We'll see," Marjorie says, rising. She starts clearing the dishes.

"You don't have to do that. Leave it to us."

Susan sees that Marjorie's crying and she turns to Ian. He rises and takes his mother in his arms. "It's the happiest and saddest day of my life," she says. "Having you home."

Although not a mother herself, the empathy she feels for Ian's mother washes over Susan giving her a taste of how a real mother feels. Isn't it true for everyone, though? A lot more happiness can bring a little more sadness. This was what was unsettling about Tijean running away. His mother will be happy to have him back on the island.

Later in the evening after they've watched the news and some t.v. with Marjorie and George the older couple ask the younger one if they want to play some cards.

"Maybe later," Susan says. "Right now I need some fresh air."

Together they go upstairs to the bedroom where Susan searches through her suitcase for her jacket. "I want to take my binoculars," she says, unzipping the smallest compartment on the outside of her case. There she finds a new pair purchased at an outdoor gear store in Toronto chosen because they're fog resistant and designed for viewing birds at dawn and dusk. She's missed dawn except for the earlier view of the sunrise through the window and the only sighting she had was of a bumblebee. Still, she wants to be prepared just in case she gets a chance to see something new.

Guiding her with his hand gently holding her elbow Ian takes her outside to a pathway through the grass that leads down to the beach. Soon it becomes too narrow for them to walk side by side so he leads. As soon as they step off the path onto the sand the smell of rotting seaweed punches through Susan's olfactory senses nearly sending her stomach into convulsions again, but she turns her head towards the offshore breeze and inhales deeply in time to settle her digestive system. Where the sand is dry large logs of driftwood sit rotting, and when she looks closely, she sees the skeleton of a large, bony fish trapped underneath one. Where the sand is wet and flat there are shorebirds skittering along the water's edge. Coming as close as she dares without sending the birds into flight she plants her feet in a spot that allows her to raise the binoculars to her eyes and hold them in a steady manner so she can gaze through them while adjusting the focus. Not surprisingly there are killdeers, the noisiest shorebird in the belted plover family. Another fatter bird has a harlequin pattern and very orange legs. "What's the one with the russet coloured back?" she asks, handing Ian her glasses.

"That's the Ruddy Turnstone," he says, handing her back her binoculars.

Again she raises her glasses to locate the strange plover. "Never seen one of those before."

"Has to be a first time for everything."

"I'm glad I came here."

"In spite of getting sick?"

"Yes." In the dusk she stops to stare across the water. "Imagine, on the other side is Britain and Europe."

"And Scandinavia further north."

"Ah, of course, all those other countries. And continents." Susan laughs. "Gosh, it's hard to imagine the size of the ocean."

"Gosh?" Ian asks with the look of someone holding back on a tease. "Haven't heard that one in awhile."

"Well, it is the first time I've been to the Maritimes. I'm gobsmacked, then, as our British tourists used to say."

"So you're impressed by this corner of the world?"

"Definitely. Speaking of firsts, I'm glad to have finally met your parents. Your mother is so pleased to have us here. But I wish she'd let me help. I hope they will visit us next winter. Then we can pay them back. I always wondered why they never visited."

"You heard what my Dad said. They've never left the farm."

"Imagine having remained in one place for decades? There are indulgences they've never experienced – room service, drinking glasses in paper sheaths, someone making your bed every morning – let alone the strangeness of foreign lands."

"Leaving is a sign of failure to them."

"Failure?" Susan stops in her tracks recalling that moment at the resort when Ian showed her the purchase of sale when he explained to her his reasons for selling. She recognized then that there was more to his move than simply cashing in on the money.

"This is God's country to them," Ian says, sweeping his arm in a strong gesture like a preacher in the pulpit. "You provide for your own here. It's seen as failure if you don't. A person only leaves out of desperation."

"So what you did was an act of desperation?"

"Yes. I was the cause of much embarrassment."

"Foolish, really," Susan says not meaning his parents, more a comment on parochial attitudes.

"Do you think she's forgiven me for leaving?"

"I imagine so. I assume mothers do. Was it your former student she said works at the pub?"

"It seems so."

"She hasn't forgiven her."

"No, she wouldn't," Susan says. "Last night Heather told me she battles that because she likes to think she's a good Christian, yet can't bring herself to forgive that 'tart' as she still calls her."

"She didn't tonight." Ian looks at her. "Call her a tart. She simply said 'her'. Maybe she's on the road to forgiveness."

"Maybe."

Susan thinks that Ian's return would help soften his mother's attitude to the past, but doesn't say so out loud. There's been enough guilt around that act already. "Have you? Forgiven her?"

Ian shrugs. "Never thought I had to. Besides, I should thank her. If I hadn't left I wouldn't have met you."

"Ah," Susan says and wonders if she, too, should thank "the tart"? Aloud Susan says, "Imagine diving into the ocean?"

Stopping in his tracks as if unable to move and think at the same time, Ian looks into the distance. "I can't," he says. "I'll stick to swimming. Though I guess you're pleased that Tijean is?"

"I am," Susan says, standing beside him. "I couldn't motivate him in the classroom, but at least I can feel good about playing a small role in getting him to do what he's good at doing – diving. I like to think that if I hadn't visited him at his aunt's." Susan laughs. "Well, I know that all sounds very tenuous, but sometimes good deeds are. Like good intentions. They're not always enough, but good deeds are, however small. As soon as I heard from my sister that he was diving I just felt a sense of relief."

"We will be judged by our good deeds," Ian says now looking into her eyes.

Susan laughs. "I hope I can muster a few more than that one."

"You can, because essentially you are a good person."

"And so are you." Susan plants a kiss on his lips.

"Thank you. I needed to hear that. Being blamed is the same as being bad."

"Displacement theory," Susan says while staying in Ian's arms.

"Which is?"

"She was being told she was bad. You got the blame. She displaced it onto you."

Ian plants a kiss on her forehead. "I can't imagine the turmoil in her head."

"No, all that hurt."

"I never intended harm to anyone."

"Last night your father said that to be offended isn't the same as being oppressed. At least you're only the offended party. Imagine how oppressed she is?"

"No, I can't."

"All in all, we're a very lucky couple."

"Yes, we are." Holding hands they turn and stroll along the beach. Dusk quickly turns to dark with the clouds rolling across the sky. In the total darkness only the sound of the waves rolling in alerts that they are beside a body of water the size of an ocean. Shivering she pulls her jacket close to her chest with her free hand. It's a different ocean here than in the Caribbean – so much colder. Still, she's looking forward to spending the summer in the Maritimes. Even if it never gets hot she knows she's going to enjoy herself with Ian and his family. There's comfort in feeling she belongs. No matter that the warm season is short, that the nights can turn cold. She feels too satisfied to be fussy about such incidentals. Why worry about ideals like perfect, balmy weather? What they have to give now is their time. They can make it up to Ian's parents, time lost together, their grieving over an expatriate son. On her part, she can offer her family a whole other holiday experience, not the exotic Caribbean, but a place in their own backyard. Such a big country Canada is. Such a paradise.

In the darkness the shorebirds are invisible, yet she imagines them along the water's edge skittering away from the incoming tide, turning over stones to find food – what the sea offers. Susan thinks of all the migrating creatures, from the smallest birds to the largest mammal. She remembers seeing the bee hummingbird and the fin whales. They instinctively follow the currents, whether wind or water, to sources of food and sites for reproduction. It's natural for them. For humans, too, only sometimes human migration is forced like the mass expulsion of the Acadians from these very shores, or the slave trade that brought the blacks to the Caribbean. Yet some individuals choose to relocate out of simple necessity or a yearning to be elsewhere. The current that sent Ian and her to the islands was simply rumour, words that stuck and gnawed at their personal foundation. Now they are back on home turf so relieved that Ian is standing beside her with tears flowing unabashedly down his cheeks. She, too, feels relief in being back in the country where she was born.

All of a sudden it brightens with a break in the storm front. Against the indigo sky a thin sliver shines so brightly Susan could believe the crescent moon is some oddly shaped star. Not only is the dark side of the moon out of view, the round shape of the planet is obscured by its brilliance. "Tonight the moon is like a star," she says. Without words Ian communes with her. His presence seems to breathe thoughts into her mind. Ian is her constant companion and they are grounded here together on this beach with the tide coming in and going out to the rhythm of a universal heartbeat.

∽

Unlike the classical prodigal son, Tijean did not return a failure, but a potential success. He had a job for the summer with the Living Classroom Foundation, a program Miss Mulrain enrolled him in in absentia with his parents approval. For now he was ready to return to school full time. His father met him at the airport on Provo with outstretched arms. Tijean was not embarrassed to return the hug. They did not speak, just laughed in each others arms. Tijean did not expect words like, "Welcome home, son," from his father, or even, "Glad to see you." His welcome was warmer for the hug without any words. It was Tijean who finally spoke, "Did Mom come?"

"No, she works today."

"I have to pick up my luggage," Tijean said.

"You have luggage?" Guy shook his head. "You didn't leave with luggage." Still, without further protest, he followed his son.

"I inherited some diving gear," Tijean said.

"How you do that?"

"From a man I met who was a diver, but he died."

"That too bad. How he die? He didn't die diving, did he? If he did, you better not tell your mother. Now she accept you're going to be a diver, she won't want to hear about anyone dying that way. Then she start worrying all over again."

"Nothing to worry about," Tijean said. "The man died in hospital. Caught a bug."

"He was your friend?"

"Yes," Tijean said, recognizing that Jake had been a friend as well as a benefactor. Tijean didn't mention the money he'd also inherited, a small amount, but enough to pay his tuition if he did pass and get accepted into marine studies.

When they retrieved the luggage they had hours to wait for a connecting flight to the island.

During that wait and on the flight Tijean shared with his father his love of diving. There was no mention of his stay with relatives. At this time in their relationship that period didn't seem relevant. Besides, they weren't Guy's blood relatives so he wasn't concerned about their well being, just preoccupied with his own son. He marveled at Tijean's knowledge and enthusiasm as the boy described what could be found underneath the ocean. "Twenty-five percent of all marine life lives on coral reefs."

"Is that so?" The verbal pictures Tijean created were colourful, as colourful as the painted crafts the Haitian lady sold to the tourists from her tiny shop on Provo. Guy had always suspected they were too bold to be true representations, but now he doubted his earlier misgivings. She had simply painted land versions of what lay hidden. As Guy entered his son's stories he felt the space that existed between the two of them close. Tijean's voice was like a switch that allowed his father to reconnect, to go deeper into that other world, a place unknown to him but one his son experienced and loved. No longer was Guy a foreigner to his son's chosen world. Guy was being given a part to play and he relished the role.

On the small airplane the pilot encouraged the passengers to sit forward to keep the weight balanced over the wings. Father and son sat behind a belonger whom Guy had known all his life. This man, Albert, was pleased to see his friend with his son knowing that Tijean had gone missing for weeks if not months. He started talking home truths to Tijean. "You learn from your Mama. You learn at home. Then you can learn from the world. The truth begins at home."

"That right," Guy said, nodding his head.

"What your Mama say different from what your Dad say," Albert continued. "You want to make something of yourself. You have to prove yourself."

"That right," Guy said, repeating his agreement.

Their words were drowned out by the noise of the plane's engine. Slowly they started to taxi down the runway. The plane's buzz sounded to Tijean like an amplified mosquito. He especially remembered that sound at night after the rains came when the insects appeared in hordes to torment him by feeding off his young skin. Turning away from his father and Albert, Tijean looked out the small window at the red mangrove wetlands below. Albert's talk reminded him of his mother when she compared his childhood to hers. She always said that back in her days things were tough, but they got through the tough times, whereas Tijean lived in the good times when they got lots of food, lots of clothes and lots of shoes. He wondered how it would be for him to return to high school. Instantly he pictured Carolyn standing outside on the cement walkway beside the green stucco building straightening his tie before he went into class. Would she still be waiting or would she have found another boyfriend?

Guy's taxi was parked at the air strip on North Caicos. They drove in silence to the resort to pick up Celianne. Unspoken between them was their shared sense of dread in facing her. They didn't anticipate a spate of her wrath. That they could handle with bowed heads and shamed faces. What they dreaded was her cold suspicions. She'd been betrayed. By them. By her family. By friends. There was no hope of her entering Tijean's world. She wouldn't ask questions about that. She'd rejected the ocean when her family fled the island of Haiti and sailed as refugees onto this one. The ocean had provided a livelihood for generations, then offered them passage to safety. Only Celianne was left feeling betrayed.

True to their anticipations Celianne did not welcome her son home with a kiss or even a hug. With a cold demeanor she got into the front seat while Tijean switched to his usual spot in the back of the taxi. She asked after her family: her sister, her nephew. When Tijean expanded his reply to describe how cold the weather was there Celianne admitted that it was the cold that kept her away. When Tijean described how vibrant and busy the city was Celianne admitted that it was the crowds that kept her on the island.

"Tell your mother about the ocean," Guy said. "He knows so much about that. All the names of the fish: Garden Eels that look like blades of grass, wrasses and parrot fish with staring eyes, triggerfish."

"Don't tell me about them," Celianne said, interrupting. "They're like dogs. They roll over and look up at you just like some loyal, stupid hound would do."

"He has some equipment," Guy said.

In the back seat Tijean sat mutely letting his father's inadequate sentence hang in the air. How did his mother know about the behaviour of triggerfish? There was no point in asking. Her distaste for the subject was evident in her tone of voice. Nothing about the ocean pleased her. Despite her censorship, Tijean only felt his curiosity pique. Jake had particularly liked triggerfish. Is that how he saw them? As the dogs of the sea? Loyal beasts to keep you company while swimming at the bottom of the ocean? Tijean smiled at the memory of Jake showing his videos. They excited him, and in turn, they excited Tijean. His mother's reluctance couldn't dampen what he'd experienced. The world below the ocean was infinite, connected right around the globe so every time he entered its depth he was a small body in touch with its vastness. Tijean settled his shoulder blades against the upholstered seat and stared out the window at the passing familiar sights of buildings that changed outside town to bush. It was good to be home. For the first time in his conscious life Tijean felt pleased to be in the company of his parents. Knowing he couldn't change his mother, he took solace in having become more intimate with his father. Beside him on the seat was the catalogue from the Marine

Centre that had arrived for him. Tijean put his hand on the cover. Inside was a whole world of studies. Could he meet the challenge? With help, yes. He'd come to accept that. There was hope for him and a future that he could freely look forward to as a diver.